MURDER AT DAWN

MURDER AT DAWN

A WINTERGREEN MYSTERY
BOOK 4

PATRICK KELLY

CHAPARRAL PRESS LLC

Published in print and ebook by Chaparral Press LLC.

Cover design by Sleepy Fox Studio.

ISBN 978-1-7342392-6-3 (Print)

ONE

An early summer storm lingered over a section of the Blue Ridge Mountains west of Charlottesville, Virginia. Lightning flashes brightened the sky, rendering otherwise unseen views visible for moments at a time. Strong winds brushed the sides of mountains and made the hardwood treetops dance to a crazy beat. Animals hunkered deep in their burrows, thankful to be warm and dry. A hard rain fell from the clouds, and the wind blew raindrops in every direction.

In the mountain resort of Wintergreen, rain pounded the roofs and sides of homes hidden in the forest. Some residents slept through the storm, oblivious of the chaos rendered mere feet from where they lay. Others awoke with a start when lightning boomed, but once their hearts settled, they rolled over to continue sleeping. A few residents, insomniacs mostly, heard every bit of the storm, and their thoughts ranged far and wide, to the positive and the negative. Optimists smiled at their good fortune. Worriers worried. A few harbored evil thoughts.

Kim Wiley, a sound sleeper, missed every bit of the storm. By the time she awoke, early as usual, the storm had passed and left in its wake freshened forests and surging streams. Kim lay on her back in bed and listened to the soft sound of her lover's breath. A warm feeling came over her as she pondered her good fortune. Kim slipped her bare leg from the covers; the room's air felt cool against her skin.

Kim had turned fifty the previous year, alone again, and she had come to believe there was a strong possibility she would spend the rest of her life that way. Kim had never been lucky with love, not for any real length of time. Undoubtedly, some of that had been her fault, but not all of it. When her birthday came and went, oddly, Kim was at peace with her pessimistic outlook for romantic prospects. She had friends and family, and she enjoyed managing the mountaintop café. And candidly, she enjoyed trading news tidbits with her friends on the mountain. Kim smiled. She was known locally as Wintergreen's chief gossip, a well-earned reputation. She traded in gossip without a guilty conscience. Information was its own currency. More than once, her information had proven most valuable.

Lily shifted in bed, still fast asleep, and Kim's thoughts returned to love. Kim realized now why lasting love had eluded her many times. Fate. It was fate that she had to suffer the pain of rejection more than once. Though keenly observant in other areas of her life, she had worn optimistic blinders when beholding previous girlfriends. Those girlfriends—who she had believed were good people—had deceived her. Kim's scarred heart beat fast with anger for a moment, but then she took a deep breath to calm herself. That was the past. She must live in the present. And the present was bright indeed.

For six weeks earlier, Lily Wolf had waltzed into Kim's life. Kim closed her eyes and relived the scene. The café was empty of customers. Nathan made sandwiches in the kitchen behind her. Kim checked the coffee urns to see how they had fared during the morning rush hour. The bell jingled to signal a customer had entered the doorway. Kim turned that way. A tall, slender blonde in her mid-forties briefly examined the display case's daily offerings. Her eyes lifted to Kim's.

"Good morning," she said.

Kim swallowed. The woman spoke with an unfamiliar accent, perhaps Eastern European. "Um. Hello."

The woman turned to inspect a shelf of locally made jams and jellies. She floated from one place to the next like a ballerina.

"Can I help you find something?"

"I'm in the market for some wine."

She was slender and moved in a way that exuded sensuality. Her bright blue eyes sparkled with mischief.

"You've come to the right place." Kim rushed from behind the counter and opened her arms toward the wine racks in the café's back corner. "Were you searching for anything in particular?"

"I want something red, but not too heavy. Maybe a pinot noir."

Kim led the way. "We have some good pinot noirs. Also, a delightful grenache."

"That sounds nice."

They lingered over the café's wine selection. Kim had learned Lily's name and that she had been living in Wintergreen for two months. She was from Russia originally but had moved around a lot for work. Lily had lived in Western

Europe for the last few years and was now in the US for an extended sabbatical. By training, she was a marketing professional, but she had grown weary of corporate life and was considering moving to the US full time.

For the next ten minutes, they stood close together and discussed wines. At one point, Lily turned suddenly, and their bare arms touched briefly.

Kim's skin tingled.

Lily laughed and said, "I'm sorry."

She had a delightful laugh, a high sound that reminded Kim of water flowing in a brook. After another few minutes, Lily selected a bottle, made her purchase, and left the café. Kim paused at the counter, her eyes lingering on the café's door. Eventually, she turned to look at Nathan. He raised his eyebrows.

"Don't say a word," said Kim.

Kim returned to her tasks and was shocked when Lily immediately re-entered the café and invited Kim to join her for a glass of the wine later.

As they say, one thing led to another, and six weeks later, Kim lay in Lily's bed at five thirty in the morning.

She rose quietly, showered, dressed, and set about making a breakfast casserole for Lily to enjoy after Kim had gone to work.

In the bed, Lily shifted, stretched her arms, and contemplated the unpleasant task she faced. She had been awake for most of the storm. Indeed, Lily had been awake long before Kim first stirred. Not wanting a conversation right away, Lily pretended to sleep while Kim lingered in bed and even after Kim had risen.

Lily Wolf was a woman of complex layers and possessed enough self-awareness to know this. At the surface, she loved Kim Wiley and everything about Kim: her smile, her sense of humor, her kindness toward strangers, even her frizzy hair. This was the only layer of Lily that Kim had ever seen, the layer that Kim believed represented the true Lily. Kim was naive. Lily had known many people like Kim in her life. And she had taken advantage of them many times.

Kim would soon witness, for the first time, Lily's deeper layer, the layer that consisted of Lily's true nature and motivations, the layer governed by reality. Lily never allowed herself to be driven by emotion.

Love. Happiness. Jealousy. Anger. They were all useless words.

Facts and logic drove Lily Wolf's actions and had done so for many years. This was about reality and survival. She had come to this place—Wintergreen—three months earlier, both tired and resigned. Weary of running and weary of deception, Lily had depleted her internal strength to fight the fight. Out of necessity, she had come here to recharge.

And it had worked. A few weeks of healthy food and exercise had restored Lily's will. And she had made an important decision: she would stay in the US. Start over. The US was a great place to lose oneself. Vast. Open. With a huge and innocent economy. Compared to Eastern Europe, money was there for the taking.

But based on new information, she needed more distance. Which is why Lily had to now undertake an unpleasant task.

There was another layer to Lily Wolf, a layer she sometimes dreamed of in deep sleep. This layer came from her youth, when she had known family and acknowledged emotions like love and happiness. This layer was of no use to Lily now. She told herself that it no longer existed. Things had happened. It was irrelevant. Facts and logic drove Lily's actions now.

Kim hummed as she worked. She checked the casserole—it needed another ten minutes—and then turned her attention to frosting a cinnamon roll. It was store-bought but would still taste yummy. Perhaps on the weekend, she'd make something from scratch. She loved to cook for Lily because Lily appreciated her cooking. To that end, Kim had brought a few essential utensils from the café. The rental home's stuff, frankly, was next to useless.

Lily had rented a three-bedroom home on Fairway Oaks Lane for several months. A great room with a kitchen, dining area, and entertainment center comprised most of the main level. Picture windows overlooked a large wooden deck and a gazebo. Beyond the deck, a small section of forest separated the house from a golf course fairway. The first hints of dawn nipped at the forest's edge.

Kim was almost beside herself with excitement. While showering, she had made an important decision. She would invite Lily to move in with her in Staunton. They had been together for over a month, and Kim was comfortable taking the relationship to the next level. Kim studied the great room. Renting this home must cost a neat fortune. Lily didn't need to spend her money on this place when Kim's home was more than big enough for both of them. Yes, it was time.

Kim's eye detected motion on the balcony above the great room. Dressed in her robe, Lily came to the edge and waved, then proceeded down the stairs. Kim's heart beat faster, as it always did whenever she first caught sight of Lily.

Once downstairs, Lily came to Kim immediately for a kiss and a quick embrace.

Lily smiled delightfully. "It smells divine in here. What have you been cooking up now?"

"Nothing much. A simple casserole. It'll be ready in ten minutes."

Lily sniffed. "I smell cinnamon."

Kim chuckled. "Yes, I baked a cinnamon roll, too."

Lily shook her finger at Kim. "I'll get fat."

"No chance. You're a rail. Coffee?"

"Yes, please."

Kim sat at the kitchen table with her knee bobbing nonstop. She hesitated to raise the subject because the decision called for a bigger occasion than morning coffee. But she had to leave for work soon and knew she couldn't keep the secret all day.

"I want to ask you a question," said Kim, the words rushing. "It's kind of a big deal."

Lily tilted her head, all ears. "Okay. What is it?"

"I want you to move in with me."

There. It was out now. Kim heaved a sigh.

Lily's eyebrows lifted. Kim's statement required further explanation.

"My place is big enough, and you could save a lot on rent. Plus, I'm falling in love with you."

Lily cleared her throat. She blinked several times.

Kim's stomach tightened. Why didn't Lily answer? They should be dancing circles by now. "Well, what do you say?"

Lily pressed her lips tightly, then said, "It's a nice gesture, Kim. I want to thank you for that. But I can't move in with you."

"Why not?"

"Because I'm leaving."

Kim's mouth dropped. Her head moved forward. "What do you mean you're leaving? When? Where?"

"I'm leaving soon. As to where, I don't know yet."

"Why?"

"It's complicated. I can't get into that part."

"I'll go with you."

Lily snorted.

"Why are you laughing?" Kim said.

"You can't come with me."

"I said I'm in love with you. Don't make fun of me."

Lily sat straight and took a deep breath. "We've only known each other a short while. Don't you think it's early to be throwing around the big words?"

Kim put her hands forward to demonstrate her commitment. "I want a long-term relationship."

"Where I come from, a month is a long time."

"What?"

"Kim, don't take this the wrong way. I like you. This has been fun."

The reality hit Kim like a tidal wave. Lily had used her like all the others. Stunned, Kim sat back in her chair. It had been fun for Lily. A month was a long time for her. She was a thrill seeker and didn't give two hoots for Kim's feelings.

Lily went into explanation mode, but she only gave it lip service. I'll always remember our time together with great fondness. Sadly, this is the way it has to be. Let's not get too emotional about it. Facts are facts.

Kim stood. She couldn't tolerate more of this.

Lily appeared amused, as if Kim's growing anger demonstrated a childishness not to be tolerated. She even said, "Kim, don't go away angry. Let's part as friends. We can kiss."

Lily stood and came around the table. She opened her arms as if to embrace Kim.

Kim's blood boiled. The wretched witch. Kim would knock that smirk off of Lily's face.

But when Kim let her hand fly, Lily's arm became a blur. Lily plucked Kim's wrist from the air, twisted Kim's arm, and wrenched it to the breaking point behind Kim's back.

Lily whispered in her ear. "I'll let you go now. Don't make this any worse than it already is."

Without another word, Kim marched from the house to her truck. She hyperventilated in the cab, boiling with anger. Kim grabbed her phone and sent Lily the most seething texts she could imagine. Things Lily should do to herself. Places she should go. What a terrible person she was. Four texts. Five. Six. Her anger knew no bounds.

Still furious, Kim started the truck and floored the gas pedal. The truck lurched forward with its tires spinning gravel. At the driveway entrance, the truck fishtailed and struck the house number sign. When the signpost snapped, it made a cracking sound that Kim never heard.

From behind the window panel beside the front door, Lily watched Kim's truck take out the signpost. She pursed her lips.

Well, that was something.

Someone would have to deal with the broken signpost, but not Lily. She'd be gone in a few hours.

Lily returned to the great room and switched on the living room lights. She was not a fan of dark rooms. Her eyes lifted to the sconces that cradled fluorescent lights near the ceiling. The light at one end was slightly irregular, as if the bulb behind the sconce may soon fail. Lily took comfort from the irregularity.

Curious, she went to the oven to inspect Kim's parting gift. Egg, cheese, and mushroom. Yummy.

Should she eat now or pack first and reward herself with breakfast later?

Later. Food always tasted better when the work was done. Lily would shower, dress, and pack everything but the money and her toothbrush. Then, she would enjoy one last meal on the back deck. The day would dawn by then. The hardwood trees and golf course were beautiful. That view, combined with the sound of leaves rustling high above her and the gentle breeze on her skin, made Lily feel something. Not love exactly, but a certain fondness. She would miss this place, Wintergreen. And if she were being honest with herself, she would miss Kim Wiley.

TWO

Several hours later, Bill O'Shea stood behind the pickleball baseline and prepared to receive a serve from his girlfriend, Cindy Quintrell. Cindy was a serious competitor, a trait he had not observed until they began playing pickleball six months ago. With shoulder-length curly hair and an attractive figure, Cindy was close to Bill in height—five foot nine—and physically fit, but not too fit. She smiled before she prepared to serve, and this distracted Bill, but in a good way, for he considered himself a lucky man to see Cindy as often as he did.

To Bill's left at the kitchen line stood Maria Metcalf—who, along with her partner, Terry Stinson—had regularly played pickleball with Bill and Cindy for the last several months. Bill and Cindy had met Maria and Terry at a social event, and the two couples had immediately hit it off. Since then, they had ventured out on winery visits, day hikes, and weekly pickleball games. Bill enjoyed Terry's company quite a lot—he was a straight talker with a dry sense of humor and a genuine smile. On the other hand, Bill sensed that Maria had a darker side than what she showed every day. On a few occasions, he had seen her eyes turn from clear to stormy instantly, and she liked to have things done her way, particularly on a pickleball court.

Terry stood a tad under six feet with broad shoulders and a powerful chest. He had a rugged face, blue eyes, and blond hair that he undoubtedly dyed to keep from turning gray. Maria was shorter than Terry by several inches but also in excellent physical condition. She wore her brown hair tied up in a complicated arrangement that defied gravity. Her thin face was pretty, and her sun-kissed skin showed little of her age. Maria was attractive, but Bill found her beauty marred by her unforgiving attitude toward others.

As they played, the four of them rotated sides so that each was teamed with each of the others. Maria bounced slightly, impatient for the volley to begin, with her feet no more than twelve inches behind the kitchen line. She often encouraged Bill to play forward, to charge to the kitchen line whenever possible, even if it meant leaving the baseline open for a well-placed lob. "In pickleball, points are won at the net," she would say. "It's not like tennis." Maria must have said these exact words to Bill a dozen times.

Maria and Terry had both recently retired from government jobs in DC and come to Wintergreen that spring for a long vacation. Once there, they liked the landscape and slower pace so much they decided to stay. They were romantic partners but lived in separate condo associations on the ridge, an arrangement that some might find unusual but seemed perfectly natural to Bill. After all, he and Cindy had dated for a year but still lived in their own homes.

Bill could not remember what Terry and Maria's jobs had been. There were many departments and agencies in Washington, and they all had their own three-letter abbreviations—CBO, DHS, DOE. Who could ever keep them straight? Was the DOE in energy or education? And what did all of those employees do?

Cindy served a long shot that landed deep in the court. Bill returned the serve neatly, and the ball soared deep into Terry's side of the court. Terry backpedaled, turned sideways, and smoothly positioned his paddle for the return.

"Come up, Bill," said Maria. "Come up." She signaled her intention with her paddle, and Bill complied.

Terry lofted the ball toward Maria's side, but she leaped high enough to successfully return the shot. Cindy had come forward and returned the ball before it landed. Bill had reached the kitchen line and hit the ball from the air. All four players were forward now, and for a few exciting seconds, the ball pinged back and forth between them. Finally, Maria won the point with a shot that narrowly missed Terry's chest.

"Ha," Maria exclaimed. "Gotcha."

"Well played," said Terry.

And those two lines captured perfectly the difference between Maria and Terry on the pickleball court. Terry played to have a good time. Maria played to win. Maria actually kept score across the games they played. She brought a small chalkboard to the court and marked a stroke by each of their names whenever their side won a game. They had played together ten or twelve times, and Bill had noticed a pattern. The score was always close between the four of them, and often, two or more of them would achieve equal scores, but if one of them did win, it was more than likely to be Maria.

This struck Bill as strange, for Maria wasn't the best player. No, but she was the fiercest competitor. Once this observation came to him, Bill began watching each of the individual players' styles carefully, and he soon came to a new conclusion: Terry's level of play changed with the score. If Terry's side was winning by a significant margin, he slacked off until the game was won or the score tightened. If Terry's side was losing by more than a point or two, he would expend more effort to return each point and make each stroke count. An avid golfer and hiker, Terry played below his athletic ability. Whose side won the game mattered little to Terry. He wanted the score to be close.

Bill did not share this observation with the others, not even with Cindy. Some observations were best kept to oneself. Bill could not discern whether Terry knew he adjusted his level of play with the score, but Bill admired Terry for his on-court behavior, whether rendered consciously or not. Bill suspected that he and Terry held similar views of pickleball. It was a game. Whether you won or lost mattered little, so long as everyone had fun.

Some considered life a game, a philosophy Bill did not subscribe to. In life, the stakes were higher. Who won and who lost mattered a great deal. On unfortunate occasions, losing in life meant losing everything.

Wintergreen's outdoor pickleball area was fenced and contained eight courts. The resort had converted three seldom-used tennis courts to pickleball courts the previous year, a brilliant move, for the new courts were popular. Indeed, nearly every morning, two or more courts were occupied, but not today. For whatever reason, the four of them were the only players at that moment. But they did have a keen spectator.

Earlier that year, Bill had decided to adopt a dog. This was not, he knew, a difficult task to accomplish, for every community had an animal shelter, and every shelter had dogs available for adoption. Big dogs. Small dogs. Old dogs. Young dogs.

"How will you ever decide?" Cindy had asked when they visited the Rockfish Valley Animal Shelter.

Bill had strolled past the available dogs twice. All of them appeared healthy and perky, save one. At the end of the line, a sickly and exhausted black Labrador Retriever sat quietly near the door to his stall. Bill winced at the healed scar on the dog's shoulder. The sign on the stall read Spot, which seemed peculiar as the dog was solid black from nose to tail. The other dogs made quite a stir with their yapping and barking and constant fidgeting. The commotion bothered Spot not a whit. He sat calmly, as if perfectly satisfied to wait for something of consequence to happen. Mealtime, perhaps.

Spot had brown eyes, and when Bill leaned closer to the fenced doorway, the dog's eyes engaged him. Intelligence emanated from Spot's gaze. And something else too—peaceful resignation. Bill got the impression the dog knew his fate and accepted it. But that couldn't be true. Dogs weren't sophisticated animals. They were driven by instinct, like their evolutionary ancestors.

"He's not as old as he looks," said the onsite vet when Bill asked about Spot's history. "My guess is three to four years old, but he's had a tough life. He had an owner once, certainly, for he's been neutered. But he's been a stray most of his life. As you can see from the scar, he's had some scraps. There are other scars too."

"And his health?"

The vet shook his head. "Worms, plus a few minor issues. We had hoped someone would adopt him and pay for the treatment because we have limited funds at our disposal. No luck yet, and we've almost given up. One of the attendants has been calling the other shelters to see if someone else can take him on."

"I see."

The vet put his fingers through the door of Spot's stall.

The dog came forward, sniffed, and then licked the vet's fingers. "You're a good boy, aren't you?"

Bill noticed the black lab was seriously underweight. Spot's fur stretched across his ribs.

"Is his name really Spot?"

The vet laughed. "No, every dog in this stall gets the name Spot."

"Oh. Got it."

Outside, sitting in Bill's Mazda CX-5, Cindy lined up the pros and cons for Spot. Mostly cons. The other dogs were younger, healthier, and easier to care for. But Bill kept seeing the black lab's brown eyes. "I'm not blaming you," the eyes said. "It's not your fault."

Which is how—after fifteen hundred dollars in vet bills and five months of good food and exercise—a healthy black lab, now named Max, patiently watched Bill and the others play pickleball from outside the fence.

Whenever a stray ball wandered toward the fence where Max lay, Max watched with great interest, and if Bill came near, Max would stand and wag his tail.

"Good boy, Max. Good boy."

Max was remarkably well-behaved for a dog who had received little formal training as far as Bill knew, other than how to play fetch. Someone had definitely taught him that game. Bill had watched a dozen YouTube videos and used those lessons to teach Max some simple words. Come. Stay. When Bill walked Max near the roads or in a parking lot, he kept him on a leash, but he saw no need the rest of the time. Max always came when Bill called and never caused trouble around other people or dogs.

At the end of a particularly hard-fought volley, Terry rushed sideways and swung wildly to hit the ball, which then soared over the fence to land near where Max lay. Max jumped up, lifted the ball gently in his mouth, and returned it to the fence. Bill approached the fence to praise Max and then realized the openings were too small for the ball to pass through.

"No problem," said Maria. "I have another ball."

"Come, boy," said Bill. "Bring it around here." Bill signaled toward the open door to the pickleball courts around the corner from where Max stood.

"That's not necessary," said Maria. "We don't need to wait."

Max observed Bill make his way toward the entrance.

"Must we do this?" said Maria, irritated by the delay.

Max turned and trotted along the fence perimeter to the corner.

"Look at that," exclaimed Terry. "He's doing it. That is one smart dog." Terry ran toward the entrance as well.

"I can't believe this," said Maria, resigned now.

Max made the corner and met Bill at the entrance.

"Good boy." Bill laughed and kneeled to stroke Max's chest. "Good boy."

Terry held his hand out for Max to sniff. "You're brilliant, Max. I've never met a dog like you."

Bill signaled that Max should go back to his observation post, and the dog turned to head that way.

"Jeez, Bill," said Terry. "You're a heck of a trainer."

Filled with pride, Bill shook his head. "Max deserves the credit. Not me."

As the two men returned to their court, Terry continued to praise Max.

Maria's eyes signaled anger at this unnecessary delay. "Now we have to play with a slobber-covered ball. Is that it?"

Bill wasn't sure how to respond. As a general rule, he preferred to avoid unnecessary conflict.

Then Terry said, "It's not about the ball, Maria. It's about the dog. That was a heck of a feat."

Maria harrumphed her residual irritation.

Terry responded to her distaste for a dog-slobbered ball with a solution. "You said you had an extra ball. Let's play with that."

Maria reluctantly dropped the issue. "Okay."

And although Bill and Maria had built a comfortable lead in the game, for some reason, Bill didn't play well after that, and they lost the game.

At the end of their pickleball session, the four gathered under the center court awning. Cindy and Maria chatted about going to an art show in Waynesboro. Terry and Bill discussed an idea they'd been kicking around to start a handyman side hustle for Wintergreen residents. Then Bill's phone buzzed.

Emily Powell, Wintergreen's police chief.

"I'd better take this," said Bill.

He answered the phone and stepped away.

"Hey, Bill. I called earlier and left a voicemail. You can ignore that now."

"What's going on?"

"We have a situation."

Which was an understatement. There had been a murder at a house not far from where Bill stood. A passerby discovered the body. Nelson County's Undersheriff Arnie Shields would arrive momentarily, and Soren Larsen, the medical examiner from Virginia's forensics office in Roanoke, was on his way.

"Maybe you could stop by for a little while," said Emily. "I'm sure Arnie will have it under control, but it never hurts to have another set of eyes and ears at the scene. Right?"

Bill was a retired homicide detective from Columbia, South Carolina. Under Emily's leadership, the Wintergreen

Police Department did an excellent job keeping the community safe. At the same time, Wintergreen had to compete with every police organization in the country for resources, and there was a nationwide shortage of experienced talent. As a result, Emily had asked Bill to help out in a minor way on a few previous investigations, a request he was happy to oblige.

"Yeah. Sure. I'm dressed in pickleball gear now, but I can be there in twenty minutes."

"Thanks, Bill."

Terry and the others had sensed the seriousness of Bill's call, and they stood together not far from him.

"What's going on?" asked Cindy.

How should he respond? Bill preferred to keep information like this confidential. But word traveled fast on the mountain, and Cindy had given him a hard time in the past about her being the last to know. So, he gave them a high-level overview.

"Murder!" said Terry. "Here in Wintergreen?"

"You're kidding," said Maria, by her tone both surprised and annoyed. "We moved here to get away from all that."

After his initial reaction, Terry swung into helpful neighbor mode. Was there anything he could do? No. If anything came up, anything at all, for example, walking Max, please let him know.

"Thank you," said Bill. "I'd better get going."

Bill put the leash on Max and hightailed it to his condo building two hundred yards away. He didn't bother to shower, just threw on khakis and a clean shirt and then drove to the murder scene.

THREE

The address was 48B Fairway Oaks Lane. Bill could have found it even with the knocked down street number signpost because of the official vehicles parked on the road—two Wintergreen squad cars and two Nelson County Sheriff cruisers—the last of which brought Undersheriff Arnie Shields and arrived moments before Bill.

A sheriff's deputy stood in front of the driveway to keep out anyone who happened to come along.

"Morning, Arnie," said Bill, and they shook hands at the entrance to the driveway. "Emily asked me to stop by. Hope you don't mind."

"More the merrier," Arnie said, with a hint of sarcasm. He was a short, thin man with brown hair graying at the temples. The murder was clearly in Nelson County's jurisdiction, and Bill was a retiree. Perhaps little more than a busybody from Arnie's perspective, but they had worked well together on a previous investigation. Bill would stick around for the moment. If Arnie wanted him gone, he'd be gone, no sweat.

Bill leaned over the broken street number signpost.

"Looks like a smidgen of black paint here. Could be from the vehicle."

"Bingo," said Arnie. "Now all we need is a vehicle, a driver, a motive, and how's the rest of that go? I forget."

"Okay, Arnie. Nice to see you too."

Arnie chuckled, and Bill figured they'd be okay.

Inside, they passed through a short hallway into a large room with a combined kitchen, dining area, and living room space. There they found Emily Powell, Officer Mitch Gentry, and a tall man in street clothes Bill recognized as a local he had passed a few times on his morning walks.

Emily pulled Bill and Arnie aside.

"This man is a Wintergreen resident named Paul Jameson," she said. "He found the body an hour ago and is a bit shaken up, but not too badly. I haven't interviewed Jameson yet. Figured you would want to be here for that." Emily addressed this last sentence to Arnie.

Arnie nodded his appreciation.

"I asked Bill to join us," said Emily, "because, you know, he's been down this road many times."

"Sure."

Arnie's one-word answer didn't make Bill feel welcome, but he'd stick around for a bit because Emily asked him to.

They moved toward the others, and Bill's eyes scanned the great room. The kitchen island was cleared save for a casserole dish, a half-full bottle of orange juice, and some breakfast pastry. On the other side of the picture windows, Officer John Hill stood on the back deck. Someone sat slumped in a chair near John.

Must be the body.

After brief introductions, Emily asked Mitch Gentry to keep John Hill company on the deck. When Mitch had gone,

Emily suggested that the four of them remain standing to preserve forensic evidence that might linger on any furniture.

Jameson was a tall, handsome man about Bill's age who moved with the grace of an athlete. Jameson's hands shook slightly, but he spoke with a steady voice. Emily asked him to explain what had happened that morning.

Paul Jameson lived alone and was a creature of habit. For exercise, he walked the same route on the same three days every week and a different route on the other days. He took Sundays off. Jameson had charted a route that equaled an exact distance of three miles. His route was a rough circle that included a portion of Blue Ridge Drive and all of Shamokin Springs Trail. The route was only two miles, so Paul added side trips down specific finger streets to reach his target distance.

"So, you come up this street three times a week?" said Arnie.

Jameson nodded. "Yes, on Mondays, Wednesdays, and Fridays. To keep myself entertained, I look for differences in the setting."

"Differences?" said Arnie.

"Yes, there are many houses on my route, but only a few people live in those houses. On some days, every detail is exactly the same as on my previous trip. The few cars are parked in the same spots. Sometimes, I don't see another person, but I usually encounter a few cars on the road. Occasionally, I see other walkers; for example, I have seen you and your black Labrador several times." Jameson indicated Bill with a nod of his head.

"That's right," said Bill, trying to be helpful. "I remember."

"You have a nice dog."

"Thank you."

"So, what happened today?" said Arnie, eager to move things along.

Jameson had noticed the broken signpost out front. He had inspected the signpost and seen the same black paint that Bill had seen. This bothered Jameson because the color didn't match that of the car parked out front.

"The woman on the back porch has been living here for about three months," he said. "I noticed her white Camry when she first moved in, and I've seen her outside maybe two or three times."

The color mismatch bothered Jameson enough for him to walk up the front steps and ring the doorbell. No one answered. He tried the door, but it was locked. Then he peered through the window by the door and saw someone sitting quite still on the back deck. He watched the person through the window for five minutes, but they didn't move. So, he came around the back to check on them.

"You did all that because you noticed a broken signpost?" said Arnie.

Paul considered the question for several seconds and apparently found it odd. "Wouldn't you?"

Bill lifted a hand to hide his smile.

Arnie asked what Paul had done when he found the body.

"I called 911."

"Did you touch anything? The body? Or something inside the house?"

"I touched her neck," said Paul. "I guess to make sure . . . but she had already lost some body heat. I knew she was dead."

"Anything else?"

Paul considered this question a few moments. "No. I didn't touch anything else. I must say, the response time was excellent. Officer Gentry was here within a few minutes of me speaking with the dispatcher."

Emily asked Jameson a few background questions. How long had he lived in Wintergreen? Three years. What did he do before he retired? Defense lobbyist.

"I was career Army," he said. "Then I found a job with the military-industrial complex."

Arnie asked some questions. Did he know the woman who lived in the house? No. Where had he seen her? Once, he saw her driving on Blue Ridge Drive. They had exchanged waves as people often did in Wintergreen. On another day, he passed the driveway while she carried groceries into the house.

After Arnie and Emily had exhausted their questions, Arnie gave Bill a begrudging nod.

"Have you noticed any other cars parked in the driveway?" said Bill.

"Yes. About six weeks ago, a red sports car was parked here on several mornings. And last week, I noticed a black truck, but that was later in the day. I couldn't exercise that morning because of a doctor's appointment."

"Did you notice the make of those vehicles?" said Bill.

"The truck might have been an F-150. But I don't know about the sports car. I'm not good with those."

"Have you seen anyone else with her?"

Paul shook his head. They had no more questions, so Emily thanked Paul for being a good citizen, asked him to keep the matter quiet until they released a statement, and told him he could go.

"Let's take a look at the body," said Arnie after Jameson had left.

When they came onto the back deck, Mitch Gentry and

John Hill, who had been speaking in low tones, turned their way.

"Do we know who she is?" said Arnie.

Emily said, "We found a small purse containing a Virginia driver's license and one credit card. Her name is Lily Wolf. The address listed is for this house."

Bill examined the body. The woman appeared to be in her forties with blond hair. She wore a green cotton T-shirt and black leggings. She was thin, with her height hard to gauge because of her position. She had been stabbed once in the back, and the knife remained there as if the killer wanted all to admire their skill in piercing the heart with one blow. A great deal of blood stained the shirt below the wound.

"What's the matter, Bill?" said Emily.

Bill stood only a few feet from the corpse, but he leaned even closer to study the knife handle. It was a bright, royal-blue color that he had only ever seen on one other set of knives.

"I've seen that knife," he said, "or at least, I've seen one exactly like it."

"Okay," said Arnie, impatient. "Let's have it."

Bill stood straight. He suddenly didn't feel well, as if perhaps he had not consumed enough water after his pickleball session. His eyes blurred, and he blinked to clear them.

Emily touched his arm. "Are you all right?"

"Yeah. I . . . I'm fine. It's just that, uh, Kim Wiley and her nephew use a set of knives with handles like that. Same color."

"Who is Kim Wiley?" said Arnie.

"She runs Café Devine," said Emily. "You passed it on the way."

"On the left after the turn? I saw it."

"Her nephew Nathan works there too," said Emily.

Bill scarcely heard the others, for his mind was reeling. What was Kim doing mixed up in this? He glanced at the corpse. Mixed up? Wrong choice of words. Murder was not mixed up. It was as bad as bad could get.

Arnie glanced at the body, then inside the house, as if trying to make a decision. He addressed Emily. "I'm going to take my guy and go to the café."

"Makes sense."

"Can you and your team wait for Soren to get here? Meanwhile, you can search the house."

"Sure."

Bill followed Arnie, who was now hustling. Arnie tromped through the house to the front door, where Bill stopped him. "Hey, do you mind if I tag along?"

Arnie's eyebrows dropped. His brown eyes studied Bill's face. "How would you describe your relationship with this Kim Wiley?"

Bill's heart sank. He knew where they were headed. "She's a friend."

"Maybe you'd better stay here. See if Soren has anything of value to add."

Oddly enough, it was at that moment that Bill recalled Kim drove a black Ford F-150, a fact he chose not to reveal to Arnie, which underscored Bill's conflict of interest. It didn't make any difference, though, not really. Arnie was a competent law enforcer. He'd undoubtedly notice Kim's truck in the parking lot.

W*ow.*

Mitch had never seen Bill O'Shea this way. Bill's face lost all its color on the back deck. He seemed terribly confused, like Mitch's grandfather did once in a while. Emily had to touch Bill's arm to bring him out of it. Then Bill had followed Undersheriff Arnie Shields into the house.

What a morning. Mitch had barely started his rounds in the cruiser when he got notice of a possible theft on Blackrock Circle. Mitch hurried over and knocked on the door, only to learn that the call resulted from a communication breakdown. The man's son had taken the bike into town for an overhaul, and the man had forgotten. Not to worry, Mitch told him. These things happened. Mitch backed out of the driveway, and the dispatcher called again. Her ordinarily calm voice had kicked up a notch. There was a reported murder on Fairway Oaks Lane. Hell's bells. What a morning.

Still on the back deck, Mitch studied Emily. She seemed lost in her thoughts, but only for a moment. Then she jumped into command mode.

"Okay. John?"

"Yes, chief."

"You're on guard duty." She pointed to the corpse. "Nothing, not a vulture, not a raccoon, not even an ant, can touch this body before the ME arrives."

"I'm on it."

"Mitch, do a visual inspection of the entire house. Find out something about this woman. Look for a surveillance camera. That would be a huge break. See what else you can learn. There must be more than a driver's license and a credit card. Find her phone."

"Got it."

Bill came onto the back deck again. His skin tone had returned to normal.

"Arnie suggested I wait for Soren," he said. "He believes I have a conflict, and candidly, I do."

"No sweat. You can help Mitch with the search if you will."

"Of course. But I don't have gloves."

"I have extra," said Mitch.

"Okay," said Emily. "See what you can learn here. I'm going to call Krista."

FOUR

Bill stared at the laptop on the dining room table. He presumed the computer belonged to Lily Wolf—the dead woman sitting on the deck with a knife in her back. The laptop would likely reveal quite a lot. The laptop was open and plugged in, but when he tapped the touchpad, the laptop demanded a password. Bill lifted the laptop and examined its bottom on the remote chance that Wolf had taped her password there. No luck, but it was worth a try. At a crime scene years ago, Bill had found the victim's password etched into his laptop. Email messages led Bill straight to the killer.

He strolled to the kitchen area. The oven was on a low temperature. Inside, he found the second half of a giant frosted cinnamon roll. A casserole dish with a lid lay on the kitchen island. Bill lifted the lid—eggs, mushrooms, broccoli, and cheese. He grimaced because the casserole resembled a dish he'd seen on display at Café Devine. The refrigerator contained scant provisions, and Bill guessed that Lily Wolf had not cared much for cooking. But someone had. A hard lump had formed in Bill's stomach. He could use a glass of water but didn't want to disturb the crime scene.

Bill walked into the living area. The furniture was reasonably new and certainly usable, but nothing fancy. Knickknacks from the local area lined a bookshelf. Decent artwork graced the walls. But there were no personal photos. In the balcony hallway upstairs, Bill found two locked closet doors that confirmed his suspicion. This was a rental home, not unusual for Wintergreen. Many owners used rental income to offset the costs of their second homes. But Lily had apparently lived here for several months, which was relatively uncommon. Most rental home guests stayed for no more than a week. Wolf had used the address for her driver's license, which also seemed strange.

Bill met Mitch at the door to the main bedroom.

Mitch smiled and lifted a key fob. "Look what I found on the bedside table. I'm going to check it out."

"Anything else?"

"Yeah. She was packing for a trip."

A single, medium-sized suitcase lay open on a window seat, nearly full with clothes, shoes, and limited beauty products. A stuffed backpack sat beside the suitcase. Bill checked the bureau and found its drawers empty. He glanced through the window at the back deck. John Hill paced nervously near the corpse. John peered through the house windows, perhaps hoping for some company. How on earth did Kim's knife wind up in the victim's back?

In the master bath, drops of water clung to the shower stall glass. A toothbrush and toothpaste lay on the sink counter. Lily Wolf had already packed everything else. Apparently, she had planned to eat breakfast, brush her teeth, and hit the road. So much for plans.

The one obvious item they hadn't found was a phone.

The sound of Mitch entering the front door came from downstairs.

"Anything interesting?" Bill asked from the balcony hallway.

"The car's not hers," said Mitch. He glanced at the notes he'd taken on his phone. "It's registered to a company—Atlantic Engineering Advisors, LLC. Does that name mean anything to you?"

"Never heard of them. It seems odd that she would drive a company car while living here for three months."

"Maybe it came with the rental house. A package deal."

Bill nodded. "That's possible. Anything else in the car?"

"Not so much as a stick of gum. Lily Wolf was a real minimalist."

"Yeah, I think she was used to traveling light."

FIVE

Kim Wiley pressed the heel of her hand against her forehead.

Hell's bells, what a headache.

She'd never felt this bad. Kim glanced at her phone. In six more hours, she could leave. At this rate, she wouldn't make it. Nathan had asked four times if Kim was okay. The last time she'd snapped.

"Just make the sandwiches, will ya?"

"Okay. Okay. Take it easy."

Take it easy? Never again. The nightmare of that morning flashed through her mind for the hundredth time. The strike. She'd never forget. If only she could . . .

The bell that hung from the doorknob jingled.

Sheesh. Not another customer.

Never in her life had Kim wished for a day with no customers.

She glanced over, and her heart rate jumped. A police officer she didn't recognize entered the store. Thin. Brown hair. Late forties. A second, more junior officer followed him. They wore Nelson County Sheriff's uniforms.

"Good morning," said the older officer. He held some rank. She squinted at his badge but couldn't make it out.

Kim's chest tightened. What did these men want? Coffee? Or were they here for another reason?

Keep it together. You've seen cops before. Lots of times.

"Can I get you something?" she asked.

"Are you Kim Wiley?"

Arnie got out of his car and stared at the wooden black bear statue in front of the café.

Hard to miss this place.

Arnie was relieved to be away from the murder scene. Twenty-five years on the job, and he still couldn't get used to being around a dead body. He'd probably miss Soren Larsen's early assessment. Let me take a wild guess, Soren. She was stabbed.

A black Ford F-150 was parked in the far corner of the small lot. Patrol Officer Dennis Fortune knelt at the rear left side of the truck. Arnie walked over.

"Whatcha got?" said Arnie.

"There's a definite scrape here. The truck lost a little paint. Looks fresh."

Things were not stacking up in Kim Wiley's favor. The blue-handled knife. The black paint. Arnie might wrap this case up today. One question did nag the back of his mind, though. Why did she leave the knife? He'd seen victims with multiple stab wounds, but the weapon was often missing from the scene. Finding the weapon became a big part of the investigation. Clever murderers would throw the knife into a deep river, bury it in a hole in the woods, or better yet, melt it down to nothing in a smelter. Then again, a murderer's behavior after the fact was hard to predict. On one case, the murderer had taken costume jewelry pieces from the victim's body and hid them in his desk drawer. You could never tell.

"Okay, Dennis, let's go inside and meet Kim Wiley. You come along in case she tries something silly. Let me do the talking. You hang back and lay low."

"Yes, sir."

Arnie opened the café door, and a bell hanging on the door knob jingled. Once inside, Arnie glanced right, where a medium-sized woman around fifty years old stood at the cash register. She had frizzy brown hair.

"Good morning," he said.

She seemed a little nervous, a common reaction when police officers entered someone's space. In the kitchen behind the woman, a younger man worked. The young man glanced at Arnie, and Arnie nodded. Arnie tilted his head to see if the man held a knife, but he was stirring the contents of a bowl.

"Can I get you something?" the woman said.

Here we go.

"Are you Kim Wiley?"

"Yes. Who are you?"

Kim Wiley had found her nerve and immediately switched to confrontation mode.

"Undersheriff Shields, ma'am, from the county sheriff's office. Could I get a few minutes of your time?"

"I'm running a café. Why are you here?"

Arnie glanced around the café. Two women had been examining jams and such on a shelf off to the side, but now they paused to see what was happening with the police officers.

"I see your patio is clear. Maybe we could step outside for a minute? It shouldn't take long."

"It's okay, Aunt Kim," said the young man in the kitchen, his voice shaky. "I'll watch the register."

Apparently, this solution worked for Kim Wiley, because she stepped out from behind the counter and led the way to the small patio. The patio had three tables with chairs for customers, all presently unoccupied. Arnie hoped Wiley would take a seat, but she remained standing.

"Ms. Wiley, I'm here on an investigation."

"What sort of investigation?"

"I'll get to that in a minute. First, could you tell me where you've been this morning?"

"Here. Working."

"What did you do earlier this morning before you came to the café?"

"That's none of your business."

"Do you own a blue-handled knife?"

Wiley seemed puzzled now. Narrowed eyes. Pursed lips.

"Why do you ask?"

"If you keep answering my questions with questions, we'll never get anywhere."

"I own a set of blue-handled knives we use in the kitchen."

"Can I see them?"

"No. What's this all about?"

Kim Wiley was a good actor, but Arnie had met some great liars in his day.

"We're investigating a crime scene."

"A crime scene. What's happened? Where?"

Arnie had all the information he needed. She admitted to owning the knives. He hadn't even gotten to the signpost, and already he was wrestling with whether to arrest her now or to ask her to come down to the station.

He said, “There’s been a murder this morning in a house not far from here.”

“A murder? Where? What street?”

“Fairway Oaks Lane.” Arnie watched her carefully. Her lips trembled. Her hands began to shake. Yes, she was a good actor.

“Who? Who’s been murdered? What’s her name?”

“I never said it was a woman.”

SIX

Krista Jackson drove her squad car down to the Rockfish Valley, took 151 to Nellysford, and parked at a white house that served as the office for a local real estate company.

Krista took pride in her career progress. For one thing, she had aced all of her criminology night courses. Then, three months ago, Emily promoted Krista to patrol officer, which got her out of the office. Now Krista was a player in a murder investigation—a bit player, certainly, but still part of the action.

Once inside the real estate office, Krista introduced herself to the elderly receptionist, a woman named Diane.

"Alex is expecting you," Diane said. She indicated the direction with her hand. "Down the hall, first door on the right."

"Thank you."

The door was open. Alex Sharp sat in an office chair with his eyes on a monitor. Krista knocked.

Alex jumped up and came around the desk to shake her hand. "Krista Jackson. Welcome. It's great to see you."

"Hey, chief."

Alex Sharp was a real estate agent and broker who had worked in the Wintergreen market for thirty years. But for six months the previous year, when Wintergreen's police chief quit to move out west, Alex had stepped in as acting chief. After that time, Emily Powell was promoted to the position.

"Not chief anymore," said Alex. "I'm a real estate broker now."

"All the same, it's nice to know you're there if we need you."

"I understand you want to see some video."

As it turned out, Alex's real estate company owned the building that housed Café Devine. Emily knew this, and that the building had two surveillance cameras mounted on its exterior, one over the main entrance and one over the café's patio. Emily had called Alex earlier to arrange for Krista to view footage from that morning.

Alex said, "Emily told me there's been a murder."

"Yes, unfortunately."

"But she said I wouldn't know who it was."

"So far, we know next to nothing about the victim."

Alex offered his chair for Krista to sit in, then said, "Maybe you should drive. It'll go much faster if you do, because I rarely touch this software. In fact, I wasn't even sure the cameras were still operating, but they are."

As a communications officer, Krista had often used surveillance software. Alex's system was a bit different but easy enough to figure out.

She started scanning the café video footage from midnight. Nothing for the first three hours, then a squad car pulled in. Officer José Rodriguez got out, toured the area to check on things, then returned to his car and drove away.

Nothing for the next three hours, then a black F-150 came tearing into the parking from the left off of Blue Ridge Drive.

Alex leaned in. "Is that Kim's truck? Looks like it, but what's she doing coming from that direction? She lives in Staunton."

Suddenly, Alex grew a lot more curious.

"Where did this murder take place, Krista?"

Krista felt as if she'd stepped on shaky ground. Emily had not given her much direction—check Alex's video and learn what she could. Emily had not said Krista should share details with Alex. If he were a regular citizen, Krista's decision would be clear. No sharing. In fact, she would have asked him to step outside while she reviewed the video. But Alex wasn't a regular citizen.

"Fairway Oaks Lane."

It took Alex two seconds to connect the dots. Someone driving from Fairway Oaks Lane to the café would enter the parking lot from the left.

"Is Kim a suspect in this murder investigation?" he asked.

"Honestly, I don't know. Nelson County's got the lead. We're in a support role."

"No way Kim Wiley murdered someone. I know Kim. We're friends. I've known her for years."

Okay. Krista had met Kim Wiley once or twice at the café when she stopped for coffee, but they weren't friends. Nevertheless, she found Alex's absolute certainty of Kim's innocence a bit naive. When Krista married her ex-husband, Tyler, at the age of twenty-two, she'd been absolutely sure they would love each other for eternity, but now, only fifteen years later, she no longer loved Tyler—that low-count cheating so-and-so. You could never know what was going on in another's person's mind. Kim Wiley had wildly wiry hair. Perhaps that signaled a suppressed psychopath lurking in the caverns of her brain. But Krista figured making that point to Alex would not advance her mission, and her criminology professor had warned her against initial impressions, so she did her best to keep her expression neutral.

Alex nodded as if he understood Krista's predicament. "Yeah. Let's keep scanning the video."

After parking her truck, Kim Wiley practically ran into the café. Nothing happened for ten minutes, but then Kim exited the café, got into her truck, and drove more slowly down the mountain to the left. Krista hazarded a glance at Alex.

He stared at the screen as if he could not believe his eyes. "Oh, Kim, what are you doing?"

Over the next ten minutes, several cars drove from left to right on Blue Ridge Drive, and one landscaping truck drove past in the opposite direction. Then Kim's truck returned, moving slowly now. After sitting in her parked truck for five minutes, Kim trudged into the café.

Krista paused the video. Alex continued to watch the screen, but Krista sensed his mind was far away.

"How did you say the victim was killed?" he asked.

Alex had left the acting chief position five months earlier. As far as Krista knew, he hadn't given the job another thought, but he was sure interested in this case.

"I don't know, Alex. Maybe you should ask Emily."

He nodded slowly. "Yeah, I'll do that."

For the sake of completeness, Krista fast-forwarded the video. Over the next two hours, traffic picked up on Blue Ridge Drive. Walkers crossed the parking lot to reach the fitness center across the way. At eight o'clock, Kim's nephew Nathan arrived for work. Customers started coming at ten o'clock. At eleven thirty, a Nelson County squad car passed from right to left. Then, a second squad car. Thirty minutes later, the two squad cars returned, and Undersheriff Arnie Shields and a deputy approached the café entrance.

SEVEN

Bill paced the living room while they waited for Soren Larsen. He and Mitch had refrained from doing a deep-dive search for fear of disturbing the crime scene. The state forensics team would arrive soon to do fingerprint dusting and so forth. Mitch kept John Hill company on the back porch. Then Mitch got a call from Emily and came inside. After Mitch had relayed what they'd found—not much—Emily gave him a quick update and asked to speak with Bill.

"It doesn't look good for Kim," Emily said, then she told Bill what Krista had discovered from the café surveillance footage.

Bill sensed Mitch watching him. Bill consciously tried to maintain neutral body language, but he couldn't resist gritting his teeth. His eyes darted to the slumped body on the back deck. What had happened here?

"Also," continued Emily, "Arnie asked Kim to come to the sheriff's office in Lovingston."

"What did she say?"

"Kim's going along with it so far."

"Did Arnie tell you anything else?"

Emily cleared her throat. "Not much."

Bill didn't push it. Emily was in a tough spot. She knew Bill was conflicted, given his friendship with Kim, and it was Arnie's investigation. Emily valued Bill's expertise; even so, she'd take care with what she told him now.

"Let me know what you learn from Soren," she said.

"Yeah. Bye."

At that moment, John Hill stepped in from the back deck.

"Hey, guys," he said.

Mitch and Bill stared at him.

"You need a potty break or something?" said Mitch.

"No, I thought I'd see what's going on."

"What's going on is a vulture on the railing is about to take a bite out of the victim. Oops. There he goes."

Hill retraced his steps in a hurry. After checking the body, he inspected the deck and the branches of nearby trees. Then he showed his fist to Mitch.

Mitch shook his head. "John has thin skin."

Bill chuckled. Cop humor. At the darkest moments, a practical joke went a long way to ease tension.

Someone made a noise at the front door.

"Yo! Anybody home?"

Soren Larsen, a medical examiner from Virginia's Western District Office in Roanoke, hustled into the main room. For his size—medium height and considerably overweight—Soren moved well. He shook Bill's hand and then studied Bill's face.

"Don't tell me," Soren said. "Bill something?"

"Bill O'Shea."

"From South Carolina."

"That's right."

"We have to stop meeting like this."

A small woman with dark hair followed Soren into the

room. She carried a kit bag. Bill recognized her as a state forensics analyst. Her name was Stowers.

After introductions, Soren said, "Okay, boys, where's the action?"

Mitch gestured to the back window.

Soren blinked several times. "Woohoo. You sure know how to party here in Wintergreen."

They all went onto the back deck. Stowers took photos of the scene, and the others stood out of the way. After several minutes, Stowers nodded at Soren, and he did his thing. Wearing gloves, he used two thermometers to test the body's temperature in several places. Then, Soren moved her arms to check for rigor mortis. Soren got down on his knees and studied her feet and ankles. Bill guessed he wanted to see how the blood had settled.

Bill hoped for a time-of-death estimate of between eight and nine a.m. This would put Kim in the clear, for she was back at the café by then.

Soren spent some time examining the victim's back. He observed the knife handle from all angles, then stood back and nodded.

"You have to give the murderer credit," he said. "That is one precise strike."

"Do you have a guess on the time of death?" said Bill.

Soren stood straight and feigned an indignant expression. "I don't guess. I estimate using a scientifically determined process." He studied his watch. "She died at approximately—and that's the guessing part—six a.m. I can confidently say that she passed between five and seven."

Damn. That is not good for Kim.

Soren turned his attention to the breakfast plate in front of the corpse. He lowered his nose to the plate and sniffed.

"Yum. That casserole still smells good six hours later. Can you imagine how it tasted fresh?"

Bill figured that for a rhetorical question.

"Is there any left?" Soren asked.

Bill looked at Mitch, who looked at John Hill in turn.

"Yeah," said Mitch. "Most of it is on the counter inside."

"Anyone claim it yet?" said Soren.

There was an awkward pause.

"Uh, no," said Mitch.

"What?" said Soren. "Hey, guys, the corpse is out here. There's nothing wrong with the food in there."

"Well," said Mitch, hesitating, "you're the forensics expert. Maybe you should ask the chief first, but if she's okay with it, then take it away."

"Oh, thanks fellas. You're the best."

"Are you going to do an autopsy?" said Bill.

"Definitely. We'll do it tonight. We know how she died, but we might find something useful for you guys. Stomach contents. Alcohol concentration. Drugs. Yeah, we'll do the whole salami, slice by slice."

A visual image that did nothing for Bill's stomach.

Officer Hill took off. Mitch and Bill stayed at the house to see if Larsen or Stowers turned up anything else of interest. So far, they had learned little about the victim. They knew her name. They had a locked laptop and no phone.

Two assistants arrived, and Soren directed them on how to move the body. Stowers was dusting for prints in the main bedroom. Mitch edged close to Bill in the living area.

"I'm curious about what's going through your mind," said Mitch.

"In what sense?"

"Do you believe Kim is innocent?"

Bill liked Mitch Gentry. Sometimes, he saw in Mitch a younger version of himself. Mitch was a patrolman with higher ambitions. The kid was smart, no question. They had worked on several investigations together, and Bill tried to give Mitch a few tips along the way. But this investigation was different.

"Innocent until proven guilty, right?"

"Sure, but the evidence is not helpful. The knife. The video."

"I believe she's innocent," said Bill. "Nevertheless, I sure would like to talk to her."

But that was Arnie's job. Bill wanted to call Kim and give her some free advice. Don't say a word. Hire a lawyer. But that would definitely cross the line into meddlesome territory. Arnie would be furious. No, before Bill could meet with Kim, she had to make the first move.

EIGHT

"So, you spent the night with Ms. Wolf," said Undersheriff Arnie Shields.

Kim Wiley sat across the table from him in a small white interview room at the sheriff's office in Lovingston. With pink-tinged eyes and a sad face, she looked a wreck. This might explain why Kim didn't question Arnie when he told her he was recording their conversation. He said he wanted to record information she shared that might help them find the killer. Kim had not objected. In Arnie's experience, criminals rarely did because they wanted to appear innocent.

When Arnie had told Kim the identity of the victim on the café's patio, Kim had fallen apart before his eyes. First shock, then denial, then an onset of grief he hadn't witnessed in some time. But was she truly grieving or marshaling a talented effort to avoid prosecution? Regardless, he had given her ten minutes to collect herself. Kim had asked if she could see the body. Not at this time. Perhaps later. Arnie had asked if she would come to the station. She eagerly agreed. Someone had murdered her girlfriend, and she was determined to help Arnie find the guilty party. He offered her a ride and said they would bring her back later. Kim considered his offer and declined. She would drive herself.

"Yes." Kim hesitated. "She was my girlfriend." Kim's lip trembled as if it nearly incapacitated her to refer to Lily Wolf in the past tense.

"Did you spend the night with her often?"

"I guess two or three times a week for the last month."

"What did you do last night?"

Kim rubbed her eyebrow. "I came over at six o'clock, and we had dinner. Take-out pizza and salad. We split a bottle of wine and watched a movie. Then we went to bed."

Arnie asked, "What movie did you watch?" A throwaway question to put her at ease.

"Um. That new Mission Impossible movie. Whatever it's called."

On the way over from Wintergreen, Emily Powell had called Arnie to share what they'd learned from the surveillance video. The sheriff was out of town for a week on business, so before meeting with Kim, Arnie had given the commonwealth's attorney an update. Craig Beaumont worked upstairs in the courthouse. Beaumont was new to the job, and Arnie had not worked closely with him on a big case. That would change now.

After the update, Beaumont had said to Arnie, "So, her knife was in the victim's back, you believe her truck knocked over the signpost, and you have video evidence of her driving from, to, and from the direction of the murder scene."

Arnie had nodded.

"Yes!" Beaumont made two fists and shook them close to his chest. "This is huge. And she's downstairs right now?"

"Uh-huh."

"Go get her, big boy."

Arnie studied Kim across the table. She chewed a fingernail, which, by the appearance of the other fingers on her hand, had not been chewed recently. He had reached the crucial point in the timeline but was determined to ease Kim into it. He would try to get her to reveal as much as possible before asking the question of no return.

"More coffee?" he said.

"No, I'm fine."

"What time did you get up this morning?" he said.

"I got up at five. I always get up early. Lily was asleep. I showered, dressed, and then made her a special breakfast. An egg casserole and a cinnamon roll. I planned to write her a note before leaving."

"You planned to? Did you speak with Lily this morning?"

Kim nodded reluctantly. "Yes, I did."

Arnie let the silence linger until it grew uncomfortable.

Kim fidgeted, then said, "We had a fight."

Arnie nodded casually, but his heart was racing. "What did you fight about?" He said the words calmly, as if having a fight under these circumstances was no big deal. Lovers fought all the time.

After a heavy sigh, Kim said, "She broke up with me." Kim wiped her eyes. "No warning at all. Just laid it out there. She said she was moving away and, uh, couldn't be with me anymore."

"Moving away? Did she say where?"

"No. Lily wouldn't give me any details. Said it was simply a fact. She had to move."

Arnie sat back in the chair and nodded to indicate they were making good progress. It was time to ease off a little bit. Kim had stated that she met Ms. Wolf six weeks earlier.

"We haven't found anything to help us contact Ms. Wolf's family. Are you in touch with her family? Or maybe a friend of hers, someone she knew before she came to Wintergreen?"

It turned out that Kim knew little about Lily Wolf's earlier life. She was from Europe, had spent her career there, and then moved to the US to make a change. Kim had no contacts from Lily's past. Arnie felt sorry for Kim. Wolf had come to town, seduced Kim, and then grew tired of her. Well, it appeared that Lily Wolf had pissed off the wrong girl.

Arnie said, "Are you aware of anyone who may have wanted to harm Ms. Wolf?"

Kim stared at him, her face a blank expression he found hard to read. At some point, Kim would realize how bad things looked for her, and then she would stop talking.

"No. I told you I don't know any of Lily's friends."

Better try a different tack.

Arnie held out a hand. "When Lily said she was leaving this morning, how did you feel?"

Kim studied the table. Her eyes appeared sad. "I was angry. I did not react well. But I didn't get it. Why did she have to leave?"

"I understand. What happened next?"

"I left."

Arnie rubbed his chin. "You said you didn't react well. What did you mean by that? What happened?"

Kim now adopted a suspicious expression. "Am I under arrest?"

"No."

"You think I did it, don't you?"

Arnie raised his eyebrows. "I'm trying to help. You want me to catch Ms. Wolf's killer, right?"

"Yes, of course."

"I need something to go on. We don't know much about

Ms. Wolf. We have her driver's license, and that's it. I was hoping you could give us something to work with."

"Okay. I get that." Kim heaved a sigh. "Truthfully, Lily and I were still in the early days of our relationship. I wanted to spend all of my time with her. I didn't want to meet her friends or family, not yet. We hiked on the AT. We drove on the parkway. We went to wineries and antique stores and cheese shops."

"Sounds like you had a fun time together."

"Yeah, it was great. And I didn't want to spoil it by digging up the past. I sensed she had some baggage she didn't want to discuss, and I didn't push it."

"Baggage? What sort of baggage?"

Kim shook her head. "I don't know. She said she was burned out from her corporate job. A bad boss with no integrity. A company with no scruples. She came to the US to get away from all of it."

"What was the company? What did she do?"

"I told you I didn't push it!" Kim's eyes flared.

Arnie raised his hands in a sign of peace. "Okay. Let's go back to this morning. You had a fight. You said some things you regret. And then you left."

"Yes."

"Where did you go?"

"I went to the café to get ready for the day."

"Did you see Ms. Wolf again after that?"

"No."

"So, you went to work at the café?"

"Yes."

"And you were there until I arrived?"

"Yes."

And that was it. Arnie had caught Kim in her first lie. But

he didn't use it against her. Not yet. He wanted to chat with Craig Beaumont first.

"How about we take a short break?" he said. "I could use it."

"Yeah. Okay. I could use some more coffee now. And I'd like to go to the restroom."

"You got it. I'll show you the way."

NINE

"I caught her in a lie," said Arnie.

"You did?" said Craig Beaumont. His eyes shone with excitement.

Few observers would call the Nelson County Courthouse opulent, but Beaumont's office was the exception. It was three times the size of Arnie's, with two large paned windows overlooking the courthouse lawn. Craig sat behind a giant and ancient desk that Arnie knew came with the office. Four large portraits of white men wearing suits from another era graced the walls. They were previous commonwealth's attorneys from Nelson County who had long since taken their last breath. Arnie didn't remember seeing the portraits on earlier visits to the office.

Craig Beaumont had grown up in Nelson County but didn't act like it. The son of a prominent farmer, Craig left the county after graduating from the local high school to attend the University of Virginia. After that, he studied law at one of the high-brow schools up north. Yale maybe? He had spent twelve years at the district attorney's office in Philadelphia, tough duty no doubt. Then, he returned to Nelson County to run for the commonwealth's attorney position. Word around the courthouse was that Craig had his eyes on higher office; however, Arnie had no hard evidence to support that rumor.

Beaumont indicated with his hand that Arnie should sit across the desk. "Tell me everything."

Craig relished Arnie's overview, especially the part about Kim fighting with Lily Wolf that morning.

"She said that?"

Arnie nodded.

"Heh, heh. We've got her now. Go on."

Beaumont's overt glee made Arnie nervous. They didn't have an airtight case. Sure, the circumstantial evidence against Kim was piling up, but they had no witness or confession. Also, forensics was still at the scene. They could find someone else's fingerprints on the knife. And to be honest, Arnie remained unsure of Kim's guilt. She had broken down upon hearing the news of Wolf's death. Only a cold-blooded killer with better-than-average acting skills could pull that off. On the other hand, mental factors might have played a role in Kim's behavior that morning. Arnie had ordered a background check on Kim but hadn't yet seen the details.

Arnie shared the rest of what he'd learned with Beaumont. Kim freely acknowledged spending the previous night with Wolf. Kim possessed limited knowledge of Lily Wolf's background. Their relationship was fresh, still in the infatuation stage. Then, he relayed the specifics of Kim's lying about not leaving the café.

"And we have video evidence of that?"

"Yes."

"Excellent." Craig stood and strolled across the office, then back. "So, Kim Wiley has a terrible fight with Wolf at the house, tears away in her truck, and goes to her café, where she retrieves her blue-handled knife. Wiley returns to Wolf's house and is astonished to find Wolf calmly eating breakfast on the back deck—a breakfast that Kim made Wolf with loving care. This incident so enrages Kim that she sneaks up behind Wolf and stabs her in the back."

"Something like that," said Arnie, although he saw two flaws with Beaumont's re-enactment. It wouldn't have been easy for Kim to sneak onto the back deck without Lily hearing her. Also, although Arnie had claimed they caught Kim in a lie, the only evidence they had was that she had left the café again.

Craig resumed pacing and said, "What did she say about the knife?"

"Earlier, she admitted that she owns a set of blue-handled knives, but I haven't brought the subject up since. I was saving that for my next session."

"Good strategy. All right, get back in there. Wrap Wiley up in her own words."

Craig had crossed the width of the office several times. Now, he paused to admire the portrait of a former commonwealth's attorney. Craig nodded as if he could see his future. Arnie suspected the rumors about Craig were true.

"Should we call the sheriff?" said Arnie.

Interrupted from his reverie, Beaumont turned toward Arnie and frowned.

"I don't see why. You know what to do. Get her to talk before she asks for a lawyer who'll put a gag in her mouth. And whatever you do, don't let her go. I want you to arrest her today."

Truthfully, Arnie had already called the sheriff and left an urgent message on his voicemail. This was a big deal, and Craig was a young commonwealth's attorney. Sure, he knew the big city ways, but this was Nelson County.

"Are you sure?" said Arnie. "It would be good to get the sheriff's take."

"If you want to call Daddy," said Craig, "call Daddy. But you don't need to. What you need to do is go back down there and get her confession."

TEN

Arnie sat behind his desk to collect his thoughts before going back in with Kim Wiley. He had called the sheriff again on the way down from Beaumont's office. No luck. Arnie couldn't afford to piddle around, because Kim Wiley was free to go anytime she chose. Sooner or later, she would fully comprehend her predicament and leave. Arnie had to arrest her before that happened. He had only arrested a suspect for murder one other time, and that had been a clear-cut case. One meth addict had killed another meth addict over a forty-dollar dispute, and Arnie had a first-hand witness.

This time was definitely different.

Arnie ran his hands down his face. Sheesh. What a job. His wife had urged him once to leave law enforcement and go into construction. If he had, he might now be a general contractor whose most significant issue was finding and keeping skilled craftsmen. But that cruise ship had left the port long ago. And frankly, Arnie had no regrets. He felt good about his contribution to Nelson County. His job was to keep the community safe. And one of the ways he did that was by arresting criminals and ensuring they were found guilty. Better get to it.

Kim Wiley's appearance had improved by the time Arnie re-entered the interview room. He again mentioned that their conversation was being recorded, and she did not protest.

"I've been sitting here thinking," she said. "Lord knows I want to help you find the killer, but I don't know how. I've racked my brain, but I have no idea who killed Lily."

"Okay. Thanks. I may have an idea." Arnie studied Kim's expression. "You'll recall I asked if you owned a blue-handled knife this morning. I asked that because we found a blue-handled knife at the crime scene."

Arnie detected no surprise or concern on Kim's face. She half shrugged.

"Yeah, so what? I took some utensils to Lily's rental house. I wanted to cook for Lily, and the knives there were so dull they wouldn't cut Jello. I used my knife this morning to chop onions and mushrooms for the breakfast casserole. I left it on the counter."

"That's not where we found it."

Kim sneered and said, "All right. Where did you find it? The dish drainer?"

Arnie leaned forward and stared at Kim.

What kind of game is she playing?

The sneer dropped off of Kim's face. She blinked several times. "Wait, are you saying . . . someone used my—"

"Lily Wolf was stabbed in the back with your knife."

Kim's mouth dropped in horror. She stammered, "My knife? They used my knife?"

Arnie nodded. "Yes. *They* used *your* knife."

She held up a hand. "Hold on a second. You believe I killed her. You think I killed Lily."

"Did you kill her? Did you do it, Kim?"

"No. How can you say that?"

"You were there. You had a fight. Things got out of control."

"No. No. I didn't kill Lily. I loved her. I told you that."

Kim had understandably grown tense. Arnie intentionally relaxed his arms and chest muscles. He adopted a sad smile. "Stuff happens, I know. I've seen it many times. It would be best if you told me what happened. How it went down. Do that, and I promise to get you the best deal possible."

She shook her head emphatically. "No. I . . . I didn't do that. I'm not perfect. I've done some stupid stuff, but I could never. I loved her."

"Kim, come on now. We know you did it. You said you drove to the café and stayed there, but we have video footage of you returning to the house. Why did you lie? You lied because you went back to the house to kill her. Now, take a deep breath and tell me what happened."

"No. This conversation is over. I'm leaving."

"You can't leave."

"Why not?"

"Because I'm arresting you on suspicion of the murder of Lily Wolf."

As Arnie recited the Miranda warning, Kim's face turned from concern to fury. Arnie couldn't blame her. He had tried to trick her by pretending he needed her help to find the real killer. No more pretending. Now Kim knew where she stood. But Arnie remained troubled. Did he know where he stood? He still wasn't one hundred percent certain of Kim's guilt. Ninety percent? Eighty percent? Probably.

One thing he knew for sure: Kim would never trust him again.

"I want a lawyer," she said.

ELEVEN

Bill and Mitch sat at the kitchen table to eat a late lunch. Earlier, Bill realized he was starving and drove down to the Market for sandwiches. He would have stopped at Café Devine, which was closer, but the police had temporarily closed the café. While Bill was gone, the forensics team finished their preliminary work and left the house.

Mitch must have been hungry too. He ate the first half of his sandwich without saying a word, and it was a big sandwich, a twelve-inch Italian with extra meat. Then he said, "We don't have much to show for two hours of searching this place, do we?"

"No."

"We have a name. We know she was planning to leave. And not much more."

"I imagine Emily has asked someone to do a background search."

Mitch, who had taken a huge bite of the second half of his sandwich, chewed massively, wiped his mouth with a napkin, and then said, "She gave it to the new kid, Brendan."

"I don't think I've met Brendan."

"He's only been with us two weeks. Straight out of school. Bit of a smart-ass, but I gather he's good with tech."

"He should be able to run a background check with no problem."

Mitch nodded. "You know what Emily said? She told me to stay right here and search this place until I found something of value. 'There has to be something,' she said. 'Find a password for the laptop or something else we can use.'"

"Okay. Sounds fair."

"Yeah, but we've been searching for two-plus hours. What if I don't find anything else? Am I supposed to stay here all night? I found her driver's license, for chrissakes."

"Mitch, it was in her purse in the living room. That's not exactly like finding the Titanic."

"What's the Titanic have to do with this?"

Mitch had something on his mind. Even a bat could sense that. During the search, he had wandered around the house and checked the same places repeatedly: bookshelves, drawers, behind the sofa cushions. A third grader would have found the driver's license in three minutes. Bill knew Mitch had talent. Heck, Mitch had once discovered a hidden compartment in a pencil holder. Now, that was clever.

"Have you looked in the attic yet?" said Bill.

Mitch's eyebrows dropped. "This place has an attic?"

"The hideaway stairs are in the hallway." Bill pointed toward the upstairs balcony, where the pull cord was clearly visible.

Mitch shook his head. "I've been distracted."

"What's going on?"

"I shouldn't tell you."

Fair enough. Bill wouldn't pry, but he would take long odds that it was personal, something to do with Mitch and Lulu. He hoped it wasn't bad news. Bill had attended Mitch and Lulu's wedding three months earlier. They should still be in the constant-hugs-and-kisses phase, total adoration.

"Lulu's pregnant," said Mitch.

"Oh. Congratulations. That's excellent news."

Mitch and Lulu weren't wasting any time. Bill believed in the old adage that young couples should wait at least a year. He and Wanda– his ex-wife—had waited two years.

"Yeah," said Mitch. "We both want a family but hadn't planned to start this early."

"I see," said Bill.

Lulu had recently enrolled in a four-year dental school program. She and Mitch both had hour-long commutes from their home in Charlottesville.

"No problem," said Bill. "You guys are young. And frankly, with Lulu's career, there will never be a convenient time. That's how it was with Wanda and me. She was a lawyer. When the kids were little, it was nonstop action. But you figure it out."

"Yeah. Figure it out." Mitch rubbed his cheek, then nodded. "After lunch, I'll search the attic."

Then Bill's cell phone buzzed, an unfamiliar number with a local area code.

"Hello?"

"Is this Bill O'Shea?"

A man named Mark Gardner—Kim Wiley's newly retained attorney—had called Bill on Kim's behalf. Apparently, Gardner was a friend of Kim's family.

"What's your deal?" said Gardner. "Are you a private investigator?"

From his tone of voice, Bill gathered that Gardner's conversation with Kim had left Gardner skeptical of Bill's credentials.

"Ah, no. I'm a retired homicide detective from Columbia, South Carolina. I live in Wintergreen now."

"I got that much. It's the next part that leaves me scratching my head. Are you working with the police now?"

"Hold on."

Bill whispered to Mitch that he would take the call outside. Mitch had taken another massive bite of his sandwich. His big jaws ground the food, and his eyes followed Bill to the door.

Once on the deck, Bill explained to Gardner that he had assisted Wintergreen in the past and that Emily had asked for his help with this investigation. Having said that, he knew his friendship with Kim left him in a conflicted position.

"I'll say," said Mark Gardner.

"What did Kim tell you about what happened?"

"I'm not going to share that with you. It's privileged. And I'm still trying to figure out whose side you're on."

"I'm definitely on Kim's side. But continuing to work with the Wintergreen PD might be of value at some point. Right?"

"You're straddling a feisty pony, O'Shea. And I don't want Kim to get trampled."

"I need to speak with her to find out what happened. Didn't she ask for me? That's why you called."

"Yes. But are you going to tell the police everything Kim tells you?"

Gardner made an excellent point. If Bill participated in the investigation, he might discover something that proved Kim's guilt. What would Bill do then? He'd feel obligated to share that intel with Emily, but doing so would hurt Kim. Gardner had figured that out in three seconds.

On the other hand, if Kim was innocent, his experience might help Emily, and Arnie, identify the real killer. He rode a feisty pony, indeed. But Bill still wanted to confer with Kim, so he made a deal with himself: If at any point during his conversation with Kim, he got the impression that she *might* be guilty, he would leave the room at once and let everyone else sort it out. This deal, tenuous though it was, gave Bill the confidence he needed to deal with Gardner.

"Kim asked for me," Bill said, "and you can't keep me from talking to her."

"Perhaps not," said Gardner, "but I'm going to be in the room the whole time."

"Fine by me."

TWELVE

Bill met Kim and Mark Gardner in a small white room in the regional jail in Charlottesville. How often had Bill entered a small white room to meet with a suspect? Countless times. But never before had he opened that door as an advocate for the defense.

Kim—appearing every bit the broken woman trying to put on a good face—burst into tears when she saw Bill. Bill strode to her, opened his arms, and gave her a huge hug. She buried her face against his shoulder and wrapped her arms around his neck. He held her that way for a long time until he finally sensed tension leaving her body. She pulled away and wiped a hand across both eyes.

"Oh, Bill, what a damn mess."

Bill turned to shake Mark Gardner's hand. Gardner was a tall, thin black man in his late fifties who wore a dark gray suit with a white shirt and a navy and red regimental tie. What was left of the hair on his head—not much—was tinged gray, as were his neatly trimmed mustache and beard.

After they sat, Mark gave them some advice. "This conversation is not covered by the attorney-client privilege because Bill is acting as a third party. We should assume someone is listening and the camera is rolling."

Bill nodded. "I've been on the other side of that trick."

Kim and Bill exchanged small talk. Bill apologized for not knowing that Kim had been in a relationship. Kim said she had wanted to keep it quiet so she could have Lily all to herself. Bill asked Kim to share what she had told Arnie that morning, and Kim relayed their three interactions, first at the café and then at the sheriff's office. Bill asked her to tell him what she could about Lily's past, which was not much.

"That's it?" he said. "Weren't you curious?"

"It became clear that Lily didn't want to share many details from her past. She mentioned living in Moscow a few times, so she might have been Russian. But she lived in Western Europe for a while too, and she spoke several languages, German and French for sure. Perhaps others."

"How about on your side?" said Bill. "Did she meet some of your family or friends? She must have met Nathan."

"Yes. Lily met Nathan a few times when she came by the café. Also, I introduced her to my sister, Jessica. The three of us had dinner in Staunton."

"Anything else?"

Kim pressed her lips tightly together. She glanced at Mark Gardner, and he nodded.

"There is something else. I didn't mention this to Shields because I forgot about it. Early on, Lily told me she was delighted to meet at least one good person in Wintergreen. I asked her what she meant, and she said she had met a man at the Edge one night and that the two of them had hung out a few times. She found him amusing at first but then grew irritated with him."

"Did she give you a name?"

"No."

Bill frowned. With a name, he'd at least have someone else to interview. "How did this guy irritate her?"

"He was wealthy and wore his riches all the time. Too clever. Too smart. No soul."

Bill asked Kim if she knew anything else to help them find this man. Kim considered the question but came up short.

"Have you seen someone driving a red sports car lately?"

"Not specifically. Of course, I've seen red sports cars, but not recently."

Thus far, Kim had said nothing that made Bill believe she was guilty. First impression? Wrong place at the wrong time. He couldn't think of anything else to ask her except the direct question. If he asked Kim whether she had killed Lily Wolf, he knew her face would tell him the truth. But what would he do if her face said she was guilty?

"We have a little problem," said Gardner. He explained that Kim had lied to Shields about leaving Café Devine after she'd first returned. Shields had recorded that lie.

"Did you go back to the house?" asked Bill.

Kim hunched her shoulders. "Yes. I went to apologize because I tried to slap her. Also, I sent her awful texts after our fight."

"Did you see her when you went back?"

"Only briefly. Lily met me at the door but didn't ask me in. After hearing me out, she said, 'Apology accepted,' and closed the door. That was the last time I saw her."

Bill recreated the scene in his mind. The first time Kim left, she was hurt and angry enough to take out the signpost. But upon returning, she was contrite. Still, Lily wouldn't let her in. Why?

"Where is your phone now?" he said.

"The police have it, but it's locked. Shields asked me for

the passcode. I told him I wanted to consult with Mark first."

"Atta girl," said Mark.

Kim had said she sent awful texts. Bill wondered how awful they were, then said, "We didn't find Lily's phone at the house. Did you take it?"

Kim shook her head.

Maybe Lily had hidden her phone in the house. Or perhaps the real killer took the phone. Why? Because something on the phone incriminated them?

"You said you *tried* to slap Lily. What happened?"

"She swatted my hand away. I don't know what she did because it happened so fast. In an instant, she had my arm wrenched behind my back. I thought she might break my arm. It hurt like hell."

Strange. Lily Wolf had some fight training. The victim grew more mysterious all the time.

"Why don't you ask me the question, Bill?" said Kim. "I can see it on your face. You want to ask if I killed her."

"Don't ask that question," said Mark.

"I didn't kill her," said Kim. "I swear it, Bill. I didn't kill her. I loved her, pure and simple. Even now . . ." Kim teared up and had to stop for a moment.

"I believe you," said Bill. "I believe you're innocent, and we're going to get you out of here."

But as far as Bill could see, Kim didn't care about prison.

"They can lock me up," she said. "What's the difference?"

"Don't say that. You don't want to go to prison for something you didn't do."

"That's not what matters," she said. Rage filled Kim's eyes. She pointed in the general direction of Wintergreen. "Someone up there killed Lily Wolf, my girlfriend. And I want you to find them."

THIRTEEN

Bill said to Arnie Shields, "We need to find another suspect, because Kim Wiley didn't do it."

After meeting with Kim, Bill had conferred with her defense attorney, Mark Gardner, and they hatched a plan to gather intel at the courthouse in Lovingston. Bill would meet with the undersheriff, and Mark would try to see the commonwealth's attorney.

Bill now sat across the desk from Arnie. Arnie had a small office and had left the door open. Down the short hallway, two deputies chatted in an open office bullpen.

"When you say *we,* who are you referring to? Last time I checked, you were a private citizen."

By his expression, Arnie was in no mood for BS. Bill could understand that—Arnie had a high-profile case on his desk and an eager prosecutor upstairs, and the sheriff was out of town.

"I meant the larger law enforcement community. Sure, I'm retired, but I'm still a Brotherhood member. And *we* all want justice, right?"

"Hmpf."

"Lily Wolf was Russian. For all we know, she was murdered by Russian mobsters."

Arnie snorted. "You seen any Russian mobsters lately? This is Nelson County, not the big city."

He had a point. Bill was making stuff up now. Never in his long career had he confronted an actual Russian mobster. That kind of stuff happened a lot more on television than it did in real life. Still, Lily Wolf didn't stab herself with the knife. If Kim was innocent, someone else was guilty.

Arnie said, in a slightly more sympathetic voice, "I understand Kim is your friend. It's hard to see good friends do bad things, but I can't manufacture a suspect. You see Russian mobsters. I see Bigfoot. But the case will be won with hard evidence and the testimony of witnesses. The circumstantial evidence is stacking high against Kim. One more piece and the whole stack's coming down around her head."

"Okay, Arnie, fair enough. I'll find another suspect who's not a Russian mobster. But do me a favor—let me assist Emily's guys on the mountain. You know I've done a lot more of this than they have, and we work well together."

Bill learned then that Arnie's eyes could grow hard. They bored into Bill. Arnie chewed his lip, then said, "That's Emily's call, for now." Arnie pointed at Bill. "But if you find one piece of evidence implicating Kim, you'd better play it straight, or I'll toss you off one of the overlooks you have up there."

Bill found that image unsettling. Arnie had a dark side. He was a good sport, but Bill had better watch his step.

Mark Gardner sat in a chair opposite Craig Beaumont and studied the wall portraits. By their attire, Mark guessed the men had served as commonwealth's attorneys in the1920s and '30s—not a great time to be a black person in America. At least these guys were post-Civil War.

On the other side of the desk, Craig typed on his keyboard, finishing a thought, or so he had claimed when he asked Mark to give him a moment. Now, Craig stopped typing, placed his hands on his desk, and smiled.

"So, you're representing Kim Wiley. I don't envy you. At least it promises to be a short trial."

"The investigation has hardly begun. To speak of trial dynamics at this point seems premature."

Craig shrugged. "We have a lot of evidence. It's her knife. She admits they had a fight. And she lied about returning to the house."

"You haven't established that Ms. Wiley returned to the house, only that she left the café again."

The prosecutor shook his head, not impressed. "How do you think the jury will read it?"

They would read the evidence precisely as Beaumont portrayed—that Kim had gone to her café in a furious state, grabbed the first weapon she saw, the blue-handled knife, and returned to kill Lily Wolf. What would forensics analysis reveal? If the knife contained traces of breakfast residue, that would lend credibility to Kim's claim that she brought it to the rental home earlier.

"Have you considered what charges you'll bring?"

Beaumont nodded enthusiastically. "Oh yeah, I'm going for it all. Murder in the first degree."

Some prosecutors worked hard to balance the crime and the punishment. Others cared for only one thing—their prosecution record. Beaumont struck Mark as the latter type. On its face, a first-degree murder charge was inconsistent with the hypothesis that an enraged Kim decided on the spur of the moment to kill her lover. Beaumont would realize that if he gave it more than a few seconds of consideration.

"Maybe we can push the arraignment hearing a few days," said Mark.

"Why would I do that?"

"Give the investigation more time to play out. I would agree to that."

"This thing's open and shut. I don't need more time. Now, if your client were open to a plea deal up front, then perhaps I could see my way to a lesser charge, but the agreed sentence would be steep. Say, twenty years without parole?"

Yeah, Beaumont knew he couldn't get murder one with the evidence he had, so he was already positioning for murder two. Hmm. It might not be the worst outcome, but Kim would never take it. Mark felt sure of that.

"Twenty years is mighty steep," he said.

Craig lifted a hand. "Murder is an awful thing. She'll need time to reform."

"I'll take it to her," said Mark. "But I wouldn't get your hopes up. She's innocent."

"Don't they all say that?"

"What bail amount will you recommend to the magistrate?"

"Bail? For murder one? No, sir."

"Kim's a solid citizen. She owns a business, and she's not going anywhere. Everything she has is here—her family, her business."

"Maybe she should have thought of that before she killed Lily Wolf."

Mark's right-hand fingers tapped their left counterparts.

Kim had told him she didn't have the financial wherewithal to post a big bail or pay a bondsman. She'd rather sit in jail.

"I still believe you should wait a few days," said Mark. "A young prosecutor like you, who puts it all out there. If it doesn't work out, you'll look silly. You know?"

Craig smiled. "I'm in a hurry. I have a big, new belt in need of a notch."

Bill and Mark Gardner stood on the courthouse's covered porch. It was a quiet day in Lovingston. Then again, Bill supposed almost every day was peaceful in Lovingston. It was a small town on the side of US Route 29 between Charlottesville and Lynchburg. Drivers who sped past on the four-lane highway hardly noticed it.

"Beaumont is a hard guy to like," said Mark. "Not big on compromise."

Bill had met prosecutors like that and didn't much care for them. Justice was a complicated process that required a lot of people to work together. When all players tried to understand the situation from the opposing team's perspective, reasonable outcomes prevailed. But my-way-or-the-highway yahoos tended to make things hard for everybody.

"What did you learn from the undersheriff?" said Mark.

"Arnie's all right. He thinks Kim is guilty, but he'll let me work with the Wintergreen folks."

"You'd better find something."

"That bad, huh?"

Mark nodded. "I could tell from the conversation with Kim that you now believe she's innocent. Good for you. I'll represent her either way. Here's my take so far—with the circumstantial evidence Beaumont has right now, eight out of ten juries would find her guilty of murder two."

"Eighty percent."

"Uh-huh. Perhaps higher. So, get up there and find something."

FOURTEEN

Brendan Baittinger thought it was cool when he started working for the Wintergreen Police Department, but after a few weeks, he wasn't so sure. His title was Communications Officer, which involved working as a dispatcher, dealing with boring paperwork, and doing occasional online research. He had to admit that handling dispatch calls was exciting. Callers were often jacked up over something that had happened. They stammered their words, and Brendan puffed up with pride as he calmed them down, got the facts, and determined what needed to be done. Then, *he* made the rescue happen by dispatching the necessary resources. He was the man.

Yeah, that part was all right, but the team? Oh boy. Less than impressive.

The chief? Emily Powell? Well, uncool summed it up. Emily knew her stuff; that wasn't a problem, but she had a husband and three—count them—three little kids. Heck, most of the time, she had dark circles under her eyes. Get some sleep, how about it.

Krista Jackson? Attractive, no question, particularly for a

woman of her age. She must be in her mid-thirties or something, with two kids in their teens. Krista had trained Brendan, which was cool, being close to a woman with long red hair and an attractive figure. But the content? Well, he picked that up in thirty minutes.

Mitch Gentry? Big guy. Lots of muscles. Not long on conversation. It was hard to sort out where Mitch stood on the IQ chart. Not as high as Brendan, certainly, but then, few people managed to scale those heights.

All in all, Brendan guessed he was unlikely to last much longer at Wintergreen. Not the right place for him. Honestly, he had to blame himself for landing there. He had accepted his first offer and stopped looking for anything more. At the time, he thought, beautiful scenery, decent pay, and low cost of living. This could work. But after a few weeks on the job, not so much.

But then there was a murder on the mountain.

Now, this is different.

The police station was now the scene for a lot of action, with people moving quickly from one place to the next. Brendan had run standard background checks on the victim, Lily Wolf, and found nothing. No police record. The bank had issued her credit card recently, and he could find no evidence that she had another card. He couldn't even find a Lilian Wolf with her birth date in the social security system. But then again, she wouldn't have one if she were a foreigner. Social media searches had turned up numerous women with the same name, and Brendan had barely started reviewing those when he got a special assignment from Emily.

She stood over his cubicle, in uniform, coffee in hand.

"I need you to do something." This was not a request. Her voice said it was important, and she needed his best.

"What, chief?"

"Locate the owner of this residence. Contact them. Ask them about their current tenant—Lily Wolf. Wolf has stayed in that house for several months. Find out whatever you can."

"Yes, ma'am."

A single call to the property owners' association had secured the owner's phone number. The area code was Northern Virginia. Brendan called and got the owner on the line, an elderly woman named King. Brendan identified himself and explained the situation.

"My tenant is not Lily Wolf," said Ms. King.

"No?"

"No. My tenant is a company—Atlantic Engineering Advisors. They've rented my house for the last three years."

Brendan typed notes as he listened.

Ms. King continued. "I haven't even visited Wintergreen in all that time. I have a property manager who handles maintenance and so forth."

"Were you aware that Ms. Wolf was staying at your home?"

"Yes. Atlantic Engineering uses the house for executive sabbaticals. They send me a note whenever a new executive comes to stay. The company is quite reliable. They pay their rent via ACH on the fourth day of every month."

"So, you haven't met Ms. Wolf."

"Oh, no. I wouldn't recognize her if I ran into her at the grocery store."

Brendan typed Atlantic Engineering Advisors into his search window. No website. He'd do a deeper search after the call.

"Have you met someone from the company?"

"No. I spoke with someone before Atlantic rented the house. Can't remember the name. They found me through the short-term rental listing and paid six months' rent up front."

Brendan asked Ms. King if she could send him a copy of the contract.

"By mail?" Ms. King asked.

"No, could you scan it, please?"

"I don't have a scanner."

"Perhaps you could text me a photo of the signature page."

"Oh, sure. I can do that."

The signature page contained a name—John Thomas. After the call with Ms. King, Brendan searched Virginia state records. He found an Atlantic Engineering Advisors LLC with a named President—Robert Johnson—and an address in Richmond. But after spending another hour banging on the internet, Brendan had learned nothing more.

FIFTEEN

"I want to keep working as part of the team," said Bill.

On the way back from Lovingston, Bill had stopped by the Wintergreen police station, and he now sat across from Emily at her desk. Behind Emily, a large monitor displayed views from a rotating series of surveillance cameras. Bill recognized the Wintergreen entrance and several other locations.

Emily studied him carefully. "I'm generally the one asking for help. Have the tables turned?"

"I met with Kim, and I believe her story. She's innocent."

Emily rubbed her chin. "And yet, the evidence points in another direction."

What would Bill do if their roles were reversed? Would he allow Emily to work a case if she was good friends with the prime suspect? Probably not. On the other hand, Bill knew Emily did not relish the sheriff's department wandering all over Wintergreen searching for clues. He was an extra set of experienced eyes she could use.

"Did you get to meet Pretty Boy Beaumont?" she asked. Her lip curled.

"No, but Kim's attorney did. He's not a fan of the new commonwealth's attorney."

"I'm not surprised."

"I gather you two have met."

Emily's snarl grew uglier. "Nelson County High, class of '99."

"Want to tell me the story?"

"I guess I'm dying to tell someone. In my junior year, Craig dated my best friend, Georgia Longtree. He treated her nicely because he wanted something. Follow me?"

"I do."

"Georgia told me that Craig loved her and wanted to marry her. I urged caution, and that worked for a while. But then summertime came, with all the short clothes and hot nights. Craig got what he wanted. After that, Georgia stumbled around goo-goo-eyed. She had no time for me."

Bill shook his head, not sure he wanted to hear the rest.

Emily said, "When the summer neared its end, Craig dropped her. I don't know whether he grew bored or couldn't resist the opportunity to hurt someone else. Maybe both. Georgia was never the same. Didn't want to study. Didn't want to hang out. She missed a lot of school. Then she started running with a different crowd, an older bunch from Lynchburg. Never made it to the spring prom. I haven't seen Georgia in twenty years. Not sure I'd even recognize her."

"He sounds like a jackass."

"The understatement of the year."

"From what Kim's attorney told me, Beaumont smells opportunity. He's confident he will put Kim away for a long time."

Which was kind of a cheap shot for Bill to take. Emily tells him why she hates Beaumont, and Bill tells her how she can ruin Beaumont's day. Well, Emily was smart. She'd see right through that. Maybe.

Emily paused, sat back, and crossed her arms. "If I let you continue to work on the investigating team, what will you do if you find evidence that hurts Kim's case?"

"That's what Arnie asked. If I find something of that sort, I'll bring it right to you. But that doesn't worry me because she's innocent."

What concerned Bill was the risk of not finding evidence to implicate someone else. He needed another plausible suspect. And the best place for him to search for a suspect was in Lily Wolf's past. He asked Emily what they had learned.

"Not much at all. I put Brendan on it."

"Brendan's the new guy?"

"Yep. He's still figuring out his life, but he's good with the tech."

Emily shared what Brendan had discovered about the house owner and the corporate tenant.

Bill said, "The two names were John Thomas and Robert Johnson? Those are very generic names."

"Brendan said there are more than a thousand Robert Johnsons on LinkedIn."

"You think it's a cover for something dirty?"

She shrugged. "I'm sharing Lily Wolf's photo with the Wintergreen community to source leads. She must have known someone besides Kim."

"That's good." Bill checked his phone for the time, after five o'clock. "What's everybody up to now?"

"I sent Mitch home and asked him to come back early tomorrow. He actually found something."

Bill looked up. "The phone?"

"No. In the bottom of Wolf's backpack, he found an interior surveillance kit with four small Wi-Fi cameras, the kind people use to spy on their nannies."

"Seems an odd possession for a minimalist."

"I agree. Anyway, Mitch is inspired. He said he's taking the rental house down to the studs."

"Good boy."

"Krista was bummed that she had to do rounds all afternoon. But someone's got to do the work. She wanted to stay after, so I sent her up to the café."

To look for what?

Then it occurred to him. Emily had sent Krista to the café to search for Lily's phone. If Kim Wiley murdered Lily, she might have thought to steal Lily's phone. If so, Kim might have brought the phone to the café and not had the opportunity to move it before the undersheriff showed up. Krista finding the phone at the café would gift-wrap a conviction for Craig Beaumont.

"You're never going to find that phone," said Bill.

"No?"

"The real murderer took the phone, ripped out the SIM card, and buried it in the woods."

"Yeah? Then Krista won't find it."

SIXTEEN

Café Devine sat forlorn. The parking lot was empty except for two vehicles, one of them Krista's squad car. Even the black bear statue out front appeared in low spirits. Someone, probably Nathan, had erected a crude sign next to the driveway: *Temporarily Closed.*

Once inside, Bill grabbed Nathan for a chat on the patio. He didn't see Krista.

"It's been a crappy day," said Nathan. "The cops shut us down and have been in and out nonstop. They say I can open tomorrow, but I can't run this place myself. Aunt Kim doesn't make much money as it is. I don't know how many days like this her bank account can handle."

"What kind of help do you need?"

Nathan scoffed at Bill's question. "Word travels fast up here. No one wants to help us now."

"You might be surprised. What do you need?"

Nathan held up a finger. "First off, someone to help me cook before we open in the morning. That's when the heavy lifting gets done. After that, I can manage the kitchen alone, but I need someone on the register who can handle coffee orders."

Bill pursed his lips. Cindy would help unless she had a conflicting catering engagement. Maybe a few others. Bill asked Nathan what time he would start. Seven o'clock. Bill told Nathan to show up at that time the next day; meanwhile, Bill would try to arrange some help.

"Now, switching subjects," said Bill. "What can you tell me about Lily Wolf?"

Nathan shook his head. "Not much. Aunt Kim's been hanging out with her a lot, but it's not like they invited me to come along. Ms. Wolf and I haven't exchanged more than ten words. My mom met her, though. Aunt Kim and Lily had dinner with Mom in Staunton. Mom didn't say much about that dinner. I got the impression it didn't go well."

"How so?"

Nathan shifted in his chair, perhaps worried he'd said something he shouldn't. "Not a big deal, I guess, but Mom believed Lily was stuck up."

"Stuck up?"

"Yeah. And disingenuous. Mom said that too."

Okay. Bill would add Kim's sister to his interview list. Kim had mentioned her sister once or twice, but Bill couldn't remember her name.

"What was Kim like recently?" said Bill.

"You mean like happy or sad?"

"Yeah. Start there."

Nathan grinned. "She was happy. Happier than I've seen her in a long time. This relationship was good for her. You know. Up until today."

The relationship was good, and Kim was happy. Bopping along, thinking everything was fine, until Lily body-slammed her. No wonder Kim got mad.

"What's going to happen to Aunt Kim?" said Nathan.

Nathan was a tall young man with broad shoulders and a soft voice. He was more worried about his aunt than his job. Heck, a good support chef like Nathan could find a new job in a week. The least Bill could do was bring some confidence to the situation.

"We'll find the real killer, and then your Aunt Kim will be free."

"Just like that, huh?"

Bill nodded. "Yep. Just like that."

Upon re-entering the store, Bill found Krista scrutinizing the wine racks.

"Hey, what's up?" he said.

Bill enjoyed working with Krista. She had much to learn regarding police procedures, but she was young, determined, and a great team player. When he first met Krista, she had been single. There had been a confusing moment when Krista thought they might become a romantic thing, but it was a crazy notion because they were in different stages of life. He had more than twenty years on her. Also, she had middle school and high school kids, and his kids were grown and gone. Still, she was fun to work with and was now dating an FBI special agent who lived in northern Virginia.

Krista said, "I searched the kitchen, the tiny office, and the event dining space without finding anything. So, I'm in the store now."

"I seriously doubt you're going to find Lily Wolf's phone."

"Oh, good. I'll tell the chief I don't have to do the work *she wants me to do.*"

Bill raised his hands to surrender. "Don't shirk your duty. But could I offer one suggestion?"

"I live for your sage wisdom."

"Nice. You wear sarcasm well."

"Thanks."

Bill's eyes were distracted by the Spanish red section. He lifted a bottle of Tempranillo. Forty-five dollars. A bit pricey. But he could really use a nice glass of wine.

"You're going to make me wait for this?" said Krista.

"Sorry. Here's what I'm thinking. Hypothetically, if I were Kim and I had killed Lily Wolf and I was stealing her phone, I wouldn't hide it in the store, the kitchen, the tiny office, or the event dining space. I'd hide it outside."

"Outside? Exposed to the elements?"

"Inside, it would be too easy for someone else—like Nathan—to discover the phone. Not good." He pointed in an upward direction through a nearby window. The sky had not been threatened by a single cloud all day. "Nice weather. Kim would have hidden the phone outside where no one would stumble across it. Then, she would have retrieved it at the end of the day."

Krista's eyes traced a path through the store and the kitchen. In the back, another door led outside. "You're not as slow-witted as you look."

Bill shrugged. "Just saying."

SEVENTEEN

As usual, Max greeted Bill at the door of his condo. Max's tail wagged furiously, and Bill sat on the couch to let the Labrador retriever lick his hands. What on earth had he done to deserve the companionship of such a magnificent animal? Max loved Bill and would show his love by lying in his bed and watching Bill for hours. His soulful brown eyes expressed his love more powerfully than words ever could.

Bill patted Max on the chest and then sat back on the couch, exhausted. He wanted nothing more than to shower and relax, but a knock sounded at the door. Cindy.

Cindy was dressed in cute shorts, sandals, and a short-sleeved top. Her lips formed a mischievous grin, and her eyes twinkled. Bill felt less intelligent than he had the moment before.

"What?" he said.

"Did you forget something?"

"Forget what?"

Cindy laughed, big chuckles that shook her shoulders. Her whole face lit up. "You do know how ridiculous that sounds."

Bill wanted to kiss her, but at the same time, he'd feel like a dumbass as soon as he recalled what he'd forgotten. He racked his brain.

"Oh, no," he said, then he checked the microwave for the time: 5:45 p.m. They were supposed to meet Terry and Maria at the Brewing Tree for beers and dinner. He and Cindy should have left the condo at five thirty. "I've been busy with this thing all day. I never even cleaned up after pickleball. And I haven't taken Max out yet."

Cindy nodded. "Figures." Then she pulled out her phone. "You grab a quick shower. I'll text them to hold tight and then take Max for a spin around the building."

Bill caressed Cindy's cheek and kissed her. "You're the best."

The Brewing Tree was a small, casual place and one of Bill's favorite breweries in Nelson County, of which there were quite a few. Located on State Route 151 a few miles north of Nellysford, the brewery made excellent use of its property, with an open gravel parking lot out front, a small stage for live music near the tables outside, and a games area shaded by tall oak trees down by the fast-flowing stream in the back.

They ordered dinner at the charming food truck out front and sat with beers at a four-top table on the covered porch. The temperature was in the mid-eighties, but the setting sun had lost its power, and a light breeze made the porch a comfortable place to sit. A trio played bluegrass music on the nearby stage. With beers in hand, they enjoyed listening to a few songs, and then the band took a break.

Maria said, "So, you're helping the police with the

murder investigation." She leaned forward. "What can you tell us about it?"

Terry gave her shoulder a gentle shove. "Bill can't share that information with us. It's confidential."

But Maria pressed forward. "I noticed that Café Devine was closed today. And I saw a sheriff's squad car parked there. I assume the two events are connected somehow."

"Maria," said Terry, irritated, "knock it off."

Bill chuckled at them. He admired their ability to argue in public and still be overtly smitten with each other. Maria, a nosy sort by nature, couldn't help herself. Maria wasn't shy. He had once witnessed her ask a complete stranger in a restaurant whether they liked their entrée because she was considering ordering the same thing. She got away with it most of the time, so why not? At least, Bill guessed, that was how she thought about it.

They would find out anyway, and Bill had already briefed Cindy on the drive over, so he gave Maria and Terry the highlights.

"No way," said Terry. "I don't believe that. Not Kim Wiley."

Maria shrugged. "You never know."

"Nah," said Terry, a bit less sure, then he turned toward Bill. "Do you believe Kim did that?"

"As a matter of fact, I don't. But no one cares what I believe."

"Is Kim in jail now?" said Maria.

"Yes, she's being held in Charlottesville."

"That's awful," said Maria, her face contorted as if incarceration was a fate only slightly better than a terminal cancer diagnosis.

Bill said Kim might be in jail for a few days or even

longer. Then he mentioned that the café would have a tough time staying open, which would hurt Kim financially at an inconvenient time. He had gone over this with Cindy earlier, and Cindy had immediately volunteered to help Nathan with the morning preparations. Unfortunately, she had a catering event the next afternoon and would have to leave before the café opened.

"We can help," said Terry.

Maria nodded. "Terry's a demon in the kitchen. He can make anything. And I know how to run a cash register. I'll have to fake my way through the lattes, but Nathan can probably teach me that stuff."

"Really?" said Bill.

"Heck, yeah," said Terry. "What else have we got to do? Read another book?"

"Boring," said Maria.

Bill expressed his appreciation and stepped away for a minute to send an update text to Nathan. By then, their food was ready. While they ate, their conversation split in two. The women discussed an upcoming event at the resort. Bill and Terry talked about the handyman concept they'd been kicking around.

They had both heard conversations that spring concerning how hard it was to get service vendors to do small projects on the mountain. This gave Terry the idea to start a business. He brought it up with Bill, and they discovered they both enjoyed doing small home projects. Nothing too strenuous. They didn't possess the skills or desire to do remodeling work, but they could handle the little stuff: plumbing jobs, light painting, television installations, etc. The next step was to develop a list of projects they were prepared to undertake and then work on a launch. Bill's only concern was that they might become too successful. He had no desire to take on a full-time job. Terry said they only had to accept the orders they wanted. Too busy? No thanks to new orders. When they first discussed the topic, Bill considered it a hypothetical notion they'd never pursue. Now, he believed it might work, but he had to catch a killer first.

On the way home, Bill brought up what might be a sensitive subject with Cindy. Although their dinner date had slipped his mind, he remembered their plan to leave for New Jersey in two days. Cindy's son, Justin, an enlisted coast guardsman, was stationed in Ocean City, New Jersey. Justin had a few days of leave, and the plan was for Bill and Cindy to join Justin and Justin's girlfriend in New Jersey for a short beach vacation.

"I doubt I'll make the New Jersey trip," Bill said.

Cindy's frown suggested that this possibility had crossed her mind. "You might solve the murder tomorrow."

Bill nodded. "Stranger things have happened. But . . ."

"I'm still going."

"You should. Justin doesn't get much leave."

Cindy gave him the side eye. "It's a good thing you're not a full-time cop. I couldn't take it."

"I'm sorry, Max," said Bill. "I'm not a good dad."

Bill said these words as he fastened Max's halter for a walk. Max waited patiently, displaying gratitude for Bill's attention, even though Max had enjoyed only two short pee breaks since seven thirty that morning. Bill hooked up the leash, slipped an extra poop bag into his pocket, and said, "Come on, boy. Let's go."

Outside, they turned left away from the parking lot and

rounded their building to the mountain's ridge on the other side. Man and dog paused to absorb the view. The crest of the hill across the wooded hollow rolled softly down from the right. Idle chairlift towers and cables ran up the cleared ski slopes. Hidden ski runs cut sweeping lines through the forests. Silence hung heavy and comfortable. The sun was setting behind Bill, casting a long shadow on the opposing mountain. Similar condo complexes occupied the ridge to Bill's left and right, all built on this spot in the mid-eighties for the same reason: the Blue Ridge Mountains view.

Bill turned right and walked Max past three buildings to an open grassy area, where he let Max loose. The black retriever ran swiftly and gracefully. With a long stride, he traversed the length of each condo building in mere seconds. He crossed in front of the Ledges and Highlands complexes to the far side of the narrow field. Once there, Max turned left over the edge and meandered down the hill, stopping frequently to sample the delightful smells of nature's small creatures. Bill had never known a more free-spirited dog, and not for the first time, he wondered about Max's life as a stray. The vet had said Max lived on his own for quite some time, perhaps two or three years. Having observed Max easily transition from the confines of a small condo to the great outdoors, Bill believed the vet's estimate might be too short.

For exercise, Bill strolled to the far side of the Highlands and returned, keeping a lazy eye on Max's whereabouts. Max never wandered too far, and Bill had concluded that the Labrador preferred to keep Bill in view. It was as if Max feared losing immediate contact with his human companion, perhaps for good reason. Max had lived with at least one other family but lost them somehow.

"Come, Max. Come."

Far down the hillside, Max lifted his head, saw Bill

waving his arm, and bounded up the slope. In moments, Max sat patiently next to Bill, panting from his exertion.

And now it was time for what Bill believed was Max's favorite game. Fetch. Pulling a rubber ball the size of a nectarine from his pocket, Bill flung it back toward the Vistas complex as far as he could. Max bounded after the ball, picked it up in his mouth at a dead run, screeched to a halt, and hurried back to Bill for another go. They played the game for the next ten minutes and only stopped when Bill had had enough. As far as he knew, Max would play fetch until the moon was high in the sky, but Bill had one thing to do before sunset.

Back at the Vistas condos, Bill paused at the edge of the ridge to search, as he had on other days, for any sign of his wild friend.

"Where is he, Max? Where is Mr. Chips?"

Late the previous summer, Bill had befriended a fat groundhog by tempting him with juicy, ripe tomatoes. In time, Mr. Chips had come to trust Bill enough to take the fruit straight from Bill's hand. Of course, one day, Mr. Chips had gone, buried deep in his burrow for the winter. This was a natural process, and Bill had researched groundhogs enough by then to not be alarmed. But spring had come and gone. Early summer was here. Groundhogs should have ventured out to eat by now. Bill worried. Perhaps Mr. Chips had not survived the winter, which had been particularly cold. Or maybe a predator had taken Mr. Chips, although there were few predators on the mountain big enough for the job. A black bear, perhaps, but Bill understood that black bears mainly ate plants. Coyote sightings in the valley were common, but Bill had rarely heard them yipping on the mountain. Maybe Mr. Chips had moved on and found juicier greens at another condo complex.

What was the world coming to when you couldn't trust your neighborhood groundhog to make it through the winter? A nonsensical question that Bill soon dropped so that his mind could return to Lily Wolf's murder. Dark forces were alive and well. He remained confident of Kim's innocence. But if Kim didn't kill Lily Wolf, who did?

EIGHTEEN

"Bill O'Shea is right," said Lulu. "It was going to be hard anyway, no matter when I got pregnant."

Lulu reached for the sugar bowl and poured a healthy teaspoonful on her cereal. Mitch could not remember Lulu putting sugar on her cereal. Wasn't that stuff already sweetened? It said so right on the box, honey-glazed. Lulu opened her mouth for the spoon and smiled at Mitch. No way would Mitch ask her that question. He wasn't that stupid.

"Then again," she said after swallowing, "it might have been a little easier if we had stuck to the plan instead of getting pregnant three months after the wedding."

Mitch said, "Well, if a certain someone had not forgotten to pick up a certain something at the pharmacy, then maybe we could have stuck to the plan."

With a second spoonful on the way to her mouth, Lulu paused and eyed Mitch.

Dumb, Mitch thought. *So dumb. I should not have said that.*

"We *could* have stuck to the plan," she said, "but someone else, who promised he would do something specific well before a certain moment arrived, got too excited and lost self-control."

Mitch turned his head to gaze out the window. Their rental home in the suburbs of Charlottesville had a grassy backyard bordered by a forest of maples and poplars. "Yeah. I'd better get to work."

"You started it."

They weren't really fighting. Mitch and Lulu often poked fun at each other in a good-natured way. But not if they had a serious disagreement. On those rare occasions, they debated the pros and cons of their relative positions rationally until one of them won the point. This was usually Lulu because she was more intelligent than Mitch, and he freely acknowledged this to himself. No problem. A giant brain still needed brawn. They made a good team, and her IQ was part of the reason he loved her, that and her luminous skin, dazzling eyes, and killer body.

Nevertheless, her accelerated pregnancy presented Mitch with a problem. Lulu was in her first year of dental school in Richmond and had more than an hour-long commute. Mitch's drive up to Wintergreen was also an hour each way. The math didn't add up, not when the baby came. They had already agreed on two important decisions. First, she would stay in school because that was her dream and a great wealth-creation opportunity. Second, he would continue to work because they needed the money to survive. Mitch's mother had offered to help by coming to their house from Waynesboro three days a week. Lulu could arrange her schedule to be home one or two days per week, and Mitch could work some nights. With a little of this and that, they could make the schedule work, but his long commute to Wintergreen would no longer make sense. Lulu could not move her dental school to Charlottesville, but he *could* get a job in town.

The Charlottesville PD had offered Mitch an interview six months earlier, but Mitch had turned them down. They may not have an open position now, but even if they didn't, other options were nearby. No, the real issue was that Mitch enjoyed working in Wintergreen. The natural beauty, slower pace, and great team made it the best job he'd ever had.

Oh, well. He didn't wish to wrestle with that problem any longer. The chief wanted him back in the rental home until he found something they could use. Time to hit the road.

"Sorry, babe," he said. "I hope you know that nothing in the world could make me happier than being with you, and I am beside myself with excitement about the baby."

She shook her head. "Every time I think you're a butthead, you go and say something like that, and I love you all the more."

Mitch stood and leaned over to kiss her on the lips. "You're calling me a sweet talker. I like that."

Lulu gave him a hard shove. "Get outta here."

NINETEEN

At seven o'clock, Krista parked her cruiser at Café Devine and studied the building. After Bill's suggestion late the previous day, she had spent a few minutes searching the perimeter but left because her boys texted her with crucial information. They were starving. What was for dinner?

Emily Powell had called an investigative team meeting for eight that morning, which gave Krista forty-five minutes to search. Krista didn't expect to find Lily Wolf's phone because of Bill's conviction that Kim was innocent. But Krista would perform a thorough search anyway because that was what a good cop must do, and she wanted to show everyone that she was a good cop. Emily had commended Krista on her performance with the online classes—straight A's so far—but Emily also cautioned Krista against overconfidence. Scoring well in the classroom was one thing—strong field work was another.

From where she stood, Krista could see the surveillance camera perched above the patio. The second camera observed the parking lot and the road.

Around the back, Krista thought. *If Kim had hidden her phone outside, she would have hidden it in the back, away from the cameras.*

The café sat at the foot of a small hill, upon which a small park provided recreational space for residents and guests. The slope of that hill came down against the back of the café such that the café's roof was close to the ground. Krista examined the gutter and its leaf screen carefully. She picked at the screen, but it held fast to the gutter. She traversed the gutter's perimeter, squinting through the screen for a hidden phone. No luck. A few long boards, leftover from a project, lay against the back wall. Krista picked her way through them with no success. The builders had formed a shallow ditch with rocks of various sizes to channel rainfall away from the foundation. Walking beside the ditch, Krista studied the stones carefully. Occasionally, she'd pick one up to look underneath. Halfway down the ditch, her phone buzzed with a text.

Skip Forrester.

I can't stop thinking about this weekend. Have a great day!

Krista smiled. She and Skip had been seeing each other for a few months. Wait, was it five months already? Her ex, Tyler, had the boys every other weekend, which freed Krista to spend time with Skip. They had met each other in Charlottesville, Culpeper, and northern Virginia, where Skip lived. Krista had enjoyed these weekends a great deal. She felt liberated, free to pamper herself with a good time—exploring new towns, dining out, and having a few glasses of wine. Skip was engaging, courteous, and attractive, which certainly didn't hurt. Plus, there were Skip's stories.

Skip started in the military, was promoted to the intelligence branch, and eventually joined the FBI. He was a special agent now and would relate old cases with the right encouragement. Krista enjoyed these stories a great deal, and she couldn't help but hope that someday, somehow, her own career would advance to the point where she could challenge her mind with similar kinds of work, not with the FBI, of course, but something at an elevated level like that.

But how did Skip feel about her? Frankly, Krista knew she was on solid ground—as evidenced by texts similar to the one she'd just received and similar gestures, like the flowers he'd sent her the previous weekend for no particular reason. Also, on several occasions, Skip told her he wanted to meet her sons. She had resisted his requests because she never knew how these things would end up, and she didn't want the boys to form attachments to someone who might not be around in six months.

How long should she hold Skip off? Was it time? Skip was ready to take that risk, but he didn't have to deal with the aftermath if things went awry later.

Wait.

With Krista's mind distracted by thoughts of Skip, she had scarcely seen the rocks of the previous five yards. She backed up a safe distance and examined the rock ditch to its end at the parking lot. No phone.

Krista retreated to the small hill behind the café and tried to put herself inside Kim's mind. Kim returned to the café after stabbing Lily Wolf. She was frantic. Kim had taken Lily's phone because it contained incriminating texts, and now she must hide it before Nathan arrived. She hurried out the back door and hid it in the first good place she found.

Not the gutter. Too hard. Not the loose boards. Too easy for someone to stumble upon. The rock ditch? Perhaps, but Kim had searched that thoroughly.

Three air conditioning compressors sat silently along the

back wall, one on the left and two on the right. Krista had passed them over because, at first glance, they afforded no decent hiding place. But now she inspected them more closely. The compressor on the left was mounted on a cement foundation. She approached the compressor and examined all sides of its base. No phone there. The second and third compressors were mounted on a wooden platform supported by two-foot-high columns. Two-by-six pieces of lumber were sandwiched between the platform and the compressors. There were two eight-inch gaps between the boards. Krista thrust her hand into the front gaps but found only empty spaces. She turned her phone flashlight on and pointed it through the gaps. No luck. She edged around the right-side compressor, rested her hip on the platform, and leaned over to search the gap on the backside.

Oh. Wow.

Krista blinked several times, astonished that she had found Lily Wolf's phone. The iPhone and its plain green case were protected from the elements in a one-gallon plastic bag. Krista touched the screen, but the phone stayed dark. Kim had probably turned it off to keep it from pinging cell towers.

Krista returned to her earlier imagined scenario, now confirmed.

Kim *had* killed Lily Wolf. She had returned to the café a second time with Lily's phone, packaged it in a plastic bag, and cleverly hid it behind a compressor.

What would Bill O'Shea have to say now?

TWENTY

Five people attended Emily Powell's roundup meeting, four in uniform, plus Bill.

Emily, Mitch, Krista, and Brendan Baittinger all stared at Bill. He understood why. The fight. The knife. The video. Kim's lie. And now the phone. The circumstantial evidence against Kim now threatened Bill's belief in her innocence.

"I know it looks bad," he said.

"Bad?" said Krista. "It was already bad. Now it's . . . What's worse than bad?"

"Very bad?" offered Brendan.

"I don't like to use the word very. It's a cheat word."

"Horrific?" said Mitch.

"Horrific doesn't fit the situation well. That's better used in describing an accident or something like that."

"Okay," said Emily. "Let's bring it back to the here and now. Bill, I'm sure you've heard the old saying—sometimes the easy answer is the right answer. Maybe that fits our crime."

"Maybe," said Bill.

He didn't want to get into it. Bill had told Emily they would never find the phone. He told Krista where to search but said she'd never find anything. Nothing Bill said now would advance Kim's position. He only hoped that Emily would keep the investigation open. If she did, they had a chance of finding a new suspect, which was critical at this point.

"Have you told Nelson County we found the phone?" Krista asked Emily.

"Not yet."

Krista frowned. Mitch studied the table. Brendan's eyes were glued to his phone. They were all wondering why Emily had not informed Undersheriff Arnie Shields of such an important discovery. Bill had the same question.

"Shut your minds on this point," said Emily testily. "I'll call Arnie after our meeting. Now, Brendan, tell everyone what you've learned about Lily Wolf."

Brendan raised his eyebrows. "I haven't learned anything."

"Yes, but tell us what you tried. Effort counts for something in this department—not a lot, but something."

He heaved a sigh. "I scanned several hundred social media profiles: Facebook, LinkedIn, even X. I found no one resembling our victim. I've searched the business records of twenty states for Atlantic Engineering Advisors but came up empty everywhere except Virginia. And I can't find any more intel on the two men connected to the company."

As he spoke, Brendan watched for Emily's reaction. The kid's fingers continued to swipe his phone screen even though his eyes were directed elsewhere, as if his phone skills operated independently of his brain.

"What tips have come in on Lily's photo?" Bill asked.

"Nothing particularly helpful," said Emily. "Several

callers have reported seeing her on the mountain, one at the Edge, and two others out hiking on the AT."

The mystery woman. No one knew her except Kim. No one had even spoken to her, except Kim. Which made no sense. Lily Wolf had lived here for three months—*someone* must have interacted with her. Someone knew her well enough to kill her. But why did that someone use Kim's knife to kill Lily? And how did Lily's phone wind up hidden outside Café Devine? It stretched the limits of Bill's belief. Unless . . .

Unless the murder had nothing to do with Lily. In the past, when Bill had pointed out to Kim that gossiping might earn her enemies, she had expressed mild outrage. Did he not believe in the free market? Yes, of course, but gossip was different. No, it wasn't, according to Kim. The ordinary citizen deserved access to a free and unfettered flow of information, and she took pride in her unique ability to facilitate that market. Nevertheless, as the reigning gossip queen of the community, Kim Wiley had alienated a few residents along the way. Could one of those injured parties have hated Kim so much they framed her for murder? No, that would take a particularly twisted mind.

Emily was handing out assignments. They didn't have much to work on, so Emily first asked Krista to make her usual rounds. Mitch was to return to the rental house and search for another few hours.

"What's my assignment?" asked Brendan.

"Research the best way to hack into a smartphone," said Emily. "I'll see if Arnie wants us to take a crack at that."

After the meeting, Bill followed Emily to her office.

"You didn't give me anything to work on. Want me to stick around?"

Emily studied his face. "I don't know. There's nothing I'd

rather do than rub Craig Beaumont's nose in his own failure, but this case seems almost done and dusted."

"I could help Mitch do one more sweep of the house."

"Yeah. Sure. That can't hurt."

TWENTY-ONE

Once inside the rental home on Fairway Oaks Lane, Mitch ran Bill through his search strategy from the previous day. Mitch had done a thorough job, and Bill struggled to offer value-added suggestions. The only places Mitch hadn't searched were the two owner's closets upstairs, which were locked.

"Let's take a look," said Bill.

The closet doors were in the hallway. The owner had not installed deadbolts, leaving only handle locks to secure the doors.

"We could probably get in there with a table knife," said Bill.

"I didn't know if I should."

Bill shrugged. "Nelson County's got the warrant. I'll do it. There's probably nothing in there but spare towels anyway."

"Yeah. Okay."

The closets smelled musty, as if they'd been closed and dark for years. Bill and Mitch went through the owner's belongings. Clothes. A set of golf clubs. Maintenance supplies.

Then Bill's phone buzzed. Rachel Dunn.

Surprised, Bill signaled to Mitch that he would step away to take the call.

"Hello," said Bill hesitantly. His voice sounded shaky. How irritating that the appearance of Rachel Dunn's name on his phone screen could knock him off stride.

"Good morning, Bill. It's been too long." She did that on purpose, spoke in a silky voice full of illicit promise.

Rachel had moved to Wintergreen the year before Bill, and he had only met her a few times, always in connection with investigations. Rachel had once made her living as a high-priced escort in DC and northern Virginia. But she had quit that profession and opened a massage therapy practice here in Wintergreen. Bill had heard from several of her clients, all women, that Rachel had a gift. Her touch soothed their aching bodies, and her sympathetic conversation soothed their minds.

"How can I help you?" he said in a steadier voice.

"I'm sure you could help me in many ways, Bill, but I'm calling to offer my assistance to you."

"Uh-huh."

"It concerns the blast email asking for information. The woman named Lily Wolf? I've met her."

"You have? Why didn't you call the police?"

The sound of Rachel taking a deep, deliberate breath came through the earpiece. "Frankly, I'd rather meet with you. And I assume you're involved."

At that moment, it occurred to Bill that Emily would prefer he send Rachel directly to her, but Emily was busy with other stuff. She had a whole department to run. And to be honest, he wouldn't mind seeing Rachel again.

"Do you want the information or not?" she said.

"Yes."

"Meet me at the Mountain Inn coffee shop. I have an appointment in thirty minutes."

Mitch collapsed onto the living room couch, frustrated with the darn rental home. He'd searched the owner's closets twice with no success. In fact, he'd probed every inch and corner he could imagine. Still, the house refused to reveal any helpful information.

Emily wanted inside that laptop in the worst way.

"Everyone writes their password down somewhere," she had said that morning. "It must be there."

Of course, he had searched beneath the dining table, where they found the laptop. Nothing. The home had an office with a desk, and Mitch had searched every inch of that desk, opened every drawer, checked the underside of every surface, and even flipped the desk on its side. Zero. He'd gone through essentially the same process with every chair, every side table, and every other stick of furniture in the whole house. He had pulled up the edges of the upstairs carpeting, peered behind every picture frame, and emptied the contents of every single drawer.

Perhaps that was the problem. Mitch had applied brute force to the search. Maybe the mystery woman would only reveal her secrets to a searcher who used their mind. What nonsense. Mystery woman.

Lulu was a mystery woman. Even after years together, she intrigued him. How could she master complex subjects like chemistry and biology yet be a total klutz in the kitchen? He laughed. Lulu couldn't scramble eggs. Fortunately, Mitch enjoyed cooking and had inherited his mother's talents in that area; otherwise, they would eat takeout six nights a week.

As thoughts of Lulu occupied his mind, Mitch's eyes wandered lazily across the ceiling to the wall sconce on the right. A brown wooden box that ran the length of the room, the sconce hid fluorescent bulbs that lit the room at night. Or so Mitch assumed. He had only searched the house in the daytime and never turned on those lights.

In a few moments, he found the switch. The bulbs flickered for several seconds and then brightly lit the room. One end of the sconce was darker, and Mitch assumed the ballast required some space. Or perhaps the bulb was darker at one end because it would soon fail.

Mitch frowned.

Surely, Lily Wolf had not hidden something in the wall sconce. But by that logic, he would have skipped over half the places in the house. No, he simply hadn't thought of searching the wall sconce. Mitch fetched a six-foot step ladder the owner kept in the mudroom closet. And then, standing on the third step, he peered over the top of the sconce and found five straps of hundred-dollar bills.

TWENTY-TWO

Krista drove up Wintergreen Drive all the way to the top, turned right on Laurel Springs Drive and took that down to the dead end, then cruised all the way back up to Devils Knob Loop. Nothing going on. Quiet. She waved at a few walkers on the road.

She had a duty to perform and was glad to do it, but still, a murder investigation was more interesting. She focused on passing details to keep her mind from wandering. To her kids, for example. Ashton appeared a bit tired that morning, and she worried he might be coming down with something.

Whoa. Look at that.

A red-tailed hawk swooped through the road ahead and into the hardwoods. Krista felt sorry for the critter—chipmunk, squirrel, rabbit—that had caught the hawk's eye. Oh, well. Maybe it got away.

Her radio sparked to life. Good grief. It was another bear call. On Blackrock Circle. Krista reported that she was on the way.

Five minutes later, she pulled into the gravel driveway of a shaded home and witnessed a catastrophe in the making. A woman in her late thirties stood beside her Toyota Highlander and shook her fist at the home's porch. Next to the woman, a young boy—about twelve—held a rock the size of a walnut. The covered porch extended across the home's front side. Upscale patio furniture on the porch exuded a sense of style and wealth. But the intended charm was lost on the large black bear and two cubs, who were more interested in what appeared to be a home delivery of several boxes.

Krista jumped out of her squad car and hustled toward the danger. Inside the house, a large dog stood with his paws on a window and barked constantly.

"Get off my porch!" said the woman.

The boy threw the rock. Fortunately, his aim was poor, and the rock bounced off the roof and fell harmlessly to the ground. The boy bent to grab another rock.

"Don't do that," said Krista.

The sight of Krista's uniform chastened the boy, and he stood silently to one side.

"Thank goodness you're here," said the woman. "Shoo those bears away."

"Ma'am, please ask your son to wait in the SUV. It would be best if you did too."

"Spencer," the woman commanded, "get in the Highlander." The boy backpedaled slowly to the SUV's door but stayed outside.

On the porch, the mother bear—whose nose was buried in a large box—ignored the humans. The bear ate hungrily and messily. One of the cubs slurped castoffs from their mother's gorging. The second cub pawed determinedly at a smaller package to one side. The second cub successfully penetrated the second package's wrapping, stuck its face inside the box, and thereby attracted its sibling's attention.

Krista recognized the mother bear. "It's Ms. Betsy. She's a regular. Got two beautiful cubs this year."

"I don't care who she is. Get her and her dirty offspring off my porch."

"Ma'am," said Krista, "what's in those packages?"

"It's a dog food delivery." The woman stood a little over five feet tall and had brown hair and a petite figure. She pointed at the bears. "Go ahead, get them off my porch."

"I'm afraid there is not much we can do at this point."

The woman dipped her head toward Krista's holstered pistol. "Shoot them."

"No," said Krista, calmly but firmly. "We don't shoot bears."

"Well, then, fire your gun in the air. Scare them away."

Perhaps a gentle reminder, thought Krista.

"There are plenty of warnings against leaving food outside. I'm sure you've seen them."

A black BMW sports car pulled into the driveway, and a man dressed in workout attire got out. He strolled toward Krista and the woman. His expression portrayed amusement.

"What have we got here?"

"Ajay," said the woman, "bears are eating our Chewy delivery."

Ajay laughed. "I swear. I leave to work out, and all hell breaks loose."

Krista was tempted to laugh as well but restrained herself.

Up on the porch, Ms. Betsy tired of the first package and swiped her paw at another, ripping off its side. This new package must have given off a delightful aroma, for all three bears hurried to consume its contents. Inside, the dog, which Krista guessed might be a boxer or a pit bull, commenced barking even louder.

"Ajay," the woman cried, "do something!" Then she

waved a hand dismissively at Krista. "She refuses to shoot them."

Ajay raised his eyebrows, approached Krista, and said, "I'm sorry. Sadie tends to get overexcited in situations like this."

"No problem. The bears will go away quietly in a little while."

"Excited?" said Sadie, storming toward Ajay. "I'll give you excited. You were supposed to be here in time for the delivery."

Ajay lifted his hands. "I ran into a prospective client and gave him a pitch. What did you want me to do?"

Sadie put her hands on her hips and pulled her shoulders back. Krista feared that a standard bear call—which she had handled without incident in the past—now threatened to escalate into a full-blown domestic dispute.

"That's a two-hundred-dollar delivery," Sadie said in a threatening tone. "I'm not going to pay for it out of my monthly budget because you were supposed to be here." Sadie emphasized the point by jabbing her finger into Ajay's chest.

Appropriately admonished, Ajay said, "That's fair. I'll cover it."

Having had her fill, Ms. Betsy now ambled quietly off the porch and around the side of the house. The two cubs stayed behind for a few seconds to scoop up remnants of the morning feast and then hurried after her.

As a closer, Sadie eyed Krista from head to toe, then said, "Thanks for nothing."

Back in her cruiser, Krista reported her status. Then Emily called.

"Got a new assignment for you," said Emily. "Meet Bill at the Mountain Inn front desk. He'll fill you in."

TWENTY-THREE

They had a laptop and a phone but no means to access either.

Brendan Baittinger sat at his cubicle and stared at the monitor. The chief had asked him to find a way into Lily Wolf's phone.

"You're the tech whiz, right?" she had said.

"Um, I guess so."

"Then figure it out."

The phone designers had made it nearly impossible to break into a phone without the passcode. Hackers got into people's phones by stealing or guessing their passcodes. Brendan had Lily's laptop, access to which would likely allow him to also open her phone, but he couldn't get into her laptop either. So, he would have to guess the passcode.

Brendan had found a security research study online that listed the ten most commonly used four-digit passcodes. Phone providers warned users that these passwords were the easiest for criminals to guess. Still, many customers chose to use them anyway.

Emily had told him to figure it out, and he didn't have any

better ideas so he tried the five most commonly used passcodes.

No luck.

The phone provider only allowed a certain number of tries before locking up the phone, and Brendan didn't want to reach that point, so he stopped, unsure of what to try next.

Then the station's front doorbell sounded.

Saved from further immediate stress, Brendan went to greet the visitor.

Art Rossi was a thin man in his fifties with dark hair and sharp eyes. He had come about the photo of Lily Wolf that the Wintergreen police had posted online. Brendan showed Rossi into the conference room and then went to fetch Emily.

"I believe we met earlier on another investigation," Emily said, after the three of them had taken seats around the conference room table.

The room was white with no windows. A large white-board with dry-erase markers dominated the wall opposite the door. Brendan was pleased to be invited but had no idea why Emily had asked him or what, if anything, he should say.

"Yes, chief," said Rossi.

"Please, call me Emily."

"Thank you. Please call me Art."

Brendan remembered the Art Rossi story. Apparently, the guy had nearly stumbled upon a murderer hiking on a trail in the Rockfish Valley. Then, Rossi got spooked by something in the woods and turned around. Mitch Gentry had told Brendan that Rossi was lucky to be alive. When Mitch told him that story, Brendan felt sure Mitch exaggerated the danger, as people often did in retrospect. Nevertheless, with Rossi sitting across the table, a chill ran down Brendan's spine.

"I considered calling in my tip on the blonde woman in

the photo," said Art, "but thought you might have follow-up questions, so I drove down."

"Thank you," said Emily. "In person often works best. Did you meet Lily Wolf?"

"No, I never met Ms. Wolf, but I saw her. At least, I think I saw her. The post indicated she was living on Fairway Oaks Lane, correct?"

"That's right," said Emily.

"Is her house on the golf course side of the street?"

"Yes, it is."

"Then it was her."

Fairway Oaks Lane ran alongside the golf course's third fairway. Art liked to tour the golf course in the morning for exercise, and his regular route took him up the third fairway. He always walked early because the golf course opened at eight.

"It's a beautiful course," he said. "And I like to come right up the middle of the fairway."

Jeez. When would Rossi get to the point? They had work to do. Or rather, Emily had work to do. Brendan had an assignment he didn't know how to carry out.

"One morning about six weeks ago, I was halfway up the third hole when I heard a man and a woman arguing."

Brendan leaned forward slightly, eager for more. Emily gave Rossi an encouraging nod.

"The man was clearly angry, but the woman not as much. In fact, I'd say she sounded amused. She laughed at one point."

"Did you hear what they said?" asked Emily.

"No, I was too far away. I started to approach the house in case the argument escalated. If he made to strike her, I would try to do something."

"Yeah. Good."

"At some point, I concluded they were having a commonplace argument. The man was a bit loud, but she didn't sound threatened. Like I said, she seemed amused."

"Did you see the man?" asked Emily.

Rossi shrugged. "I didn't get a good look. He was tall with brown hair. A little on the flamboyant side."

"Okay."

"I saw him one more time a few minutes later. I had reached the top of that hole and made to cross Fawn Ridge when suddenly, a red convertible roared past on Blue Ridge Drive. The car was speeding, going fifty at least, and I'm almost certain the man driving the convertible was the man from the house."

"Did you get the make of the car?"

"Yeah. An Audi. He had the top down."

And at that moment, Brendan realized he had witnessed an important turn in the case. Until then, they had only one suspect. Indeed, they had no evidence that anyone other than Kim Wiley had known the victim. Art Rossi's statement gave them a second person. Brendan knew Emily would go to great lengths to identify the tall man with the brown hair and the red convertible. Yeah. They might have another suspect.

TWENTY-FOUR

Bill entered the Mountain Inn and found Rachel Dunn playing with her phone at a table near the coffee bar. She wore a magenta massage tunic with black scrub pants and white tennis shoes. Rachel noticed Bill approach and stood to offer her hand for him to shake. Her hand was warm and strong.

He had not seen Rachel since the winter, and his memory of Rachel's beauty had faded. After brief greetings, neither spoke, and they stood close together, somewhat awkwardly. Rachel had a long neck, gray eyes, and blond hair that she wore up. She had full lips and a smile that could take a man's breath away if he didn't pay attention.

"Um," he said. "Can I get you some coffee?"

"Yes, Bill. Thank you for asking. I'll have a large latte with whole milk."

Bill hurried off and returned a few minutes later with her latte and a black decaf for himself.

They chatted first. Rachel's massage business continued to grow, picking up a few new customers every month. She had increased her prices modestly to counter inflation, and not a single customer complained. Soon, she would have a full book and stop accepting new customers until she found a competent assistant.

"Ever thought of becoming a masseuse, Bill? I'm sure you'd be great at it."

"What makes you say that?"

"You have strong arms and hands. And you have a nice smile. Massage is a customer service business. Strong hands, a caring touch, and pleasant conversation are all you need."

"I've never considered it. Probably not my thing."

"Suit yourself."

Bill wanted to ask Rachel if she had lived up to her promise to run a clean business—no happy endings—but doing so would imply a lack of trust. And though he was curious, he also believed that everyone deserved a second chance, including Rachel.

He asked what she'd been up to outside of work. She had taken up the game of pickleball. What a coincidence. So had he.

"No kidding," she said. "Have you ever joined the open play on Saturdays or Sundays? I'm usually there one day or the other, sometimes both."

"Not recently. Cindy and I play with another couple once or twice a week."

Rachel nodded. "Oh, yes, Cindy. How is Cindy?"

"She's fine. Still busy with her catering business."

"Are you two serious now? Do I hear the faint sound of approaching bells?"

Bill's face grew warm. He scratched his neck. "No. Nothing like that. We're together, that's all."

Rachel's eyes searched his as if to read whether Bill's relationship with Cindy fully met his expectations. It did, for the most part. What relationship was perfect? None. And sustaining a relationship required precisely that wisdom.

Had Rachel ever married? Bill doubted she'd had the opportunity, given her earlier occupation. And in any case, he wouldn't ask.

"Thank you for reaching out," he said. "How did you know Lily Wolf?"

"I didn't know her. I met her once at the Edge. I met her and a man named Nick Pappas at the same time."

Wintergreen presented few nightlife options for a single woman like Rachel. And so, Rachel was a regular customer at the Edge, a restaurant and bar near the ski slopes behind the Mountain Inn. Rachel knew most of the workers by name and vice versa. On a typical night, Rachel would sit at the bar, where she could converse with the bartender and patrons occupying the other stools.

On the night in question, the combination of a wedding and two business retreats made for a busy night at the Edge. Rachel had struck up a conversation with the woman on her left and the man on her right. The woman—Lily Wolf—had moved to Wintergreen recently for a long-term sabbatical. The man—Nick Pappas—was a resident on the mountain.

"This dude was super-rich," said Rachel, "and he made sure I knew that in the first five minutes. He founded a tech company that invented a new piece of security software. According to Nick, his brilliant marketing strategy compelled every IT department in the country to buy their product, and he subsequently sold the company for hundreds of millions."

Bill scratched his chin. Where did he go wrong? How did these people come up with these ideas? Why wasn't Bill born with a creative mind like Pappas? Never mind. More to life than money. And Pappas hadn't won the long race yet. He might check his phone one day, forget he was driving, and find himself tumbling down a cliff.

Rachel continued. Rachel and Lily Wolf and Nick Pappas had struck up a lighthearted conversation. They had dinner and a drink. Then another drink. When Pappas ordered a third round, Rachel switched to club soda, but not Lily. Lily matched Pappas beverage for beverage. Two martinis. Then wine. Of course, Rachel knew what Pappas was up to in the first five minutes—married and on the loose while his wife was out of town.

"How did you know he was married? Did he wear a ring?"

Rachel shook her head. "He took the ring off before going out. I knew what that looked like, and Lily did too."

"What happened?"

"It became clear that Nick wanted companionship for the night. He would have gone with Lily, or me, or both of us for that matter."

Bill swallowed. Rachel must get lonely some nights. Wasn't that why she frequented the Edge—to meet others, to have a conversation with a fellow human, and perhaps more than conversation? He was working up the nerve to ask the next question when Rachel saved him the trouble.

"Lily went to the restroom, and Nick came out with it. 'What do you say we get out of here?' Or something along those lines. I made up an excuse, but the truth was I didn't want to sleep with another jerk. I've been with a lot of jerks in my life, always for money, and now I don't have to."

Bill gave Rachel a congratulatory smile. "Good for you. And what about Lily?"

"She had other ideas."

Lily returned from the restroom, and the two of them—Nick and Lily—began leaning on the bar to converse across the space that Rachel occupied. With the message clearly received, Rachel soon said her goodbyes and left. At the door, she turned back to see that Nick had already moved one stool over. Lily didn't mind. Nick said something, and she touched his shoulder and laughed.

"I didn't feel sorry for Lily," said Rachel. "She had a look I recognized—a woman on the make. Nick believed he was seducing her, but it was the other way around. She wanted something specific from him, and I'm certain she knew how to get it."

"You think they went home together?"

"Definitely."

"What else can you tell me?"

Rachel shook her head. "I haven't seen her or Nick since. But I can tell you one more thing about her."

"What's that?"

"In DC, many of my clients were from other countries. Most of them spoke English well, but they spoke it in different accents. I learned to recognize accents from all over, and I'm almost certain that Lily Wolf came from Russia."

TWENTY-FIVE

Krista shifted the cruiser into reverse, backed out of the Mountain Inn parking spot, and pulled onto Wintergreen Drive headed up the mountain. Bill O'Shea sat next to her. Generally speaking, Bill was a relaxed person. He smiled often and laughed easily, but now his left hand was a fist he rubbed against his cheek repeatedly. Then he scratched the back of his neck. Krista understood his anxiety. Bill wanted his friend Kim Wiley—their only suspect—to be innocent.

But to fit this new guy—Nick Pappas—for a jailhouse jumpsuit, Bill would have to prove he had used Kim's knife to commit the murder and then hidden Lily's phone behind the café to frame Kim.

No way. Not in a year. Kim was as guilty as Oswald. Time to move on, Bill. You can always make new friends.

Even so, Krista was pleased that Emily had asked her to accompany Bill to the interview. Why had Emily picked her instead of Mitch, who had found fifty thousand dollars hidden in the victim's house? Maybe it was a gender thing. This guy Pappas was a player, apparently. Put a female cop in the mix to throw him off his stride? Krista was probably overthinking

Emily's logic. Maybe it was just her turn. Either way, it beat the heck out of minding bears.

Bill bit his thumb. His stomach felt tight, and he had a tiny headache that he hoped would go away soon. He breathed deeply and told himself to relax. Finally, he'd caught a break.

They passed Blue Ridge Drive, and Krista turned left on Devil's Knob Loop. The cruiser's powerful engine engaged, and they climbed the summit. Near the top, Krista pulled into a driveway on the left, and Bill recognized the house. Once or twice a week, he hiked around the Devils Knob Loop road for exercise, and he had watched construction crews transform what had once been a modest home into a full-blown mansion with a two-car garage. Bill and Krista approached the garage windows. The bay on Bill's side was empty, but on Krista's side, light from the window revealed a red convertible sports car.

At the massive front door, Bill and Krista waited after pressing the doorbell. Emily had called ahead to say they were coming. After a short wait, a handsome man opened the door and gave them a big smile. He wore nice jeans and a denim shirt. Nick Pappas exuded confidence. With an olive complexion, dark hair, and a strong body, Pappas possessed the physical attributes required to play the male lead in a Greek drama. His face resembled a young Sylvester Stallone.

After brief and pleasant introductions, Pappas led them into a vast living room. Bill paused to take in the view of mountains cascading down to the Rockfish Valley.

"Wow," Bill said, "that's a heck of a sight."

“Yeah,” said Pappas, “it’s the main reason we built our second home here.”

“How long since you moved in?” said Bill, for no reason other than to prolong the small talk. He knew from Rachel—and Art Rossi’s statement—that Pappas had spent time with Lily Wolf. They would get to that shortly, but a little chitchat would help Bill form a more rounded impression of the man. Bill soon found that Pappas needed little encouragement to brag about himself and his great success.

After selling his company—for an amount he enunciated clearly as six hundred and thirty-seven *million* dollars —Nick decided to find a beautiful place to live and then golf every day for the rest of his life. Upon studying the matter more fully, Pappas concluded he would need two more residences. Wintergreen worked well for six months of the year, but Nelson County winter golf was a no-go. So, when the Devil’s Knob golf course closed this fall, Pappas would set out to find a winter paradise. No rush. The world offered many fabulous winter golf destinations, and Pappas intended to sample the menu extensively before deciding.

“Wintergreen was an easy call,” he said. “Our original home is in Virginia Beach, and my wife still works there. Maeve spends her week in the city and comes here for the weekends.”

“Nice,” said Bill. He nodded to show his appreciation of the fabulous life Pappas had constructed.

Pappas may have detected a trace of insincerity in Bill’s expression, or perhaps Krista standing stoically in her uniform threw him off. In any case, his smile disappeared. He offered them a chance to sit on living room furniture near the picture windows. Bill and Krista sat on the couch, and Pappas sat in a nearby armchair.

"I gather from Chief Powell that you want to discuss Lily Wolf's murder."

"Yes," said Bill. "How well did you know Ms. Wolf?"

"I didn't know her well at all."

Nick Pappas rushed his words, and Bill suspected he had practiced that line. Bill exchanged looks with Krista, an exchange he knew Pappas would notice.

"I see," said Bill. "Do you drive a red Audi convertible?"

At first hesitant, Pappas eventually said, "Yes."

"Maybe you should modify your earlier statement about not knowing Ms. Wolf. Because we have a witness who saw you with Lily Wolf at her rental house."

Fear entered Nick Pappas's eyes. For a moment, Bill believed they had him. Pappas might lawyer up now, which Bill would interpret as a confession.

"Wait. Someone saw me and Lily together at her house?"

"Yes," said Bill.

Krista casually cleared her throat.

Technically, Art Rossi had not identified Nick Pappas as the man on Lily Wolf's back porch, but he had seen a red Audi convertible, and that was close enough.

Bill said, "Our witness said you and Lily Wolf were arguing on her back deck one morning six weeks ago. What was the argument about?"

For some reason, Pappas appeared visibly relieved. Why? Bill made a mental note to give that more thought.

Pappas rubbed his hands together. "Okay, this is a tricky subject, given my situation."

He glanced at Bill and then Krista, as if searching for understanding. Bill tried to appear sympathetic. Krista's stare showed Pappas no mercy.

Pappas continued. "I met Lily one night at the Edge when Maeve was in Virginia Beach. We had a few too many drinks, and then we hooked up." Pappas grimaced. "I'm not proud of this."

"What happened then?" said Bill. "After the first night."

"We started hanging out once or twice a week when Maeve was gone." Pappas's eyes darted to a hallway, then he added hastily, "Always at Lily's place. Never here."

"Go on," said Bill.

Nick shrugged. "It was never going to work long term. It was a tryst. A fling. We both knew that. Lily didn't seem to mind. She was into the mystique, but she grew upset when the inevitable parting of the ways occurred. That's what your witness saw on the back deck. It was not a huge deal, a little tension over the breakup. That's all."

"The witness got a different impression from the argument. They said Ms. Wolf appeared amused. Laughed even. You were the one who was upset."

Pappas pushed his lips out, then shook his head. "No. They got the wrong impression. She might have laughed nervously once, but believe me, I wasn't upset about the breakup. Lily was fun, and we had a good time, but she could also be kind of irritating."

Krista shifted in her chair, her eyes not quite seething. She said, "The witness saw you speeding after the encounter. They believe that anger affected your driving."

Pappas chuckled. "Nah. I always drive too fast. Sorry."

"Did you meet anyone else when you were with Ms. Wolf?" said Bill. "One of her friends, perhaps? A business associate?"

"No. No one at all. Like I said, it was a casual fling. After the one night at the Edge, we met at her house exclusively. We didn't go out to dinner or anything like that. I'd show up. We'd chat awhile, have a few glasses of wine, and then, you know."

"Do you have any idea who might have wanted to kill her?" asked Bill. It was the same question framed differently, but sometimes you got lucky.

"No. If I had to guess, I'd look for another romantic interest. Seducing Lily was no great task. After we split, I wouldn't be surprised if she found someone else to hang out with."

What a jackass, Bill thought.

If he didn't need him as a suspect, Bill would prefer to never lay eyes on Pappas again. But he did need him.

"Where were you early yesterday morning?" said Bill.

"I wasn't on the mountain. I had a big dinner the night before at the Boar's Head in Charlottesville. I spent the night there. I'm sure your security cameras captured me leaving from and returning to Wintergreen."

What a strange thing to say. Nick Pappas had practiced that answer. No doubt.

"Do you have any more questions?" said Nick.

Bill glanced at Krista. He had monopolized most of the interview.

"We found money hidden in the house," said Krista. "Fifty thousand dollars in one-hundred-dollar bills. Any ideas?"

Pappas raised his eyebrows. "Fifty thousand dollars? I don't know anything about that."

Krista took a few moments to type a note on her iPad. "Okay. Good. Thank you for your time."

"I wonder if you could do me a slight favor," said Nick.

"What's that?" said Bill.

"I realize this is a serious investigation and that you need to track down every lead. But I hope you can keep my brief affair with Lily Wolf under wraps. I've never done this kind of thing, and I never will again. But if my wife found out, well, I don't know how she would react."

"We'll do what we can," said Bill, although he knew Pappas had cheated before and would again. That was not Bill's business. Sooner or later, Pappas's wife would find out if she hadn't already. Perhaps one day, Maeve Pappas would get her fair share of six hundred and thirty-seven *million* dollars.

Outside, they got in the squad car without saying a word. When they were out of the driveway and descending the hill, Krista said, "He's lying about the money."

"Yeah. No question. But is he lying about the rest?"

"Why did he bring up the surveillance cameras?"

Exactly. Krista was a quick study.

Bill said, "I can only guess that the footage will show his red convertible leaving and returning when he said it did."

"And that gives him a solid alibi."

"It would appear so."

Which didn't help. Not at all. But for now, Bill put the alibi to the side and tried to scenario-play Pappas as the murderer. First, Bill assumed Nick had a motive for killing Lily Wolf, maybe something to do with the money. Somehow, Nick realized that Lily was now seeing Kim, and he schemed to frame Kim as the murderer. Pappas arrived at the house early, watched Kim leave, waited until Lily was eating on the back porch, and then stabbed Lily with Kim's knife. Then what? He planted Lily's phone at the café? It was a stretch, and he'd get nowhere with Arnie Shields unless he had proof.

~

Krista dropped Bill off and then made another casual loop around the mountain's north side. Being in the neighborhood already, she turned left on Fairway Oaks Lane to study the rental house from the driveway.

What had happened on the morning Lily Wolf died? Until the interview with Nick Pappas, Krista had been ninety-nine percent sure Kim Wiley was the murderer. Every bit of evidence they had pointed in Wiley's direction. But now they had Nick Pappas. What a slimeball. At first glance, she had found the man attractive. But once he opened his mouth—ewww! Whether he had killed Lily Wolf was a different question. But they could write him down as a suspect. Pappas knew Wolf. He had an affair with her that ended recently. And he knew something about the fifty thousand dollars.

The fact that they had another suspect introduced a kernel of doubt in Krista's mind concerning Kim Wiley's guilt. And that meant that Krista, as part of the investigating team, had to work harder to find the truth.

Dang. This work was fascinating and impactful. Sitting in her idling squad car in the driveway of a crime scene, Krista was thrilled to be a police officer.

TWENTY-SIX

"Is there any more of the pepperoni left?" asked Mitch.

Brendan Baittinger, standing at the side table next to the pizza boxes from the Market, lifted a lid. "Yeah. One slice left."

"I'll take it," said Mitch.

"I thought five slices was your limit," said Krista.

Mitch scowled. "I've only had three, and I don't want it to go to waste. Food waste is a big contributor to climate change."

Krista appeared dubious of Mitch's true intentions.

Emily had assembled the same cast for the second roundup meeting of the day. She sprang for pizzas and sodas to keep their spirits and energy high. Bill wished she had thrown in a big salad as well, but what the heck—it was free.

"Let's bring it in, kids," said Emily. "Mitch, summarize where we are."

Mitch—whose communication skills had developed considerably in the time Bill had known him—gave a quick report. They had made two significant discoveries in short order—the money hidden in the house and the existence of a second suspect. But they had yet to prove whether the two were connected. Nick Pappas admitted knowing the victim intimately but claimed their affair ended six weeks earlier. Also, they had Lily Wolf's laptop and phone, both locked.

"Brendan has had no luck hacking his way into the phone," said Emily, "and he has no better chance of getting into the laptop. Does anyone have any great ideas?"

Bill, all thumbs with technology, shook his head. Mitch studied his fingernails. Krista stared at the ceiling.

"That's unfortunate," said Emily, "but we'll carry on."

She then handed out assignments. With no new leads, Krista and Mitch would return to their regular duties. Brendan would review surveillance footage of Wintergreen's entrance to verify Nick Pappas's alibi.

Bill said, "We should identify every vehicle that entered or exited Wintergreen all night before the murder and all morning afterward."

Emily frowned. "Every vehicle? That's a lot of work, Bill."

Brendan leaned forward. "I can streamline the process. We have access to Virginia license plate records. I can cross reference that with a list of Wintergreen property owners to identify residents. Most of the service providers drive trucks with logos on the side. That analysis might leave us with relatively few unidentified vehicles."

Emily blinked several times. "You can do that?"

"Yes, chief. Should take me a couple of hours."

"All right. Go for it."

Emily asked the group for any other ideas. No one volunteered anything. She said she had a scheduled call with Soren Larsen shortly and would share whatever useful information she learned. Before dismissing the group, Emily drummed her fingers a few moments, then said, "Brendan has some more information."

All eyes turned to Brendan, who glanced nervously at Bill.

"Emily asked me to run a background check on Kim Wiley yesterday, but, um, I didn't get around to it until this morning. Aside from a few traffic violations, I found nothing for the last twenty years."

Bill nodded. Didn't surprise him at all.

"But the older records tell a different story. In the nineties, Ms. Wiley had a few run-ins with the police."

Bill's stomach twitched. "Run-ins?"

"Started off as a wild child, nothing too serious. DUI. Pot charge, dismissed. Public brawling."

"Public brawling?" said Bill.

Brendan's eyes widened at Bill's skeptical tone. "The report indicates alcohol was involved."

"Keep going, Brendan," said Emily.

"There was an assault charge at one point. A domestic situation, apparently. Her girlfriend at the time claimed that Ms. Wiley slapped her. Ms. Wiley said it was a misunderstanding. The girlfriend changed her story later and dropped the charges. The report notes that Ms. Wiley volunteered to seek counseling."

Bill realized his mouth was open and closed it. This was not the Kim Wiley he knew. They had sparred verbally many times but always in good fun. He couldn't remember her ever getting angry. Then again, his interactions with Kim were low stress and low stakes. He had not witnessed how she managed tough situations.

"I'll have to report this to Arnie," said Emily. "This won't help Kim's situation any."

No. Not at all.

As the meeting broke up, Bill felt a bit dazed. Emily asked what he would do next, and he told her he planned to drop by the café to visit Nathan.

"And then I'll go see Kim. Find out why the hell she didn't tell me that stuff earlier."

"Yeah, okay."

He almost forgot his other idea, the long shot not worth bringing up in the meeting. Before running it down, he wanted to talk with Krista. He caught up with her in the parking lot.

"I'd like to reach out to Skip," he said.

Krista nodded. "Sure, but how does the FBI figure into this?"

"I have a feeling about Lily Wolf. We believe she's Russian. Also, from Kim Wiley's description of their altercation, I gather Lily had some fight training. And she hid fifty thousand dollars in the house. Maybe the FBI, or the CIA, knows who she is."

"Want me to call him?"

Bill nodded. "Given your situation, Skip might be more inclined to help you than me."

TWENTY-SEVEN

"Hmm," said Undersheriff Arnie Shields. "Fifty thousand dollars and a new suspect. You guys have been busy."

On Emily's computer monitor, Arnie appeared thoughtful. They had joined the scheduled call a few minutes early, allowing her a chance to share the latest intel.

"But that doesn't prove Pappas killed anyone," said Arnie. "Wiley is still our poster girl for Murderer of the Week."

"I agree. And there's more."

Emily shared what they'd learned from Kim Wiley's background check.

"Domestic abuse?" said Arnie. "Beaumont's gonna dance the tango. And he doesn't strike me as much of a dancer."

"He's not."

Long pause. Emily should not have said that, certainly not in that tone.

"You know Craig Beaumont?" Arnie asked.

She couldn't lie about it. Arnie was too quick.

"Yeah, we both went to Nelson County High."

"And you guys were friends?"

"Let's just say I don't envy you having to work with him."

Arnie fiddled with his ear. "It sounds like there's a story in there somewhere."

"Which you're not going to hear."

He held his hands out in supplication. "Come on. We have a few minutes. Give me a little gossip."

Emily told Arnie the abbreviated story of Craig Beaumont dumping her friend. On the credenza behind Arnie was a picture of him with a smiling boy carrying a fishing pole and a large fish. Arnie was a family man, and his expression grew shaded as Emily told the story.

Of course, she shouldn't have told Arnie, not after so many years. Maybe Craig had changed. *No,* she decided, *there was not much chance of that.* People earned their reputations. If others shared that reputation in the back channels, they had it coming.

The picture wobbled, and a new rectangle opened to reveal Soren Larsen's smiling face.

"Afternoon, boys and girls. Who are we calling a butthole today?"

Darn. Soren had heard Emily's last few words.

Arnie threw a hand to the side. "You wouldn't know him. A local vendor. Rips everyone off here in the county."

"I always wonder how those guys stay in business," said Soren.

"Limited options," said Arnie. "You have to call someone. What do you have, Soren, that we couldn't see with our own eyes?"

Soren shrugged. "In terms of consumption, boring stuff. No drugs. Mushrooms are making a comeback. I thought perhaps the two of them had gotten into psychedelics and taken a wrong turn. Nope. No cocaine. No meth. She consumed most of a bottle of wine the previous night. And as you know, she had recently eaten a partial breakfast."

"What about the knife?" asked Arnie. "Any fingerprints or residue from the casserole?"

"No. The knife was clean. No fingerprints. No breakfast residue."

"Anything to note regarding cause of death?" said Emily.

"Very simple, and impressive. The murderer struck a fierce blow. The knife missed her spinal cord by an inch but then pierced her heart. She bled out in no time. Game over."

"Doesn't that seem *too* impressive?" said Emily. "It almost sounds like this was done by a professional. Kim Wiley runs a café."

Soren sat still, expressionless. The silence dragged on. Then he said, "Was that a question for me? That's above my pay grade. I share facts. You guys do the detecting. I will say this, though. The knife was extremely sharp. Like a razor. I wish I had knives like that at home."

Soren sometimes wandered from the task at hand to make irrelevant comments. Emily found him colorful. Arnie was a different story.

"What else do you have?" Arnie said.

"Two tattoos. She has a wolf on her left hip, not merely the face but the entire animal. Fierce. Nicely done. She used a talented artist."

"That's interesting," said Arnie. "Her name is Wolf, at least her English name. What's the other tattoo?"

"It's a word tattooed on the underside of her left forearm," said Soren. "Actually, it's a name in the Cyrillic alphabet. One of my guys had it translated. The name in English is Kobryn, which is a town in Belarus close to the Polish and Ukrainian borders."

"Kobryn, Belarus," said Arnie, no less confused than if Soren had named one of Saturn's moons. "Anything else?"

Soren pursed his lips, studied his notes, and said, "Ah, yes. She was shot, years ago. The wound is in her thigh. The bullet went clean through her muscles. Very lucky."

"Hmm," said Arnie. "Her luck ran out, didn't it?"

TWENTY-EIGHT

"Good afternoon, sir. May I help you?" said Maria Metcalf, from behind the register at Café Devine. A few steps back, Terry Stinson stood stirring something in a bowl in the kitchen area. He gave Bill a smile and a wave.

A woman and a man Bill didn't recognize perused the wine racks. The store was otherwise empty.

"Can I get a latte?" he asked.

"Oh, yes. I've been fully trained."

Maria turned right and stepped toward the coffee machines, and Bill followed her along the front side of the counter.

In a lower voice, he said, "How's business?"

"Not good. These two folks are short-term guests, so they're not up on current events. We've had a few locals asking after Kim, but not many."

"Not too surprising," said Bill.

Maria responded at once. "I'm disappointed, frankly. Aren't friends supposed to help each other in times of trouble? Why do our servicemen fight to protect our freedom if we're going to treat each other like this?"

"You have a point."

"Damn right."

Genuinely upset, Maria focused on the latte. She had a temper, as he had witnessed on the pickleball court. But this time, Bill empathized with her reaction. Some people, like Maria and Terry, naturally responded to an opportunity to ease a friend's suffering. Others, who might tell themselves they were charitable, never left their house.

Terry wiped his hands and came forward to say hello.

"I don't want to take you away from your duty," said Bill.

Terry waved off Bill's concern. "It's slow. I'm doing make-work, baking cookies that we may not need. I've also been giving our business idea some thought. How good are you with HVAC?"

"I know beans about HVAC."

"Me neither. I'll take that off the list. Wallpaper?"

"I can do wallpaper. I can't pick it out, but I can hang it all day long."

Terry whipped a notebook out of his back pocket. He clicked a pen and scribbled a few words. "We can make this thing work. When can you start?"

Bill made a face. "I'm kind of busy with this investigation."

"Oh, sure. Not now. A week, a month, a year. Whatever works."

Maria arrived with Bill's latte. "Are you working on that handyman concept again? You'd better watch it. You'll work yourself into a full-time job."

"No problem." Terry smiled to signal that he had this thing wired. "It's all in the model. We enter how much we want to work, which dictates how many jobs we'll accept." He leaned forward to whisper. "It even affects the pricing. Low supply drives higher prices."

Maria chuckled. "Oh, yeah. You've got it all figured out. Careful, Bill. Keep an eye on him. He's had other business ideas."

Terry quickly responded, "Now, that delivery business was on its way. If we hadn't decided to move, I'd be counting money right now."

Even Bill laughed at that, and then he said, "Where's Nathan?"

"He's in the office with his mom, Kim's sister," said Terry. "Have you met her?"

"No." But Nathan had mentioned that his mom had met Lily Wolf. Bill wanted to hear about that meeting—he needed whatever data he could get about the victim.

"How's the latte?" said Maria, as if curious whether she'd learned enough from Nathan to make a decent beverage.

Bill sipped the latte—quite satisfactory—and gave his report. "This is the best I've had in here. It's definitely better than Kim's."

Maria burst out laughing. "That's such BS. But thanks all the same."

At that moment, Nathan and Kim Wiley emerged from the back office.

What in hell? How did Kim get out? No, that can't be.

Bill blinked twice, shook his head, and realized the woman behind Nathan was *not* Kim Wiley. This woman's hair—though the same chestnut brown—was straight and silky compared to Kim's wiry mop. Also, this woman dressed more nicely. Whereas Kim always wore jeans and an apron, her sister wore nice slacks and a buttoned shirt, as if dressed for a corporate meeting. Her face was a near carbon copy of Kim's—rounded, smooth complexion, with a slightly smaller nose, perhaps altered surgically. And her eyes were more severe than Kim's, whose were often filled with mischief.

Then, three things happened all at once. Nathan's cell phone rang, and he stepped away to take the call. The wine shoppers brought their choice to the register, which distracted Maria. And the front door's bell signaled the arrival of a new customer, who immediately asked Terry about the sandwiches in the display case.

Bill found himself standing directly across the counter from Kim's sister, still a bit distracted by the likeness. He smiled, a break-the-ice tactic that generally worked but not with this woman.

"Who are you?" she said, all business.

"Bill O'Shea. A friend of Kim's." He extended his hand for her to shake. She scrutinized his hand as if weighing the benefit of not appearing rude against the cost of touching his unclean appendage. She took a risk, shook hands for the briefest of moments, and introduced herself as Jessica.

"You're the detective," she said.

"Retired."

"Have you found something to get Kim out yet?"

Jessica spoke in a loud, clear voice, easily heard by the others in the store, making Bill uncomfortable.

"Um, no. Not yet."

"I can't believe the damned cops have locked her up."

Jessica's eyes, serious to begin with, were now shooting fire in Bill's direction. The wine customers stared at Jessica in horror. Maria did her best to distract them with a question. Terry launched into a detailed discussion of the dessert choices available in the display case.

"And these people up here?" said Jessica in a slightly lower tone. She turned her withering gaze toward the customers at the register and then toward the one with Terry. "They haven't got the decency to support Kim in her time of need."

It occurred to Bill that Jessica and Kim possessed the same quick temper. Was it a genetic trait or acquired through circumstance? Then, a strange notion entered his mind. Could Jessica, who was clearly protective of Kim, have somehow been involved in the murder? No, surely not. Then again, during his twenty years as a homicide detective, he had witnessed the unbelievable many times.

Nathan had told Bill on the afternoon of the murder that his mother developed a negative impression of Lily when they first met. How negative? Bill's mind formed a frightening image of Jessica spying on Kim and Lily through the window of the rental home. Jessica held a blue-handled knife in her hand.

No, that made no sense. According to Kim, the knife was already in the kitchen. Kim had brought it to the house earlier. Then, an even more disturbing thought occurred to Bill. Perhaps Kim and Jessica had plotted to murder Lily as a team. He shook his head. Better say something soon. Jessica had begun to scrutinize him as if he were the student in class who needed extra help.

"Could we chat somewhere for a few minutes?" said Bill. "Nathan mentioned that you met Lily Wolf. I'm trying to learn more about her."

Although Jessica initially adopted a disdainful expression, she granted his request.

"Okay. We can talk in the office."

TWENTY-NINE

Krista sat in her idling squad car in one of the ski parking lots below the Mountain Inn and recalled the first time she'd met Skip Forrester. Bill had brought Skip into a murder investigation the previous winter. Krista had been nervous when they first met, and rightly so, given that she was a lowly communications officer and he was an FBI special agent. Next thing she knew, they were careening down the mountain in the high-speed pursuit of a prime suspect with her behind the wheel.

Whew. Krista's heart rate jumped. What a day that was.

She had been naive then, but she and Skip had come a long way in the last five months. A long way. They had plans to meet in Charlottesville on Friday night. She had the weekend off, and the boys would stay with Tyler. Skip had picked out a new restaurant, a seafood place not far from the downtown mall. They would have a glass of wine first, stroll to the restaurant for a meal and another glass of wine, and then head back to the hotel, where they were not, repeat *not,* staying in separate rooms. And how did she feel about that? Well, good, actually. She was thirty-seven, financially independent, and doing a first-rate job of raising her kids. But she did get lonely once in a while, and the thing with Skip, whatever she wanted to call it, certainly helped with that. Gave her something to look forward to. Uh-huh.

A concrete mixer rambled past on its way up the mountain, startling Krista from her daydream. Time to get to work. She speed-dialed Skip.

"Hey, babe," he said, after picking up on the first ring. "What's up?"

Babe. Were they at the babe stage? Was that a disrespectful term or merely a term of endearment?

A term of endearment, she decided, which did not wholly allay her concern. Skip had clearly crossed the term-of-endearment bridge, but had she? No. Not consciously. And when she did, what would she call Skip? Babe? Sweetie? Hon? Jeez.

"Um, hey, Skip. Believe it or not, this is a work-related call."

"Work-related? I'm intrigued."

Krista filled Skip in on the investigation and their difficulty researching Lily Wolf's background. Bill O'Shea suggested she call Skip to see if he had access to information they didn't.

"Bill asked you to call me?" said Skip.

"Yes."

"Why didn't he call me himself?"

Kim had asked herself that same question and reached the same conclusion that Skip did now.

"I know why," said Skip. "He asked you to call because he knows we're seeing each other, and he believed I'd be more likely to help you than to help him."

"Are you? More likely to help me?"

"Of course I am. But that's beside the point. Please do this for me. Tell Bill that I am not in debt to him any longer. He is in debt to me."

"You bet."

Krista let silence take hold of the conversation, knowing that Skip would re-engage soon enough.

"Okay," he said. "Give me what you have on Lily Wolf."

Krista shared their limited intel. She heard Skip tapping on his keyboard. He must be in the office.

When Skip spoke, it was as if he were thinking out loud.

"Sounds international. The Russian accent. No US background."

"Okay," said Krista, to fill in the blank space.

"You'd be better off consulting the CIA than us," said Skip.

"I don't know anyone in the CIA," said Krista, then she gave it two beats for good measure. "Do you?"

More silence. From what Skip had told her, he never got to the bottom of his case file. Here she was asking him to do more. She felt a little guilty, but apparently, Skip would make the time. More typing.

"Hmpf," he said.

"Hmpf? What does that mean?"

"It means I found something interesting. It'll take more time for me to get useful intel."

"I'm sorry. I didn't mean to create a lot of work for you."

"No problem. Now I'm curious. I *do* know some CIA guys, but I want to make sure I call the right one."

Skip promised to call back when he had something, and they switched topics to their upcoming weekend getaway. They discussed a possible hike near the Skyline Drive. He had searched for live music and found a show that seemed interesting.

"I have a somewhat awkward question for you," he said.

"What's that?"

Krista hoped he wouldn't bring up the boys again. Skip had asked twice whether the four of them could spend a day together. She had said she would consider it both times but then never responded.

"You remember that nightgown thingy you wore last time?" said Skip.

Oh. That.

"Want me to bring it again?" she said brightly. Men were so easy to please.

"If it's not too much trouble."

"No trouble at all."

After the call, a warm feeling entered Krista's chest, and she realized the feeling came from more than a physical attraction. She was genuinely fond of Skip.

But what did their future entail? Her infatuation had graduated to fondness. Fondness could grow into love. Then what? Marriage? Then what? Skip was thirty-six. Did he want to have his own family? Kids? If they married in a year, waited a bit, and then got pregnant, how old did that make her? Thirty-nine? How did she feel about that?

THIRTY

Café Devine's back office was no more than a small room with a small desk. Jessica Smith offered Bill one of the simple cushioned chairs. The room was so small that when Bill sat, his knees brushed against Jessica's, and he edged his chair backward against the wall, creating a gap of a mere two inches. Jessica didn't seem to notice, perhaps because of her high state of agitation.

She said, "I can't believe they've arrested Kim and are holding her in jail. It's total BS."

Bill pushed his lips out, unsure why Jessica was so angry. "Are you familiar with the facts of the case?"

Jessica assured him she was because she had visited Kim in jail, and Kim gave her the highlights.

Bill said, "Then you know that the facts implicate Kim. That's why the police have arrested her."

"But they're wrong!"

Jessica made this statement with such passion, Bill wondered if she might have evidence he did not possess.

"How can you be sure?"

"Because she's my *sister.* And my sister is not a murderer."

Okay. On the face of it, Jessica had no more to go on than Bill: faith in Kim's innocence. He gave Jessica a moment to catch her breath and took a different tack. He had heard from Emily that the judge at Kim's arraignment agreed to a bail amount of one hundred thousand dollars, well below the quarter million requested by the commonwealth's attorney, Craig Beaumont.

"It might as well have been a million," said Jessica. "Kim doesn't have money like that."

"She could hire a bail bondsman," said Bill.

Jessica nodded. "I brought that up and offered to pay the fee, but she won't take it." Jessica shook her head as if often perplexed by her sister. "Kim says jail is no worse than some motels she's seen. Now, how can I help you get her out?"

"Nathan mentioned that you met Lily Wolf."

Jessica made a face like she'd bitten a rotten peach. "Yes. Kim brought her to Staunton for dinner. I didn't like her much."

"Tell me about her."

"Useless. Lily was as useless as all of Kim's other girlfriends. Kim has a real talent for picking losers. Whenever Kim falls in love, it's a downhill journey to a bad place."

"Can you be more specific?"

Jessica took her time fashioning a response. Her eyes grew tense, and Bill sensed Kim's choices of romantic partners had caused problems in the past.

"If, for once, Kim would find a girlfriend who had a decent job, I'd be happy. I wouldn't care how old she was, how pretty she was, or where she came from if she could keep a job."

"I gather you were unsatisfied with Ms. Wolf's means of employment."

"Correct. I'm in real estate, Bill. I sell houses. I work hard at it, and it pays me a good living. I'll never be the US president. I'll never win a Nobel prize. But I'll pay my bills until the day I die."

Bill nodded. He had a healthy measure of admiration for hard workers.

"I asked Ms. Wolf what she did for a living and got vague answers. Consultant. What sort of consultant? Business consultant. What industry? Growth industries. Crap like that. I asked what she was doing here in the US. Sabbatical. For how long? She was flexible and might stay in the US for a long time. How will you make money here? Freelance consulting." Jessica lifted her arms in frustration. "It went on and on like that. Finally, I gave up and ate my food. I figured she was another loser like all the others, and the relationship would end badly." Jessica closed her eyes, inhaled deeply, and clenched her hands. "And now we have this mess."

"You figured the relationship would end badly?"

"Hmm."

"What do you mean by that?"

Jessica studied Bill's face, her attention drawn away from Kim's predicament. She pointed at him. "You're good at this stuff, aren't you?"

"I try."

Jessica drew another big breath and let it out slowly. "What I mean by end badly is that Kim calls me in tears when her lover leaves. Kim loses her job because she's too depressed to work. Kim drinks too much wine. On and on and on."

"What about violence? Does Kim become violent when she's depressed or drinks too much wine?"

"Why do you ask that? I already told you she didn't kill Lily Wolf."

"I remember. But earlier in life, Kim did become violent. Didn't she?"

Jessica pressed her lips tightly together, then said, "I feel that when you ask a question, you often already know the answer."

"The background check on Kim revealed a pattern of conflict. I want to hear your version of her past."

Jessica stood as if she wished to walk across the room, but the small office afforded her only enough space for two steps. Then she turned back. "Kim had what I will mercifully call an exuberant youth. But like a drunk who gets behind the wheel, Kim's exuberance sometimes caused her to veer into a ditch. Kim's party nature and her uncanny ability to find attractive lovers who are otherwise scoundrels often got her into trouble. And the police were called on more than one occasion."

"Did anyone get hurt?"

"Not seriously. Kim and a girlfriend got into a physical altercation at a party. They were both drunk, and both sustained mild injuries. The police were called. Kim and the other woman made up after they sobered up. But the girlfriend left for good a month later."

"When did this happen?"

"Oh, gracious." Jessica rubbed her forehead. "Ages ago. Twenty years, maybe? Longer even."

"And recently?"

"Kim's grown up. She lost her wildness with age." Jessica smiled sadly. "Haven't we all?"

"She's never married?"

Jessica shook her head. "I think she gave up on the idea.

Kim told me once that she knew she'd die alone. Before Lily, she hadn't had a real date in five years."

Bill nodded to indicate his understanding while sorting out what to ask next. Although she had expressed frustration with her sister's romantic past, Jessica clearly cared for Kim, or she wouldn't be here. Jessica was the protective sibling fretting about the downstream effects of Kim's latest romantic involvement. Jessica cared little for Lily Wolf, despised her even. How far was Jessica willing to go to protect Kim from her own bad choices? Murder?

As he had with Nick Pappas, Bill momentarily assumed that Jessica killed Wolf. How did that scenario unfold? Was Jessica capable of carefully plotting the dreadful deed? Had she watched her sister leave the rental house, then tiptoed into the kitchen, grabbed the blue-handled knife, and stabbed Lily on the back porch?

No. That didn't add up. Why use Kim's blue-handled knife? Maybe Jessica didn't realize the knife was Kim's. Still, it seemed an awfully extreme measure.

On the other hand, Bill could imagine Jessica coming to the rental home to have a frank conversation with Lily Wolf. What were Lily's intentions? A quick fling before she moved on to the next happy place? Don't mess with my sister. She doesn't deserve it.

Perhaps that conversation had not gone well.

"Mind if I ask what make and model of car you drive?" said Bill.

Jessica frowned.

"We're searching video footage of all recent vehicle traffic. I want to be able to identify yours."

"I own a Mercedes sedan, E350, white."

The real estate business was apparently good in Staunton.

"When was the last time you drove up here before today?"

"Gosh. Long time. Months. I came up for the New Year's Eve show."

Bill put a hand out as if to beg her pardon for his next question. "Where were you early yesterday morning?"

Jessica raised her eyebrows. "You have me down as a suspect?"

"I hope you understand that I have to check certain boxes."

Jessica laughed. "I'm flattered. And honestly, I'm not sad to see Lily Wolf go, although I would have preferred her to leave alive. To answer your question, I was at home until eleven yesterday morning."

"Anyone with you?"

"No. Not unless you count my YouTube exercise instructor."

If it came to that, and Bill didn't think it would, they could verify whether someone at Jessica's home address had watched an online exercise video that morning. For now, he would drop the line of questioning.

"Can you think of anyone who might have wished Lily Wolf harm?"

Jessica folded her arms and considered Bill's question. "I don't know of anyone specific, but I'd suggest you look for someone Lily wronged in the past. Kim can't see beneath a person's skin. She only sees their appearance. She only hears what they say. When Kim first told me about Lily, she was gushing with emotion, but it was clear that Kim didn't know her well. Kim couldn't answer the first question. Where was Lily from? Russia, she believed. What did Lily do for a living? Kim didn't know and didn't care. How did Lily wind up in Wintergreen? Nothing. None of it made sense."

Jessica paused to breathe and then locked eyes with Bill. “In my line of work, and in yours, I suspect, you need the ability to read a person’s intentions. Kim couldn’t see it, but I could. Lily Wolf didn’t care what I thought, and she didn’t care about Kim. Lily Wolf only cared about herself.”

THIRTY-ONE

When Bill left the café, he phoned Kim's lawyer, Mark Gardner. Bill wanted to meet with Kim again and thought having Gardner attend would be helpful. Gardner had a light afternoon and would rearrange his schedule to accommodate Bill's visit, provided Bill would give him a thorough update.

"I'm walking a thin line sharing intel with you that I got from a police investigation," said Bill.

"Aren't we all trying to get to the truth?"

"Yeah. I guess that's why I want to chat with Kim again."

The regional jail guard brought Kim into the interview room in handcuffs. She wore an orange jumpsuit, and her hair, unruly on the best of days, was badly mashed to one side.

"Can you take those off?" Mark asked.

The guard frowned.

"Come on," said Mark. "She's not going anywhere."

"I can't imagine anyplace I'd rather be," said Kim.

The guard snorted, shook his head at Kim's attitude, and uncuffed her.

After the guard left, Bill asked Kim how jail suited her. It wasn't her ideal vacation, but sometimes you had to take what you could get. She had learned a few things from the woman in the next cell, and the food was okay.

"We need to discuss a few things you neglected to share with me earlier." Bill relayed this in a voice that said he was none too happy.

Kim glanced at Mark to see if her attorney knew why Bill was angry. Mark shrugged.

"Like what?" said Kim.

"Like your police record, for starters."

"Oh, that."

"Yeah, that."

Kim dipped her chin into her chest and rubbed the back of her neck. "I'm sorry. My bad, for sure. But that was a long time ago. I'm not like that anymore."

"Not like what anymore? Confrontational? Prone to violence? None of this stuff looks good, you know."

Kim went on and on with her apology. Bill grew tired of listening. Mark didn't say a word, which struck Bill as peculiar until he figured it out.

"You already knew all of this, didn't you?" Bill said to Mark.

Mark shrugged again. "How do you think I came to be a friend of the family? In Kim's defense, that *was* a long time ago. Didn't you do a few stupid things when you were young?"

Bill pouted but then acknowledged that what Mark said was true.

Mark said, "What else did you want to discuss with Kim?"

"Lily Wolf's phone."

Kim fidgeted in her chair. A sinking feeling entered Bill's chest. If she confessed now, admitted that she'd killed Wolf in the heat of passion, Mark could negotiate a plea deal with a reasonable prosecuting attorney. But Craig Beaumont wasn't reasonable.

"What about Lily's phone?" said Mark.

"The police found it hidden behind the café."

Kim frowned.

"Did you take Lily's phone?" said Bill.

"No. I don't remember seeing her phone."

"Don't lie to me."

Kim threw her hands out to her sides. "I'm not."

"Then how did it get there?"

She raised her eyebrows. "You're the detective. You tell me."

Bill pointed a finger at her. "Kim, you're one smart-ass comment away from me walking out that door. And then Mark's going to be the only friend you have."

Kim's eyes grew big, and she launched into apology mode again. Then she started crying, which made him feel like a louse. After all, she was the one in jail.

"Bill, I'm not lying to you. I didn't kill Lily, and I still want you to find out who did. I have no idea how they did it, but the killer must have taken Lily's phone and hid it to implicate me."

"Yes, but who, Kim? Who would do that?"

Clearly, Kim didn't know. They covered the same ground they had during Bill's earlier visit, including Lily's remarks to Kim that she had been involved briefly with someone else on the mountain earlier. Bill now suspected this person was Nick Pappas, but by Nick's statement and Kim's recollection, that relationship had ended over a month ago. The review of video footage would verify Nick's alibi, or not.

Kim continued fidgeting, still nervous, and Bill picked up on it.

"What?" he said.

"There's something else I haven't told you."

"Now would be the time."

"I sent Lily a text that morning after our fight. It was not a nice message."

Bill exchanged glances with Mark. Could this situation get any worse?

"The message said 'I wish you were dead.'"

Mark, who struck Bill as a rock of a defense attorney, folded his arms and frowned.

"I didn't mean it," said Kim. "That's why I went back to the house, to apologize for that message. But Lily wouldn't let me inside. She laughed at me."

Kim was on the verge of tears again. What kind of person was Lily Wolf? To laugh at an apology at such a time. Bill decided that he would not have liked her. He placed his hand on Kim's, and she grabbed him as if he were a lifeline.

Kim had nothing further to confess, and they began to wrap up the conversation. Kim appeared distraught, and Bill tried to buoy her spirits. He even joked about the food, but it didn't help much, so Bill said, "Kim, don't give up. I believe you're innocent, and I will prove it."

~

Outside in the parking lot, Bill brought Mark up to speed on the potential suspect, Nick Pappas.

"That's something," said Mark. "If you can put him at the scene, we'll have a chance for reasonable doubt."

"We have a long way to go in this investigation. Are you going to stop by the courthouse to see Beaumont?"

Mark frowned. "No point. Not yet. Beaumont sees this as his ticket to the moon. He's not going to trade it in for a rollercoaster ride."

THIRTY-TWO

On the way back from Charlottesville, Bill took a detour down Route 29 and stopped by Saunders Brothers Farm Market to see if the early peaches were out. Oh, yes. Fresh peaches were on display under the overhang out front—bushels, pecks, and smaller portions. The market offered two varieties—Rich May and Early Redhaven. Bill lifted a Rich May and gave it a sniff. Yum. They were firm yet for eating, but two or three days on the kitchen counter would take care of that. He selected a small basket of peaches and then stepped inside, where he found a jar of strawberry preserves he couldn't live without. He was about to leave when the ice cream counter caught his eye. What the heck. He was supporting the local economy.

Back in his Mazda, he savored the creamy texture of the treat. Then his phone buzzed.

Skip Forrester, his contact at the FBI.

With a mouthful of ice cream, Bill tried to say, "Hello, Skip," but the words came out mushy.

"Are you eating?" said Skip.

"Ithe Scream."

"Want me to call back?"

Bill swallowed. "No. No. This is about Krista's request?"

"Yeah. And while we're on that subject, I wish you wouldn't use my girlfriend to get to me."

"Did it work?"

"Well, yeah, but—"

"Wait. Are you officially boyfriend and girlfriend now?"

Skip cleared his throat. "Let's not get too technical with the terminology."

"Whatever you say."

"And I'd appreciate it if you didn't tell Krista I called her my girlfriend."

"Sure."

Personally, Bill hoped the relationship worked out. He was a big fan of Krista's and thought Skip was a decent match for her. Smart. Good job. Not bad looking if you were into tall, slender men with prematurely gray hair. Which apparently worked for Krista, given that the two of them had been hanging out for several months. And Bill knew from experience that Skip was a solid investigator.

"Did you dig up anything new on Lily Wolf?" Bill asked.

"Plenty."

While Bill worked on his ice cream treat, Skip shared his newfound knowledge. Skip's initial search of FBI records for Lily Wolf turned up little, just a phone number at the CIA. He called that number and got a recording asking him to leave a voice message. He left his name and FBI badge number and said he was seeking information on Lily Wolf. Two hours later, a man returned Skip's call. The man would not give Skip his full name; he called himself John and said he was with the CIA.

"Cloak and dagger stuff, you know?" said Skip. "And I don't think his real name is John."

"Okay. Wow."

Skip continued with his briefing. John said he knew Lily Wolf. He claimed she was a CIA asset. Skip told John that Lily Wolf was dead, and John grew agitated. Then John wanted to know everything Skip could give him. Skip gave John the high-level outline of the murder, which was already public information in Wintergreen. John went silent for a minute, then asked Skip who was investigating the murder. Skip shared that Nelson County had the lead with the local community police doing some legwork. Skip also mentioned Bill's involvement.

"I hope that's all right."

"Yeah. Fine. Actually, I'd like to talk with John."

"Good. John doesn't want to confer with anyone who works in an official police capacity, including Krista. But he will meet with you."

What was that all about? It probably had something to do with turf. Generally speaking, the CIA was supposed to stick to its playground—international dirt. US soil was the FBI's purview.

"I gave him your phone number," said Skip. "You should expect a call."

Holy smokes. What an unexpected break.

Lily Wolf was a CIA asset, which might explain a lot. Her accent. Her fight training. Maybe even the money. But why was she holed up in Wintergreen?

"Anything else?" said Bill.

"No. I mean, yes. Not the Lily Wolf thing. It's something else."

"All right. What's up?"

Then silence. Bill had nearly finished the ice cream. He scraped his spoon around the cup's bottom edges. Still nothing from Skip.

"You still there?"

"Yes. It's about Krista."

Oh. Okay. Skip was now searching for a different kind of intel.

"She's hard to read," said Skip. "We've been seeing each other for five months, and I can't tell where we're going."

"Do you want to go somewhere specific?"

"Yeah, I do. Not a specific destination necessarily, but I want to know that we're progressing. I want us to be more than once-a-month weekend pals. And I can't tell what Krista wants."

Hmm. Relationship advice wasn't Bill's thing. After all, he was divorced. Nobody wanted to hire a coach with an overall losing record.

Bill said, "You're in a better position to gauge Krista's intentions than I am."

"I'm too close. You've known Krista longer. Has she said anything to you?"

"If she had, I wouldn't betray her confidence."

"I'm not asking you to do that. But I've done you a favor. Help me out."

Truthfully, Bill had given this particular question zero thought. But it was easy to see that Skip and Krista were coming at this thing from different places. Though they were approximately the same age, they had vastly different backgrounds. Skip had never married, had no kids, and was well on his way career-wise. Krista was divorced with two teenage boys and was still new to her career.

Bill shared this perspective with Skip and added that he

believed this might affect Krista's willingness to move forward quickly.

Then Bill said, "My advice is to chill out and let the relationship take its course. Don't try to force it."

This seemed to work for Skip, who said, "Makes total sense. Definitely. I can do that."

THIRTY-THREE

"I wish you were coming," said Cindy.

After his conversation with Skip Forrester, Bill had texted Cindy to see if he could stop by in thirty minutes. Sure. Once he got to Cindy's condo, she invited him into her bedroom, where she was packing for the trip to New Jersey. She would leave in the morning and be gone for four days.

"Me too," he said. "I've never been to the Jersey shore."

Bill sat on Cindy's bed and inspected her room. Though he'd been in her bedroom on other occasions, Cindy's previous invitations had come with an assumed agenda that focused all of his senses on her and her alone, not the furniture or wall hangings or personal items on her bureau.

Now, as Cindy packed her bathing suit, shorts, tops, and other assorted clothes, Bill inspected the contents of her room and asked questions. She had found the four small paintings of owls at the local artists' shop in the Rockfish Valley Community Center. The porcelain bowl was a prized find from an antique store in Crozet. The bedside lamps came from an online store. He didn't mention the framed photos of her two children on the bureau.

"Did you stop by the café today?" Cindy asked.

Bill chuckled. "Yeah, Terry and Maria were doing a great job holding things together."

"They were awesome this morning. They don't know Kim well, but they pitched right in."

"I'm glad we met them," said Bill.

"How is Kim holding up?" she asked.

"She started off strong, but after spending a day and a night in jail, the cracks are starting to show."

"Are you making progress with the investigation?"

Bill shrugged as if to say it was hard to tell. "Each case is different. Some cases solve themselves. The murderer steps forward, confesses their guilt, and it's all over except for the paperwork. Other cases take years. This one feels like it's in the middle somewhere. We went downhill for a while but may have caught a lucky break today."

Cindy asked whether he could provide more details, but Bill said he'd better not. Soon, Cindy finished with that phase of her packing, and he followed her into the main room. He hoped they could spend time together since she'd be gone for four days.

She stepped close to him and put a hand on his chest. "I'd ask you to stay for dinner and, you know, but I still have a lot to do, and I need to leave early in the morning."

"Oh, sure, that's what I expected. Plus, I have to take Max out. He's been cooped up most of the day."

Their goodbye kiss lingered as if they knew they should not take their time together for granted—everyone's story ended eventually.

~

Back at his condo, Bill told Max to get ready for a long walk. The black Labrador obediently struck a downward dog pose as part of his prep routine. Bill arranged the peaches on the kitchen counter to ripen.

Maybe Mr. Chips would like one of those peaches right now.

Then Bill recalled that he had yet to see Mr. Chips this year. He hurried onto his balcony in hopes of spotting his groundhog friend. No such luck.

"Okay, Max, it's just us two tonight. You ready?"

Outside, with Max on his leash, Bill turned left, and they began to ascend the hill via the parking lot. He had in mind taking Max up to the dog park behind Café Devine, around the fitness center to the mail hut, and then to the ridge, where he would set Max free to run.

As usual, Max spent a healthy amount of time sniffing various scents like flowers, other dogs' markings, and invisible rodent trails. Max stopped to study a squirrel standing under a tree with a nut in its hands. Unlike other dogs Bill had known, Max did not lunge at the leash in an attempt to catch the squirrel, and Bill thought he understood why. First, Max didn't need the squirrel for food since Bill fed him every day. Also, Max knew he had no chance of catching the squirrel. Perhaps there had been a time in his life as a stray when Max needed to catch a squirrel or go hungry. Max may have learned then that chasing a squirrel sitting under a tree was a no-win proposition. Better to lie quietly in a low place and wait for a lazy squirrel to get caught in the open.

Bill leaned over to rub Max's head. "Where have you been, Max? Huh? Where did you live? What did you do?"

No answer.

They reached the upper end of the Vistas' parking lot and

crossed into the Cliffs complex. Suddenly, a dog set off a furious barking frenzy. The barking came from an open third-story window. Bill knew the guilty party, a poodle named Curly, who belonged to his friend Frieda Chang. Bill tried to calm Curly by calling out to him, but Curly continued making an obnoxious racket. For his part, Max led Bill to the sidewalk in front of the Cliffs building, sat on his haunches, and gazed with mild interest at the upper end of the parking lot.

Bill turned his eyes that way.

Holy Peter, Paul, and Mary. It's a bear.

A large black bear hauled a white plastic trash bag out of an open dumpster and shredded the bag in seconds.

Curly barked and barked.

Max sat unperturbed.

Bill's heart pounded.

The bear rifled through the trash bag's contents, slurped at something of interest for a few seconds, and then began ambling down the parking lot in their general direction.

Curly barked even louder.

Max sniffed.

Bill calculated the distance between them and the bear. The bear drew closer but paid them no mind. Instead, the bear was keenly focused on the dumpster across the parking lot from Bill and Max. Though Curly continued to bark, Bill ignored that noise and focused on Max's reaction to the bear. Max turned his head uphill toward the obliterated trash bag and sniffed again.

The bear tried both doors on the new dumpster but found them locked. The bear then turned toward Bill and Max, perhaps to assess whether they posed a threat. Bill held his breath. Max didn't move. Apparently, the bear found them to be of no consequence and ambled toward the next dumpster farther down the hill.

Bill and Max observed the bear try unsuccessfully to open those doors. Then, the bear continued on its journey. It occurred to Bill that this may be a regular routine for the bear. There were probably twenty dumpsters on the ridge. The bear was like a gambler playing a slot machine. Sooner or later, pulling the handle would pay off in delicious, golden trash.

Max rose and continued his journey up the hill. Max was not a pacifist, Bill realized. Instead, it was as if he had a sixth sense for detecting danger. The bear meant them no harm, and Max knew this from the start. How Max knew this, Bill couldn't fathom. But Bill did know that if the bear had meant them harm, Max would have reacted differently. On a walk one sunny afternoon, they had come upon a rattlesnake on one side of the path. When the snake coiled, it turned Max into a monster, and it was all Bill could do to drag Max away.

Yes, Max had seen violence during his time as a stray. Bill knew this because the fur on his shoulder barely covered a vicious scar.

Bill watched now as Max calmly ascended the hill.

"Where have you been, Max?" he asked. "What did you do?"

It saddened Bill to realize that he would never know.

THIRTY-FOUR

Brendan Baittinger was authorized to work extra hours until he finished analyzing vehicle traffic on the mountain. According to the chief, getting the data was more important than the overtime cost. So Brendan had stayed until eleven at night, went home to grab a few hours of sleep, and returned at six a.m., two hours early for his regular dispatcher shift.

Despite his skepticism toward the department's lack of a cool vibe, Brendan had to admit this investigation was exciting work. After the previous day's team meeting, Bill O'Shea—an old dude whose precise role Brendan had yet to figure out—stopped by his desk to give him a long list of search parameters.

"Unless that's too much for you," Bill said. "Given that you're new, I wouldn't want to strain your abilities."

"I can handle it."

Bill had nodded. "I guess we'll find out."

Brendan had started by requesting vehicle license data from the Wintergreen Property Owners Association. The WPOA recorded license plate numbers when they first issued

Wintergreen stickers to owners for vehicle bumpers. Unfortunately, Brendan soon learned this data lacked integrity because owners often changed cars without updating the records. Nevertheless, Brendan created a query to compare license tags read by the license plate recognition camera to those in the WPOA sticker database. Then, he copied the owners' names next to matching tag numbers.

This left Brendan with sixty-three unidentified vehicles that had entered and/or exited Wintergreen during the search period. Most of these vehicles were licensed in Virginia, though a fair number came from North Carolina or Maryland, and a few hailed from as far away as Florida or Texas. Brendan put the out-of-state vehicles to one side, as they would be the hardest to track down. He matched many of the remaining Virginia tags to Wintergreen owners by accessing DMV records and comparing names to a list of owners.

One of the owners' names was Nick Pappas. O'Shea had said finding this vehicle was critical to verifying Pappas's alibi, so Brendan switched his screen to the actual video of the car. At 6:43 p.m. on the night before the murder, a red Audi R8 convertible with the relevant tag number left Wintergreen. Brendan soon found video evidence of the same car returning at 11:15 a.m. the next morning, well after the murder occurred. Nick Pappas had stated the truth, at least about his car's movements.

Brendan then inspected the names associated with Virginia tags from non-owner vehicles. He was on the lookout for Jessica or Nathan Smith. Jessica's name did not appear during the search period. Nathan Smith's Ford Focus entered Wintergreen at 7:48 a.m.

Wait. What's that?

Brendan blinked several times and double-checked the data. After entering the first time, Nathan Smith's car had left

Wintergreen at 12:30 p.m. and returned once more forty-four minutes later. Brendan made a note to mention this find to Emily.

He then searched the footage to inspect all of the unknown vehicles with Virginia and out-of-state tags, of which there were twenty-four. Fifteen of these were associated with service businesses who had arrived at Wintergreen in the morning—landscapers, plumbers, painters, etc. The remaining vehicles were not noteworthy and probably belonged to resort guests. But there was one that Brendan found interesting—a black Lincoln Continental entered Wintergreen at 4:24 a.m. and left again at 7:13 a.m.

Brendan's heart rate quickened. He turned back to the DMV system. The Lincoln was registered to a business named Virginia Easy Ride LLC. The car was identified as a commercial vehicle registered to provide intrastate for-hire services. The record included a business owner's name, a phone number, and an address in Charlottesville.

It was 7:45 a.m. He'd better update the chief before his dispatcher shift began.

Emily Powell sat behind her desk with a cup of coffee and read incident reports from the previous day. Sheesh. More bear calls. They had more than doubled year-over-year. The previously widespread mange had run its course through the bear population, and the bears were making a solid comeback. Emily chuckled when she read Krista's report. Krista had a talent for slipping sarcasm into her incident descriptions. Apparently, an owner had expressed dissatisfaction with Krista's explanation of their policy against shooting bears. Krista promised to work on her communication skills.

Emily's cell phone buzzed. Speak of the devil.

"Good morning, Krista," she said.

"Hey, boss. Listen, I'm sorry. I'm stuck at home with a sick kid."

"That sucks. You think it's COVID?"

"No. Ashton's puking all over the place. I believe it's norovirus. It's going around his school."

"Heaven save us. Thank goodness my three are healthy, for now."

"Anyway, my mom will spell me at noon. I'll be in shortly after that."

"Don't worry about us. We'll manage."

Krista asked if there were any developments on the case. No. Emily asked whether Krista had learned anything from her call with Skip Forrester. Maybe. More to come on that front.

A shadow appeared at Emily's door. Brendan Baittinger waved to indicate he needed a minute.

Emily told Krista she had to go, and they signed off.

"Come in, Brendan. What do you have?"

Brendan shared the interesting vehicle search results. First, Pappas's vehicle data matched his alibi. Next, following the murder, Nathan Smith's car had left Wintergreen and then returned. And finally, a mysterious Lincoln had visited around the time of the murder.

Emily frowned.

"That's odd. So, Nathan came to work, left Wintergreen at twelve thirty, then came back forty minutes later?"

Brendan nodded. "His car did."

"Okay. We'll discuss that at the next meeting. What do you make of the limo?"

"Maybe someone ordered a ride to the airport?"

Possibly, thought Emily, *but why did the limo stay for nearly three hours?*

"Did you check the weather cam by the overlook?" she asked.

"Yes. The limo passed the cam a few minutes after entering Wintergreen and returned a few minutes before leaving. He was at the top of the mountain somewhere."

Emily pushed her lips out. The limo had been on top of the mountain for a period that bracketed Lily Wolf's time of death. Probably nothing important. But you never knew.

"Your shift will start soon, right?" she said.

"Yes, ma'am."

"Okay. We've got to figure out why the limo was up here. Make a call or two when you get a break in the action this morning. Get ahold of the owner."

Brendan nodded.

"Track that sucker down."

"Yes, chief."

THIRTY-FIVE

After taking Max out for exercise, Bill showered and ate a hearty breakfast of scrambled eggs, a bagel with cream cheese, and blueberries. He checked the peaches. Not ripe yet. He poured another cup of coffee, and his cell phone buzzed: an unidentified number with a northern Virginia area code.

"Hello?" he said.

"This is John."

Car noise indicated John was driving. It had to be Skip Forrester's CIA contact. Only a spy could be that rude.

"Okay."

"Am I speaking with Bill O'Shea, formerly of the Columbia, South Carolina, PD?"

"Uh-huh. I've been expecting your call."

"Good. Give me the scoop on this Lily Wolf situation."

Bill scratched his head. He walked to the floor-to-ceiling window that overlooked the mountains. Two turkey vultures circled the air above the forest.

"I don't have much scoop. Ms. Wolf is dead. We think she

might have been Russian, she had a wolf tattoo on her leg, and I gather she was on your payroll. Honestly, I was hoping you could give me some information."

"I won't talk to the police."

"That's fine. I'm not with the police."

Which, strictly speaking, was true. Bill was not on the payroll in any official capacity. And though he was coordinating efforts with the Wintergreen PD, he didn't feel the need to share all of those details. For crying out loud, CIA John wouldn't even share his last name.

More traffic noise. It sounded as if another driver honked their horn. CIA John honked back.

"Okay," said John. "Here's the deal. I can't confer with Nelson County or Wintergreen PD. But we do have an interest in how this thing plays out. So, I propose a scratch-each-other's-back arrangement. You share. I share. Make sense?"

"Yep."

"I understand Nelson County has a suspect in custody."

"They do, but I'm convinced they have the wrong person."

"Why is that?"

Bill's face grew warm. He made a fist with his free hand.

"So far, *John,* I've been doing all of the sharing. How about you tell me who the heck Lily Wolf was?"

More road noise, then, "Yeah, fair enough."

CIA John opened up. Lily Wolf, real name Liliya Volkova, was born of modest means in Belarus but did exceptionally well in school. In her twenties, she moved to Russia, where she attended university and studied linguistics and government. Lily had gifts of charm and beauty and used those gifts to cultivate a network of influential people in the oligarch community. Over time, she expanded her network to include people in both Eastern and Western Europe, not only businesspeople but also politicians and people within the military-industrial complex.

Then, one day, Lily approached the CIA with a proposition. She would provide intel in exchange for money. The agency gave her a probationary offer, paying small money at first. Over time, she proved her value, and her compensation grew.

"But some people inside the CIA didn't trust Lily because she had no philosophical grounding. Autocracy, democracy—it was all the same to her. Some field agents asserted that Lily worked both sides. She gave us good stuff, to be sure, but she might have sold intel to the Russians as well. No one knew for certain."

Bill opened a sliding door, and the sounds of children playing rose from the ground below. A little dog barked. Over on his bed, Max snored. John's story sounded like a spy novel. How in the world did this stuff come to Wintergreen?

CIA John got to that part next. Something big had happened, and Lily was in the middle of it. A Russian oligarch was killed. Then, two Polish field agents died under suspicious circumstances. At the end of it all, the CIA gained a treasure trove of intel on Russian weapons development. Lily's supporters hailed her as a hero. Her detractors called her a traitor. No one knew where the Russians stood.

"She wanted out," said CIA John, "and we agreed to help her in a limited fashion. We gave her an ID. We put her up in a safe house . . ."

"In Wintergreen."

"Yes. Wolf was only supposed to be there for a month—six weeks at the most—but she stayed on. She claimed she had no money, had frittered it away, and needed to raise a new stake. Lord knows how."

"Then what?"

"Then nothing. She was quiet. Lily's handler should have insisted that Lily move farther away from DC, but the handler got busy. Other stuff came up. Next thing I know, Skip Forrester calls, and I get a new assignment."

"Did the CIA do this?"

"No. No chance."

CIA John's answer sounded more like an official denial than a genuine conviction. Would John even know if the CIA had ordered Lily's assassination?

"There may be someone inside who wanted her gone," said John, "but operating on US soil is considered a career-limiting move. No one up top would sanction that."

Then why was John sharing his intel? He clearly wanted something from Bill.

"I'm headed your way," said John.

"Why? If the CIA is clean, what do you care? Let it play out."

"We have to keep close tabs on this. We have the safe house, which we'll have to relocate now. Plus, Lily was an asset. And . . ."

"And what?"

"I need your help. I'm convinced her murder was not the CIA's doing, but there could still be a link."

Jeez. Bill was glad he'd never worked for the federal government. There was always another twist. If only they could keep things simple.

"What link?"

"I gave you the highlights of her latest adventure, but Lily's been working for us for fifteen years. There have been other incidents. Other conflicts. It's possible that a former CIA person wanted her dead."

"I see. You want me to work other suspects for you."

"Thanks for volunteering. I've got an analyst back in DC working on this. She'll have something soon. Let's meet for lunch."

THIRTY-SIX

On his drive to Wintergreen that morning, Mitch Gentry got a crazy notion that he couldn't shake. He was born in Augusta County and used the name Augusta, plus his birth year, as the password for his laptop and bank account. What if Lily Wolf did the same?

Mitch checked his watch. Krista Jackson had called in absent that morning, and Mitch would sub for her patrol shift starting in a few minutes. One of Krista's kids had norovirus. Jeez. Lulu and Mitch had seven months to go. When Mitch was younger, he considered seven months a long time, but his frame of reference had changed. A friend of his compared having kids to riding a speedboat and throwing an anchor off the back. Mitch's shoulders felt tight. He couldn't remember the last time he'd called in sick, but if their baby became ill and Lulu had an important test, he would have to stay home.

After punching in at the police station, Mitch got ready for his patrol shift and stopped by the chief's office on the way out. He knocked on the doorframe, and Emily Powell looked up from her screen. Her expression instantly changed from intense concentration to a relaxed smile. How did she do that? With so many competing priorities, Mitch would pull his hair out by the roots. Emily had three kids, yet somehow, she managed. Maybe he could too.

"Hey, Mitch," she said. "What's up?"

"Morning, boss. Sorry to bother you."

"Not a problem. Come on in."

Mitch explained his idea concerning Lily Wolf's password.

"That's what you use?" she said after he'd finished.

Mitch nodded.

"I do something similar, but I use Virginia instead of Nelson County, and I use the year of my high school graduation."

"I guess everyone has a different idea for their password. Kind of a long shot, huh?"

"Probably. But what else do we have?"

So, after Mitch left, Emily opened Wintergreen's evidence room—little more than a closet since they seldom had evidence to secure—and retrieved Lily Wolf's laptop. Ms. Wolf had cared enough about a town named Kobryn to have it tattooed on her arm, and they had a birth year from her driver's license. Back at her desk, Emily wrote down four variations of the name Kobryn and the year 1978, using upper case and lower case for the first letter and two and four digits for the year. Then, she took the paper and the laptop to the dispatcher's station.

Brendan was on the radio. An SUV with a flat tire had pulled onto the shoulder of Wintergreen Drive, and John Hill had stopped to help. Brendan wrapped up that conversation and turned to Emily.

"Any luck with the limo service?" she asked.

"No. I left two voice messages. It's an office phone."

"Keep trying. And do a search on the owner to see if he's got a different number."

"Yes, ma'am."

"Here. Try these passwords on the laptop."

After Brendan had tried and failed to open Lily Wolf's phone, Emily decided she should have joined Brendan in that endeavor. Whether successful or not, having two witnesses observe the result left a better fact pattern in case someone, like Craig Beaumont, should question their methods later.

Brendan studied the four combinations of letters and numbers. "Huh. You think someone would use something so obvious?"

"Why? What do you use?"

Brendan's face flushed. "Um. My dog's name, but I spell it backward. And I add her birth year and an exclamation point."

"Great. I'm glad you're more security-conscious. Do you know the name of her dog? No? Try these instead."

And then, to Emily's great astonishment, Brendan accessed Lily Wolf's laptop on the third try.

"Damn," he said. "It worked. Oh, sorry."

Emily ignored Brendan and leaned closer to the screen. Lily Wolf had organized her toolbar on the bottom. Emily asked Brendan to click on the browser icon. Only two tabs were open; one was for email, and the other showed a video screen of a movie on pause. Emily recognized the movie as an old rom-com starring Sandra Bullock. Hmm. Wolf had good taste in movies.

"Pull up the email," she said.

The email messages were in a foreign language using the Cyrillic alphabet. Perhaps Russian.

Brendan said, "I can translate those using an online tool."

"Do that later. Check the photos icon."

Brendan clicked the button, and an image consumed the entire screen. Brendan jumped back in his chair.

Emily frowned and leaned closer to the screen.

The photo was of Lily Wolf and a man in bed, naked and engaged in an activity that could not be mistaken for anything else.

Brendan, speechless, edged his chair farther from the screen.

"Try not to think of it as porn," Emily said.

"Yes, ma'am."

Emily touched the escape button, and the image shrank into a library of photos. There were several dozen similar images of Lily Wolf and the man.

The radio crackled, and Brendan hastened to answer what turned out to be a routine check-in.

Emily scanned the photos and zoomed in on one that showed a clear shot of the man's face. She didn't recognize him, but she could guess his name from his dark hair and olive complexion.

Yep. We may have figured out where the money came from.

THIRTY-SEVEN

Bill met Mitch in the parking lot of the resort fitness center. Nick Pappas had requested that they interview him at the outdoor swimming pool. Inside, two young women sat behind the check-in, their eyes wide at the sight of Mitch in his uniform.

"How y'all doing?" Mitch said.

They smiled and politely returned his greeting. Bill was a regular at the fitness center and recognized the women. He said they had a meeting with a member by the pool, and the women waved them through.

The resort's large outdoor pool had four swim lanes and a deep end. A man, a woman, and two young children played together at the pool's shallow end. Nick Pappas—the only other person present—sat by himself at the far side of the deep end. He wore nice khaki shorts, a buttoned short-sleeved shirt, and deck shoes—not exactly pool attire.

He stood to shake their hands, all smiles. "Thanks for agreeing to meet me here."

"Let me guess," said Bill. "Your wife is at the house."

Nick grimaced. "She came up early. I didn't expect her until Saturday."

Bill found it audacious that Nick believed he could get through this without disclosing the facts to his wife. Depending on how this interview went, Nick might be in jail the next time his wife saw him. Nick suggested they move to a nearby round table with seats for four.

"Where is Officer Jackson?" Nick said after they'd been seated.

"She couldn't make it," said Mitch.

"Shame. I thought she was nice."

I'll bet you did, thought Bill. *What a turd.*

Of course, Bill wanted to pin the crime on Pappas to clear Kim Wiley. They had discovered a motive for Pappas, but as for the rest, they had more work to do.

"Additional facts have come to light," Bill said. "Maybe you can help us out."

"Okay. I don't know how. I told you everything I know."

"Perhaps not. We were able to access Ms. Wolf's laptop, and we found photos of you and her in an intimate setting."

Pappas's shoulders collapsed, and he closed his eyes. "Jeez. Lily promised to destroy those."

"Wolf blackmailed you, didn't she?" said Bill. "Fifty thousand dollars."

Nick's eyes darted from Bill to Mitch as if calculating his odds of successfully deceiving them.

"It's not worth lying," said Bill. "We'll get you one way or another."

Nick nodded his begrudging agreement. "Yes, she blackmailed me. And yes, I paid her the fifty thousand. What else was I to do? It was a pittance for me."

Mitch bit his lip. Fifty thousand was much more than a pittance for Bill and Mitch.

"That angered you," said Bill.

"Obviously."

"And you worried that she had kept the photos despite her promise. So, you went back to see her two days ago in the early morning."

Nick jerked backward. His eyes widened. "Is that what you think?"

"Yes."

"No, I didn't do that. I didn't go see her."

Bill had no proof that Nick Pappas returned to the rental home, but when you pushed a suspect, they occasionally broke.

"Wait a second," said Nick. "You know I didn't go back there. You guys are thorough, so you've already checked my alibi. You saw my car leave Wintergreen. Why are you hassling me now?"

Not so fast, rich boy.

"You hired a limo to bring you here in the early morning. The limo dropped you off a short distance from the house. You walked to the house to do what you did, and afterward, the limo took you down the mountain."

Pappas's brow furrowed in confusion.

"I didn't do any of that stuff. I haven't been to that house in over a month."

If Pappas was acting, he could have won an award.

"What did you do overnight?" said Mitch. "Can someone verify your whereabouts?"

Nick's eyes turned cagey, flitting back and forth. His knee began bouncing.

Oh, boy. Here we go.

"Yes. I was with someone. She can verify that we were together." And then Pappas had the nerve to give them a sly grin. "We were together *all night* and *all morning.*"

"Uh-huh," said Mitch, clearly unimpressed. "I need her contact information."

Pappas pulled his phone out and read the information to Mitch. Then he gave Bill and Mitch some advice.

"You guys should be looking at someone from Lily's past. She was a charmer up front but then changed into a snake. I consider myself a savvy guy, but she had me completely fooled. I'd bet big money she's done stuff like that, or even worse, on other occasions. As I said, for me, fifty thousand was no big deal. I was willing to walk away. But there are many people out there who aren't as forgiving."

"Thanks," said Mitch. "We'll give that consideration."

Mitch could pull a straight face if he wanted to. Pappas had no idea how much Mitch despised him.

Pappas smiled again. "And, uh, like our last conversation, we're keeping this on the down low. Right? My wife and I, you know, we have enough problems as it is." Pappas searched their faces for an affirmation but must have concluded he had not closed the deal. "I haven't yet made my annual contribution to the police fund. I'm feeling generous."

Mitch's eyes narrowed. He moved closer to Pappas. "Are you offering me a bribe?"

"No. No. It was an idea. That's all."

"Let me give you some advice. When driving around the mountain in your red convertible, stay below the speed limit."

Outside in the parking lot, Bill and Mitch conferred.

"You can get in a guy's face, can't you?" said Bill.

"Too much?"

"No, I like that look. Mad Mitch. A patrol officer has to

throw his weight around once in a while. But not all of the time. It's a delicate balance."

Mitch adopted a thoughtful expression, as if filing Bill's comments away for the future.

"What did you make of Pappas?" said Bill.

"I don't like the guy, but I have a feeling his alibi will check out."

"Yeah. Me too."

"And that leads us back to Kim Wiley, right?"

"Not necessarily."

Bill had chatted with Emily before the interview with Pappas. He relayed his plan to meet CIA John for lunch, and Emily told him about Nathan Smith's mysterious round trip off the mountain on the morning of the murder.

"How did Nathan manage that?" Mitch turned toward Café Devine, which was close by. A short wooden bridge crossed a stream separating the two facilities' parking lots. "Wasn't Undersheriff Shields at the café?"

"Arnie had already left to take Kim to Lovingston. Emily wants us to chat with Nathan."

"Makes sense." Mitch checked that his shirttail was appropriately tucked. "I knew Nathan in school."

"No kidding."

"Yeah, we played ball together. He was a good guy."

THIRTY-EIGHT

They reached Café Devine's parking lot, and Bill paused to take inventory of the vehicles: Nathan's Ford Focus, Terry Stinson's Honda CRV, Jessica Smith's Mercedes, and another SUV he didn't recognize. He ran through the list of vehicles with Mitch.

Mitch snapped his fingers. "I've got it."

"Got what?"

"What if Nathan's mom, Jessica, came up in the limo to disguise her movements? She killed Ms. Wolf, but something went wrong, and she couldn't get back to the limo. So, she hid until the sheriff's department cleared out and got Nathan to drive her down the mountain."

This scenario had occurred to Bill, but he considered it unlikely.

"Okay," he said, "but answer me this. In your scenario, after Jessica Smith killed Lily Wolf, why did she leave Kim's knife in the victim's back? That didn't help Kim at all."

"She freaked out. Jessica planned the act up front, but afterward, she lost her wits and left the knife. She thought the limo driver would realize something weird was happening, so she ditched him and came here to hide. She recruited Nathan's help later on."

"And Wolf's phone? If Jessica brought the phone up here, why didn't she take it? Why leave it hidden behind the café?"

Mitch pushed his lips out. "It does sound far-fetched. Doesn't it?"

It did. Still, it *was* possible, so Bill would test the hypothesis.

"When we get in there," said Bill, "we'll split them up. You take Nathan into the back office. I'll bring Jessica out here on the patio."

"Yeah, okay." Hesitant voice.

"What's up?"

"Nathan and I have a little history. In high school, we went after the same girl. He wound up with the girl, and I met Lulu."

Bill laughed and slapped Mitch's arm. "You won that contest, hands down. Ask him the question. He may have a perfectly logical explanation."

Again, Mitch said, "Yeah, okay," but he sounded more confident this time.

Inside, Bill found Maria Metcalf at the register and Terry Stinson behind her in the kitchen making sandwiches. Bill introduced Mitch, and the four of them chatted for a minute. Apparently, Nathan and Jessica were in the back office. Two customers inspected items in the local crafts area.

Maria said in a mischievous tone, "Terry's found a new career. He likes playing chef more than golf."

Terry nodded pleasantly. "At least someone gets to eat. What good does my playing golf all day do for anyone? Chasing a ball from here to there is fun but also a waste of time."

Maria leaned across the counter and lowered her voice. "Have you made progress on the investigation?"

"Maria," said Terry, "that's confidential."

Her partner's objections did not deter Maria. She remained poised to receive intel, her eyes expectant. At that moment, she reminded Bill of Kim, who never allowed him to leave the café without sharing a bit of community news.

"Have you taken over Kim's role as gossip queen as well?" asked Bill.

"Someone's got to do it."

Terry grumbled from behind the sandwich counter.

"We're making slow progress," said Bill. "I can't say any more than that."

"How is Kim holding up?" asked Maria.

Bill said, "Yesterday, she looked like she'd spent the night in jail. She probably looks worse today."

"Maybe I could bring her some beauty products."

Bill glanced at Mitch, who raised his eyebrows. They needed to keep moving because Bill had a lunch date with CIA John.

"Maybe," he said to Maria, "but call the jail first to see what's allowed."

Bill and Mitch walked back to the office, where they found Nathan and his mother. Bill asked Jessica if she would accompany him to the patio to discuss a follow-up question concerning Lily Wolf.

The small office was scarcely big enough to contain the two large men, who had both played high school football. Mitch played linebacker, and Nathan played various line positions. After Bill and Jessica left, Nathan sat in one of the two chairs. Mitch couldn't fit in the second chair without bumping into Nathan, so he remained standing. He leaned against a bookshelf and tried to appear casual.

The air was tense between them. Or maybe that was Mitch's imagination. Nathan smiled weakly. Mitch decided to address the old history first.

"You still keep in touch with Haley?"

Nathan chuckled. "No. We haven't spoken in years. She moved to Richmond. I heard you and Lulu got married."

"Best thing that ever happened to me."

"Congrats. Lulu's a nice person. You're both nice people."

Mitch realized there was no lingering ill will between them. They had both moved on.

"I need to ask you a question about the morning of the murder," said Mitch.

Nathan frowned. "What's up?"

Mitch explained that in their search of video footage, the police had seen Nathan's car do a round trip off of the mountain after the murder.

"Why did you leave the café?" Mitch asked.

Nathan wouldn't look at Mitch. He rubbed his hands on his thighs. "I, ah, had to get my meds."

Mitch tried to keep the surprise off of his face. By Nathan's appearance, he was as healthy as a two-year-old thoroughbred.

"Your meds?"

"Uh-huh. I get anxious sometimes. In high school, I took anxiety medication all the time. I don't have to now, but that morning was intense. After the cops left, the café was closed, and I was a near wreck. So, I zipped down to my apartment in Lyndhurst and took a pill."

"That's it?"

Nathan nodded.

It occurred to Mitch that you could know a person for a long time but not know them well. He had been to hundreds of football practices with Nathan and never knew he was on medication.

"When did your mother first get here?"

Nathan paused to think. "Yesterday, a little after noon."

"You two are spending a lot of time here in the office."

"Yeah. Mom's teaching me how to read the books. I want to run my own restaurant, but I need to learn the back-office stuff. Mom bitches about Aunt Kim. She says we could make more money if Aunt Kim did a better job of managing the business."

"What kind of restaurant?"

Nathan gazed at the wall that separated the office from the café. "Something different. I've been researching pizza ovens. They're not that expensive."

Mitch would bet his last quarter that Nathan Smith had nothing to do with Lily Wolf's murder. The guy was ten years out of high school, making sandwiches in his aunt's café. But he had dreams for the future that did not include prison.

With both of them seated in patio chairs around a table, Jessica Smith smiled pleasantly at Bill. It was a nice day, mid-seventies, light breeze, puffy clouds floating in an azure sky. A mockingbird serenaded them from a shagbark hickory behind the café. Jessica was an attractive woman in her early fifties. Too young for Bill, certainly, and he was romantically committed to Cindy. But still, with a bottle of wine to share and some snacks, the two of them might have a delightful conversation. Instead, he was investigating a murder to clear Kim's name. Such was life.

"It's quite a thrill that you consider me a suspect," Jessica said.

"More a person of interest than a suspect. During our last conversation, you expressed great anger toward Ms. Wolf. It would help if you had a verifiable alibi."

"Would you like for me to invent one? A husband, perhaps? I had one once. We lasted eighteen years before we grew excruciatingly bored with one another."

"Someone hired a limo on the morning of the murder. The limo drove up here, spent over two hours, and then drove down the mountain."

Bill observed Jessica's expression carefully. Her face registered no concern, only mild surprise. He didn't believe Jessica was acting, but if she was guilty, she might have anticipated the limo question and prepared for it in advance.

"Do you believe the murderer was in that limo? Oh, I get it. You think I might have hired the limo to disguise my movements."

"The thought crossed my mind. Briefly."

"Sorry. I didn't hire a limo. You can check my credit card receipts."

"Also, after the undersheriff and Kim left that morning, your son drove off the mountain and then came back."

Jessica, who until that moment had playfully jousted with Bill, suddenly turned cross.

"Nathan had nothing to do with this."

"Nothing to do with what?"

Frustrated now, Jessica searched for words. "With . . . With . . . the murder of Lily Wolf. He never even had a conversation with her."

"Do you know why he drove off the mountain?"

Jessica chewed the inside of her mouth. Her eyes burned.

"No, I don't, but I'm sure there's a logical explanation."

"I hope you're right."

Bill checked his watch. He needed to go.

"When you had dinner with Ms. Wolf, did she mention knowing someone else on the mountain?"

"Why do you ask? You have another suspect, don't you? That's good."

"Please answer the question."

"No. I don't remember Lily discussing anyone else."

"Okay. That's all I have. But stay tuned. Wintergreen PD will get in touch about those credit card records."

Once again, Bill and Mitch compared notes in the parking lot beside Mitch's squad car.

"I believe Nathan's story," said Mitch. "I don't think he was involved."

"Yeah, well, someone is lying."

Bill checked his phone. He had barely enough time to make his lunch appointment with CIA John. They were to meet at noon at the Blue Mountain Brewery on 151. Emily had called for a team meeting at two o'clock. Hopefully, by then, the new kid, Brendan, would have figured out who hired that limo. Bill felt sure it was a key element to the case.

THIRTY-NINE

Bill walked hesitantly toward Blue Mountain Brewery's main entrance. The brewery was on several acres of land abutting Route 151. A sidewalk at the front led to a merchandise booth, an outdoor wooden deck with seating, and a dozen tables on a brick patio. Small groups occupied half the outdoor tables, but no men sat alone.

How was Bill to find his contact? He didn't have a description and couldn't very well ask the hostess for CIA John. Once inside, Bill told the hostess he was meeting someone and would have a look around. She seemed okay with that, and Bill strolled into the large room on the right. An elderly man sat by himself, surely too old for intelligence work, but maybe? Bill approached the man's table and had nearly reached it when a similarly-aged woman came from the restrooms and sat with the man.

Bill searched the other two dining areas with no success. He paused at the bar area and pulled out his phone to text CIA John. He entered his passcode and accessed the message screen. Then, someone tapped him on the shoulder.

A man in his early forties stood before Bill. He had blond

hair, was medium height, and wore brown-framed glasses and casual clothes.

"I'm John. You're Bill. I have a table over here."

John had not been seated at the table when Bill passed it a few moments earlier. Bill guessed that sort of talent was required for the job. See but not be seen. He despised the secrecy. Bill had never been good at office politics, disliked paperwork, and detested meetings. It was a wonder he had kept his job for three decades.

Once seated, John focused his attention on the menu.

"Any recommendations?" he said.

John seemed to know that Bill had been to the brewery several times, although Bill had not shared that information.

"The food is good. I've never been disappointed. The Reuben is great."

"Excellent. The Reuben it is."

John put his menu down and waved at their server. He ordered his sandwich and a Full Nelson IPA. Bill ordered a chef's salad and a Diet Coke.

CIA John examined the room's interior and nodded. "It's nice out this way. I've been to Charlottesville but not beyond."

"You should get out of the city more, but don't feel obligated to come to Wintergreen. It's a long drive."

John frowned, perhaps trying to ascertain whether Bill had hidden a message in his words. In their last conversation, CIA John had shared a lot of information with Bill. Bill hoped to get a new suspect's name from John now, so he needed to play nice. Bill tried a genuine smile, and that seemed to please John.

"Anything new with the investigation?" John asked.

Bill shared what they had learned about the limo and the blackmailing of Nick Pappas. He omitted the part about

Nathan Smith leaving the mountain and didn't mention Jessica Smith.

"Your turn," said Bill. "Did your analyst find anything?"

CIA John nodded. "Yeah. I've got two names for you to work."

Bill grew tense, and he leaned closer to John. This was it. There must be a CIA connection to Lily Wolf's death. What other answer made sense? Jessica Smith, an overly protective sister gone mad with rage? No. Nick Pappas? The rich guy in over his head with a blackmailing Russian spy? A stretch. That led a rational detective to only one conclusion: Kim Wiley murdered Lily Wolf. Unless CIA John came through.

"You have my undivided attention," said Bill.

"Here goes. The first name is Paul Jameson. He's retired but still works as a part-timer for the agency. He's essentially a caretaker for the safe house."

Of course, Paul Jameson, the concerned neighbor, who stumbled upon a murder. Bill had witnessed his interview that morning. Cool as could be. On Paul's usual morning walk, he had noticed the broken signpost and approached the house to investigate.

"Paul checks to make sure residents have what they need and don't get into trouble," said John.

"He discovered the body."

CIA John frowned and consulted his phone. "Jameson worked in Europe for fifteen years. He handled assets, but we have no record of him directing Lily Wolf. Still, there's a good chance they worked together at some point."

"Maybe she crossed him," said Bill, "and he carried a grudge into retirement. As caretaker of the safe house, he meets her, pretends all is well, and waits for the right moment to make a move."

CIA John nodded. "It's not a bad theory. Wolf's real name is Liliya Volkova. You know what Liliya means?"

"I assumed Lily."

"Correct. The lily flower represents innocence, sweetness, and purity. Which makes no sense in light of her behavior. Unless you focus on the word pure combined with the name Volkova. Wolf. Pure Wolf. That suits her perfectly. Lily Wolf made a lot of enemies in the field. And I'm afraid Paul Jameson may have been one of them."

Okay. That made a lot more sense. Jameson bides his time and keeps a close watch on those who visit the rental home. At some point, he realizes Kim Wiley is visiting Lily regularly, and he makes a plan. The timing of Lily and Kim's argument was pure luck. When Paul sees Kim leave the second time, he makes his move. Goes into the rental home while Lily is eating breakfast outside. He finds the blue-handled knife and does the deed. Then he grabs Lily's phone, hikes it up the hill, and hides it behind the café. Yeah. That could work.

"You mentioned that you had two names," said Bill.

"Yep. The second name is Maria Metcalf."

Whoa.

Suddenly dizzy, Bill raised a hand to his forehead.

"Do you know her?" said John.

"Yes. We're friends. We play pickleball together."

CIA John rechecked his phone. "According to my intel, she only moved to Wintergreen four months ago."

"That's right."

"Anyway, I'd bet money on Jameson. Metcalf was CIA, too, but not a field person per se. We're not positive that Maria Metcalf even knew Lily Wolf, but she was stationed in Belarus for a few years, so there's a good chance their paths crossed."

Maria? No chance. Not Maria. Then Bill recalled Maria's temper on the pickleball court. She could get riled in a hurry. And she had been mighty curious about the case. Could that be why Maria had volunteered to work in the café? To stay close to the action? Keep an eye on Bill to see if he showed any signs of suspicion?

"So, you'll take a run at both of them?" said John. Without waiting for an answer, he added, "I want you to report to me as soon as you learn something."

"I can do that."

"And I don't want the local police involved."

Bill scowled. "What? No, that doesn't work."

"I'm not kidding."

"Neither am I. I'm not going rogue on this. I need the backup."

CIA John frowned.

"Furthermore," said Bill, "there's an innocent woman in jail, and the only way I'm going to get her out is by finding the real killer. When I do, the police will be the first to know."

FORTY

Bill listened politely as Emily queried Krista about Ashton's health. It had been over a decade since he'd had a sick kid at home. Five of them sat around the Wintergreen conference table. Once again, the other four—Emily, Krista, Mitch, and Brendan—wore their uniforms. Bill wore khakis and a buttoned shirt with the sleeves rolled up. While the women discussed the speed with which the norovirus symptoms advanced and then retreated, Brendan worked on his laptop. For his part, Mitch paid rapt attention, perhaps taking mental notes on how to deal with similar situations in the future.

Soon enough, Emily asked Bill what he'd learned at lunch with their distant cousin from the CIA. Bill briefed the team.

"So," Emily said, "let's assume the bad guy is Paul Jameson. Paul had it in for Lily because of old infractions committed in Europe. Paul stakes out Lily Wolf's rental home. He sees Kim leave in a huff and knock over the signpost. Now, he decides to implicate Kim by using her blue-handled knife to stab Ms. Wolf. Is that your theory, Bill?"

"Something like that."

"Here's what doesn't make sense," said Krista. "If the murderer staked out the house, they would have moved on Lily after Kim left the first time. In which case, Kim would have found Lily dead or interrupted the killer when she came back."

Krista has a sharp mind for this stuff, Bill thought. *She'll make a good investigator.*

Mitch said, "Maybe the murderer didn't arrive at the house until after Kim had already come back. Or perhaps they were waiting for Lily to do something specific, like sit down to eat breakfast."

"We may never know," said Emily. "But one thing we can safely assume is that the murderer hid Lily's phone behind the café. How did they do that without us seeing their car?"

They kicked this around for a while. Bill had already developed his theory. The murderer had ascended the hill on foot. The rental house backed up to the third-hole fairway. The killer had hiked up that fairway, then stayed on the golf course or switched to the wooded path nearby. From there, they could have come out to Blue Ridge Drive or, more likely, climbed the stairs by the pro shop and come up behind the café that way.

Emily pulled her ear. "I'll bet there's a surveillance camera on one or more of those homes backing up to the fairway. It was dark, but we might get lucky. Krista?"

"Yes, chief."

Emily gave Krista the assignment of searching the route for cameras. Krista would coordinate with Brendan to contact owners with cameras to get a look at their footage. Bill and Mitch would interview the new suspects.

"Be careful," said Emily. "One of these guys might be a killer."

Throughout the discussion, Brendan continued working on his laptop without saying a word.

Emily said, "You still with us, Brendan?"

"Yes, ma'am. Coordinate with Krista to track down homeowners with surveillance cameras."

"What are you working on, anyway?"

"Trying to find another number for the limo service. They're still not answering."

"Keep at it. Questions, anyone? No? Good. Bill, you got a second?"

Emily had one question she saved until the others had left the room. Did Bill trust his CIA contact?

"I wouldn't say trust exactly. It's more of a mutual dependency. I want to find the real killer, and he wants to know if the CIA has a problem. We need each other to accomplish our tasks."

"And if we find the killer? What will CIA John do then?"

"I don't know. But we can't let him whisk our suspect off to nowhere-land. That won't help Kim."

"Hey, Krista," said Mitch. "You got a second?"

Mitch had followed Krista outside the front door of headquarters. They stood on the sidewalk in front of Krista's squad car.

"Is Ashton going to be okay?"

Krista smiled. "Oh, yeah. He's a tough kid, and he's finally realized that girls are pretty. It'll take more than norovirus to keep him away from them."

"Well, I don't know how you do it. It seems like a lot of work."

"Yeah, it is. But you get used to it."

"Do you really?"

Krista cocked an eyebrow. "You got some news you haven't shared yet?"

Mitch admitted that he and Lulu were going to have a baby. Krista congratulated Mitch and then gave his arm a light punch. She kidded him about being in a rush, and Mitch blushed. Then Krista returned to his question.

"Here's how it works, Mitch. You have kids, work, your marriage, and other stuff. It's impossible to get everything done. The only way to stay sane is to decide upfront what doesn't get done. You have to prioritize what's most important. For me, the kids have always come first. Then work. Kids and work. And that doesn't leave much time for anything else."

FORTY-ONE

Bill drove separately in case Jameson wasn't home. Paul Jameson lived in a two-story wooden home on the Crawford's Edge finger street off Shamokin Springs Trail. Flowers bloomed brightly in beds out front. The unoccupied driveway was exposed aggregate. On the left was a self-standing garage with two bays.

Mitch approached the garage and peered through the bay windows. He shook his head. They approached the house and rang the bell twice. No answer.

"You stay here in case he comes home," said Bill. "Park up the street and text me if he shows. I'll come running."

"What are you going to do?"

"I'll stop by Maria Metcalf's place. She's a friend."

"Maybe we should go together."

Bill shook his head. "The CIA contact believes Jameson is the guy. We can't afford to leave his house unobserved. I'll pop over to see Maria. If she's there, I'll ask for an alibi that we can get someone to check. If she's not, I'll come right back."

Mitch screwed his lips into a bunch.

"Don't freak out," said Bill. "I'll call you as soon as I'm done. If I don't call in twenty minutes, send the cavalry."

"You damn sure better call."

Maria Metcalf lived in the High Ridge condos down Blue Ridge Drive from Bill's place. It only took a few minutes for Bill to reach her complex. He parked next to Maria's green Subaru, which didn't necessarily mean she was home. She could be out for a walk or on an excursion with Terry. They might still be at the café, for that matter.

So, after pressing her doorbell, Bill was pleased to hear footsteps approach the door.

When she recognized Bill, Maria burst into a smile and gave him a quick hug.

"Hey, stranger. Gosh, I haven't seen you in three or four hours. What's up?"

"Not much."

A stupid answer, Bill realized too late.

"Just stopped by to shoot the bull, huh?"

Maria smiled knowingly, and then it hit Bill. Hairs stood on the back of his neck.

"You've been expecting me."

She pulled her tongue from the roof of her mouth. "You're a smart guy. I figured you'd get around to me sooner or later. Come in. Let's get comfortable."

Maria offered coffee or water. Bill declined. He kept an eye on her hands, a function of training. She sat on the couch and gestured toward a side chair.

"I never knew you were in the CIA," said Bill.

"If you tell someone you were a spy, one of two things happens—they don't want to see you anymore, or they can't stop pestering you for war stories. Most of us make something up."

Bill didn't doubt Maria's word on that subject. He had encountered similar behavior when others learned he was an ex-cop. Now, he could empathize with the non-combatants. He and Cindy had dined with Maria and Terry five or six times. Maria had hosted a small May Day party for close friends. He had sat in this very room and enjoyed wine and charcuterie, never suspecting her true past. What had Maria done as a spy? Had she killed for her country? Had she killed recently?

"Did you know Lily Wolf? Did you meet her when you were stationed in Belarus?"

Maria raised her eyebrows. "You've got some good intel, Bill. Who did you talk to?"

"I don't know, and I don't care. But I do care about Kim Wiley. So please answer the question."

Maria's face soured. "Yes, I knew her, but not well. I met Liliya Volkova twice at embassy functions. She wore slinky dresses with plunging necklines, quite the attraction. The men eyed her with desire. Real charmer, too. Everyone's favorite. I wasn't immune to the attraction. We only exchanged a few sentences, but when she turned away—and she had to because others were clawing at her—I was disappointed. I wanted our conversation to continue."

"What did you do for the CIA? Did you get involved in fieldwork?"

"Don't you mean dirty work? Violence?"

"Yes. That's what I mean."

"It's not like in thriller novels. Most of the work is done on computers. They give the hands-on assignments to ex-military types."

"I don't doubt you, but you haven't answered the question."

Maria took a deep breath. "I had a few moments in the field that I don't share with Terry."

"Ever use a knife?"

Maria's temper flared. Who needed a knife when they had eyes that could cut right through you?

"Enough of this," she said. "I told you I didn't know Lily well, and I certainly didn't kill her."

"Where were you on the morning of the murder?"

"I played pickleball with you and Cindy and Terry. Remember?"

"How about earlier that morning?"

"I was in Richmond. I went to see my sister the day before and spent the night at her house. I left early to return here for our pickleball date."

"I'll need her contact information."

Borderline furious, Maria hurried to fetch her phone and share her sister's contact information with Bill. As she did, it occurred to Bill that Maria had answered the alibi question instantly, as if she knew it was coming.

Afraid he had lost a friend, Bill tried to recover with chitchat. They had a regular date to play pickleball the following day that Cindy would miss. Bill said he could still play singles with Terry unless the investigation got in the way. In no mood for idle banter, Maria said she'd pass the message along and then showed Bill to the door.

Bill had silenced his phone during the interview. Once outside, he noticed that he'd missed two calls from Mitch.

FORTY-TWO

Krista parked her squad car in the rental home's gravel driveway. Even though the forensics team had left long ago, yellow barricade tape remained across the front entrance to keep the curious away. Krista walked around the house to the back deck and examined the table where Lily Wolf had died. A passerby would never know. No blood stains on the chair, table, or flooring. Of course, the internal bleeding had been fatal.

She looked toward the back door and tried to imagine the killer's movements. They gained access through the front door. Perhaps Wolf had forgotten to lock it after Kim's second departure. They saw Wolf eating her breakfast outside, grabbed Kim's blue-handled knife from the kitchen counter, and crept through the back door and behind Wolf to strike the blow.

What then? A professional would have scanned the exterior and interior for surveillance cameras and breathed a sigh of relief when they found none. Where had they found Wolf's phone? Perhaps on the table beside her. Maybe inside. Once they had the phone, they would have turned it off to keep it from signaling their position to the nearest cell tower. Krista strode to the far end of the deck. Stairs led down to a small lawn area. At the far end of the lawn, a seldom-used trail wound through a narrow section of woods to the golf course.

Once on the course, Krista turned to her right. Two men stood on the green a hundred and fifty feet away. One man eyed his putt several times by turning his head to the hole and back to his ball. The second man watched Krista with great interest. She waved, and he waved back.

Krista had never played the game, but the weather—temperature in the low seventies and not a cloud in the sky—struck her as perfect for golf. Turning to the left, she scanned the fairway for other golfers and found none. Maybe her luck would hold out. She strolled the left side of the fairway until she reached the next house and used that home's connecting trail to get close enough to scrutinize its exterior. No cameras.

She repeated the process for two more homes with the same result. However, the following home did have surveillance cameras, and Krista stood at the property line to estimate the distance from the nearest camera to the golf course. At least a hundred feet, perhaps more. The camera might have captured an image of the killer if they walked along the course's nearest edge, but not if the killer was smart enough to stay in the middle of the fairway. That was the last house on the left side, and Krista started to cross the fairway but then heard a noise from the tee box to her left.

Three women stood at the red tees fifty yards uphill. Two of them stared at Krista. Krista waved them through. A woman in a yellow sweater cupped her hands.

"Better stand back in the woods! We've been known to hit wild shots."

"Thanks for the warning."

Krista edged behind a thick trunk but needn't have bothered, for the women each hit solid shots that remained in the clear.

The women hopped into their golf carts and met Krista halfway across the fairway.

"You're working on that murder investigation, aren't you?" said the woman in the yellow sweater.

"Yes, ma'am."

"A friend told me Kim Wiley did it," said a woman in short sleeves who rode in a cart by herself. "They have her locked up in Charlottesville. Isn't that right, officer?"

"I'm sorry. We're not allowed to discuss ongoing investigations."

"Makes sense."

"I can't believe Kim would do a thing like that," said the third woman.

"Rumors," said yellow sweater. "Don't pay attention. They'll get the right person soon. Wait and see."

The women thanked Krista for serving the community and rode their carts to where their balls had landed. Krista played spectator while they hit their second shots, and then she crossed the fairway to repeat the process for homes on the opposite side. The first few residences had no cameras, but the two houses closest to the tee each had surveillance cameras. And they were closer to the fairway than the home on the other side. In fact, if the cameras were in operating order and the killer had taken the cart path, Krista would bet at least one camera captured the killer's image.

The hill inclined steeply as Krista approached the blue tee. She paused to catch her breath and turned to survey the third hole, which doglegged sharply from left to right. Krista couldn't see the green, but she knew the basic contours of the hole. She imagined the killer leaving Lily Wolf's back deck and entering the golf course. If the killer knew the homes with surveillance cameras, they could have weaved their way up the hole undetected. But if unaware of the surveillance, the killer might have made a costly mistake.

Once she caught her breath, Krista called Brendan at the station to report her findings. Together, they sorted out the addresses of those homes with cameras so that Brendan could contact the owners. Then Krista continued up the hill to Fawn Ridge Drive and crossed it to reach the end of the second hole. At that point, the killer had a choice of staying in the fairway and risking triggering cameras from the homes on the right side or switching to a gravel path that cut through the narrow section of woods between Blue Ridge Drive and the golf course.

The fairway was occupied by another group of golfers, so Krista chose to walk the path first. She could search the fairway's other side later. The path inclined gently, and Krista hurried, virtually certain no cameras could see her. Vehicles occasionally motored past on Blue Ridge Drive twenty feet to her left. Condo associations lined the ridge across the road. She passed a tall man walking a small white dog, and they exchanged brief hellos. Through the woods on the right, the golfers hit approach shots. One went wild and struck a tree behind her. The man who hit the wild shot laughed and pulled another ball from his pocket.

Another hundred yards up the path, a gap between oak trees afforded Krista a clear view of the Overlook Condos across the road. She stopped to scan the buildings. Krista had answered a bear call once at the Overlook Condos. A bear had climbed into an open dumpster and found something worth eating. Krista had encouraged residents to remain safely near their buildings, and soon enough, the bear left.

Krista now remembered something from that visit to the complex. The Overlook Condos had surveillance cameras over every entrance. Using her phone, she zoomed in on the nearest building until she found the surveillance camera. She frowned at the poor line of sight through the foliage bordering the complex. Krista continued farther up the path and soon found an even larger gap in the trees.

Whoa. What do we have here?

Krista took several shots of the surveillance camera mounted above the nearest Overlook entrance. The camera had a clear shot of her from fifty yards. She turned around to view the golf course through the trees. If the killer had used the fairway, they would have escaped the Overlook surveillance camera, but if they used the path, the camera might have caught something.

Krista reached the end of the path and called Brendan again, explaining what she had found.

"Find out who has that Overlook surveillance footage. It might be the property manager."

"I'm on it."

"Any luck with the owners?"

"One guy said their cameras aren't hooked up. They use them for deterrence only."

"Great."

"A second owner is supposed to send me a link to online footage. I can't reach the third owner."

Krista searched the other side of the fairway but found no other homes with surveillance cameras. Then she toured the two routes from the upper end of the path to the café. No cameras there either.

She called Emily with an update.

"What's your conclusion?" asked Emily, after Krista had shared her search results.

"If the killer knew what they were doing, they could have hiked from the house to the café without being captured."

"That's not much help."

"But if they made a mistake, if they walked past that house or on the path along Blue Ridge Drive, there's a good chance we'll have something."

"Okay. Come down and review that home's footage with Brendan, then go see the property manager."

"Yes, chief."

FORTY-THREE

Two houses down from Paul Jameson's place, Mitch leaned on the front bumper of his squad car and fretted about his update call with Emily. She was none too happy that Mitch had let Bill leave to interview Maria Metcalf by himself. But what could Mitch do? As a citizen, Bill had an ideal life because he wasn't bound by the rules. He didn't have to call in his every move, follow protocol, or file paperwork. On the other hand, Bill was old, at least sixty, and his kids were grown and gone. Mitch wouldn't change places with Bill for anything. Lose Lulu? He'd rather die. So he might as well stop whining and do his job.

Crawford's Edge inclined gently for a hundred yards from where he stood before intersecting with Shamokin Springs Trail. A cement truck rumbled past on the bigger road. A squirrel entered the road in front of the squad car and stopped to glance at Mitch. Mitch waved at him, and the squirrel scampered away. High in the sky, cirrus clouds had formed. A FedEx truck turned on Crawford's Edge and made two deliveries. The driver, who Mitch recognized, waved as he passed.

He must have been behind schedule; otherwise, he would have stopped to exchange a few words.

Mitch checked his phone. He'd been standing there for fifteen minutes. Bill had said he'd be back in twenty.

A white SUV pulled onto Crawford's Edge and stopped.

After Emily's roundup meeting, Brendan checked the Wintergreen database and learned that Paul Jameson drove a Toyota Sienna.

Mitch squinted. Was that a Toyota?

A lone driver sat in front, not moving. He was tall. Paul Jameson was tall.

Mitch's heart skipped a beat.

Suddenly, the SUV reversed back onto Shamokin Springs and turned to face right. The SUV's tires screeched, and Mitch jumped.

Holy crap! He's running!

Back in the car, Mitch punched the accelerator, and the cruiser roared up the hill. By the time he reached Shamokin, Jameson was a quarter mile farther along. Mitch turned right to follow and called in his pursuit. With his adrenaline cranking, Mitch held his speed at fifty. Faster than that was downright unsafe. Jameson didn't feel the same way, and the gap between them increased. Mitch updated his position and requested backup.

He kept Jameson in sight until they reached the intersection with Blue Ridge Drive. Jameson ignored the stop sign, speeding through the turn, and Mitch lost sight of the SUV.

Damn it. He's going to get someone killed.

After the turn, Mitch punched it to sixty and kept his eyes glued to the road for any sign of pedestrians. The road curved to the left and climbed the mountain. Mitch glimpsed the SUV when Fawn Ridge came into view. The SUV turned right again.

The SUV was out of sight when Mitch reached Fawn Ridge. He accelerated again, and his tires squealed. After two hundred yards, he came to the T-intersection with Laurel Springs Drive.

Mitch heaved. His skin was clammy underneath his gear.

The SUV had vanished. Which way did Jameson go? Left led up the mountain toward Wintergreen Drive and the only exit. But Jameson could never escape via that route. The police would block the entrance. To the right, Laurel Springs Drive rolled down a mile and a half to a dead end.

However, there was a jeep road that extended beyond Laurel Springs all the way down to Rockfish Valley. The jeep road was unpaved most of the way and closed off with metal gates in two places. Did Jameson believe he could escape by crashing through the gates? Or maybe, in desperation, he would attempt to flee on foot.

Mitch roared down the hill to the right and updated his position. Two squad cars were on the way and would block Jameson if he had headed in the other direction. Mitch zipped past finger streets. Ravens Roost Lane. Osprey Court. Valley View Lane.

The road was primarily straight but steep. Houses sped by. Mitch slowed down to pass a woman walking with a German shepherd. No sight of Jameson. Mitch told himself to breathe.

More streets rushed by. Great Owl Lane. Warrior Run. Stoney Cove Lane.

Mitch approached the little parking lot on the left that accessed a connector path to the Appalachian Trail. Jameson could have pulled in there to try to hitch a ride out on the Blue Ridge Parkway. Mitch pulled to a stop and examined the parking lot closely. No sign of the white SUV. Mitch's foot slammed the accelerator.

He was nearing the end. Up ahead, the road parted to

create a small island with one-way traffic on each side. If clever, Jameson could have stopped out of sight on the other side to wait. Upon hearing Mitch's squad car, he could let Mitch begin to circle the island and then mirror Mitch's movements on the other side and climb back up the hill unseen.

Mitch stopped in front of the island. He wrinkled his nose, swore at Jameson, and drove slowly around the circle's left. No sign of the SUV. The dead end was another quarter mile down the hill. Mitch readied himself for a footrace through the woods. The jeep road was overgrown with weeds, so he would soon know if Jameson had been foolish enough to take that route. Mitch cruised down the hill at the speed limit, rounded the last curve, and came upon Jameson's SUV pulled across the jeep road entrance.

Paul Jameson leaned on his front bumper, smiling.

Mitch called in the update and got out.

"Good afternoon, officer."

"Are you Paul Jameson?"

Jameson nodded. "Yes."

"Why were you driving at twice the speed limit? Trying to get away?"

Jameson held out his cell phone. "Sorry. I was trying to get a better signal."

Better signal. What a bunch of hoo-ha.

"Are you going to give me a ticket?" said Jameson.

"My boss wants to talk with you. Will you follow me to the station?"

Jameson smiled again. "No problem."

"Don't try to drive away. You'll only make it worse."

"I got it."

FORTY-FOUR

On the drive down to visit the Overlook Condos property manager, Krista received a cell call from Skip. At first, he asked whether the lead he had given Bill would help. Yeah. Maybe. They were working on it now. Then they traded chitchat. She told him Ashton had been sick with norovirus. Skip expressed genuine concern. Was Ashton okay? Did she need anything? Yes, Ashton was fine. No, she didn't need anything. They discussed their upcoming weekend. Skip asked whether she wanted to watch a UVA tennis match, see a movie, or go for a hike. Let's figure it out as we go along. Good. Be spontaneous. That's cool.

She pulled onto a long driveway near the Devils Backbone Brewpub and told Skip she had to bounce.

"Okay. See you soon, babe."

"Looking forward to it . . . Skip."

And so, as she walked toward the small white building that housed the property manager, instead of considering the importance of the surveillance footage she would review, Krista's mind was on her upcoming weekend with Skip. Dinner. Drinks. Other activities.

She shook her head and told herself to snap out of it.

Her Uncle Charlie had given her a piece of advice long ago.

You can't do everything.

She had work to do right now.

The surveillance footage Brendan had sourced from an owner provided no useful evidence. If the killer had walked up the golf course, they were smart enough to stay out of that camera's line of sight. Hopefully, she'd have more luck with the Overlook's surveillance footage.

Twenty minutes later, Krista sat in a closed room with a laptop computer, scanning black-and-white video of the Overlook parking lot and a gap in the trees beyond Blue Ridge Drive. She started at the time stamp of five forty-five a.m. and watched the video at speed until a vehicle passed from right to left. It was a white truck, not Kim's. After ten more minutes of footage, Kim's black F150 sped up the hill. Krista slowed the video. Fourteen minutes later, Kim's truck drove down the mountain again, then returned after an even shorter interval.

The purpose of Krista's review was to test the hypothesis that the killer had struck *after* Kim left the rental house the second time. Then, after the murder, the killer took Lily Wolf's phone and hiked to the café. Krista forwarded the video at four times the normal speed for ten minutes of footage, then switched to real-time and settled in to carefully observe the gap. It was a tedious task. A slight breeze moved leaves gently on the screen, but otherwise, almost nothing happened. After fifteen minutes, an unidentified pickup truck hauling a flat trailer crossed the screen from left to right. Five minutes later, a light-colored sedan climbed the hill. Krista yawned.

Then, twenty-five minutes after Kim's truck had driven

past the final time, something moved across the gap. The movement lasted about two seconds. Then the boring view reappeared, leaves moving gently in the breeze. Krista wasn't confident that she had seen anything. She backed up the video and watched that section again.

Movement. Definitely. A figure walking uphill had crossed the gap in the hardwoods. Krista watched that section several more times. She could not see the person clearly. They appeared to be of medium height and weight, perhaps a woman, maybe a man. The figure wore dark clothing and a head covering.

Krista continued watching the video for the next hour to see if the figure returned. No success. The day dawned, and a woman with two large dogs crossed the gap from right to left.

Krista leaned back in the chair and sighed. They'd have a heck of a time proving anything with that evidence. Someone had climbed the path at the right time. The video would not identify that person and would certainly not tell them whether the person carried Lily Wolf's phone. Perhaps the only purpose the video served was to strengthen the conviction of someone who wanted to believe a murderer had taken the phone up the hill. Whether that was a positive development, Krista couldn't say.

FORTY-FIVE

Emily sat in her office and tried to figure out what to do with Lily Wolf's email correspondence. She knew for sure it wouldn't help them solve the case.

Brendan had forwarded the translated messages a short while earlier. There were only twenty-three emails in total. Lily Wolf had apparently created a free account upon arriving in Wintergreen. She neither sent nor received official messages concerning business of any sort. In fact, she only corresponded with one person—her brother, Anton. Anton lived in Belarus with his wife and three children. Lily requested and received recent photos of the children. The oldest was a boy in his late teens who had left home to attend a school of higher education. The two younger siblings were girls. Vera was about fifteen and enjoyed acting in the school's theater production. Milana, younger, played volleyball.

When will we see you again? her brother asked. Lily replied that it was difficult to say. She had told them she was in the US and would settle in a new location soon. Once settled, she could send them enough money for a visit. Anton expressed great excitement at that possibility.

An uncle had died, and Anton took his entire family to the funeral. This was apparently in their hometown. They had visited with Lily's parents for several days. Her parents expressed concern about her being in the US. It was far away.

Emily allowed herself a moment of feeling. Eight thousand miles away, Lily Wolf's brother had no idea that she had died. How would Anton find out? Would Anton find out? Or would he fret for months and then eventually assume the worst?

The moment passed. Emily heard a commotion down the hall. Mitch had returned with Paul Jameson.

FORTY-SIX

"So, you lied about Lily Wolf," said Bill.

Paul Jameson shrugged. "I'll admit that I left out certain pieces of information that you might have considered material."

Bill grunted his dissatisfaction with that answer.

He, Emily, and Paul Jameson sat in the Wintergreen PD conference room. Paul had freely admitted that he was still in the CIA's employ, although now as a part-time contractor. He served as the caretaker of their safe house, and as such, he had touched base with Lily Wolf several times during her stay.

"Why did you run today?" said Emily.

"I saw Officer Gentry waiting near my house, and I assumed you had figured out my true past. I needed instructions from my supervisor."

"Uh-huh," said Bill. "What did your supervisor tell you?"

"She told me to be honest. She said the whole thing had entered *snafu* territory and that you were in the best position to sort it out. We certainly can't."

Bill studied Jameson's facial expressions and body

language. The guy was a trained liar. He sat comfortably in the conference room chair as if he had all day and no wish to be anywhere else. But his heart had to be cranked. He was now at the top of their murder suspect board.

"Tell us what really happened on the morning of the murder," said Emily.

Jameson sniffed nonchalantly. "I didn't just happen to notice the busted signpost. I went there purposefully to check on her. But when I saw the signpost, a feeling of dread came over me, and my instinct was right. She was long since dead by the time I got to her. I called my supervisor. She told me to stay put and called back ten minutes later. I was to report it and let the locals sort it out because the agency couldn't do anything. The hope was that you would find the murderer quickly, and the issue would peter out."

"Did you move her phone?" said Bill.

Jameson shook his head. "I didn't see a phone. And my instructions were to leave everything as is. Call in the murder and then back away. When Nelson County arrested Kim Wiley, the mystery appeared to be solved. But apparently, you guys felt the need to keep digging."

"We like to get to the truth," said Emily, "even if it's not the easy answer."

"My compliments," said Paul.

Far too smooth, thought Bill.

Jameson's responses rolled off his tongue as if he had practiced them. He, his supervisor, and the rest of the CIA wanted the whole thing to blow over as soon as possible. If Kim Wiley was sent to prison as a consequence, too bad. She got caught up in the skirmish.

To heck with that.

Bill said, "You mentioned that as caretaker, you had contacted Lily Wolf several times during her stay."

"Yes."

"How many times did you visit her?"

"I don't know. Four or five times."

"Was it four or five?"

"I don't know. I don't keep a careful record."

"That's surprising. Didn't your supervisor want to know every time you visited Ms. Wolf?"

For the first time, Jameson appeared less comfortable. He shifted in his chair. Emily leaned back to let Bill drive.

"I find it curious that, given you had only visited her a few times, you happened to drop by on the morning of her murder. Why did you choose that particular day to visit?"

Paul shot Bill a look of distaste, as if he liked Bill less than he had a few moments earlier.

"Okay. I visited Lily a lot, more than four or five times."

"You knew Lily Wolf before she came to Wintergreen. You knew her in the field."

Jameson's eyebrows furrowed. Bill had struck a nerve.

"You hated her, didn't you? She did something to you."

Jameson's eyes burned, and a chill went up Bill's spine. The man had changed in an instant. He was back in Eastern Europe.

"You don't know anything," said Paul.

"Tell me."

Then, as quickly as he had turned into a hardened cold-war veteran, Jameson's face turned sad. He heaved a sigh.

"Yes, I knew Lily Wolf. Liliya Volkova. No, I didn't hate her, although many in the agency did. They viewed her as an asset to be used, kept on the payroll for as long as she gave us something of value, and then tossed to the side, ignored, forgotten, unless she came up with something new. Some said she played both sides. Maybe so. But how was she supposed to play if no one was on her side?

"When I first met Liliya, she was in her twenties, and I was already in my late forties. Unlike several in the agency, I never considered her a potential romantic partner. She made a play for me once, but I saw right through it. For her, it was an opportunity to gain leverage and nothing else. I laughed at her. She grew angry at first but then laughed with me. After that, we were friends. And believe me, she didn't have many of those in the CIA.

"Three years ago, I retired and came here to play the part-time caretaker. It was mildly amusing and low-stress. And I told myself I could keep my hand in the game. Six months ago, I heard something big had happened in my old stomping ground. A major coup for Liliya. But my boss said Liliya had given something away in the process. A few names. When Liliya got here, I asked her about it. She said it was all BS. But with Liliya, I could never be sure of the truth."

Jeez.

Cloak-and-dagger stuff. Bill was glad he had worked as a regular cop in a normal city in the homeland. He didn't like every cop he'd worked with, but they always had each other's back.

Bill leaned forward. "You said on the morning of the murder, the busted signpost triggered a feeling of dread. Why? It might have been nothing more than a minor mishap."

Jameson's hands squeezed the table's edge. Bill got the sense Paul was wrestling with what to say. How much truth did his boss want him to share?

"I was worried because I ran into someone here in Wintergreen. An operative from my agency days in Eastern Europe. Someone who hated Liliya. Maria Metcalf."

"Maria Metcalf?" said Bill.

"Yes."

Bill waited. Paul paused, not sure how much to tell. Bill was prepared to wait a long time. Not so with Emily.

"Come on. Come on. Come on," she said. "We haven't got all day. Tell us about Maria."

"Like I said, she hated Liliya. I don't know exactly why. It was partly personal, I think. They got into a loud verbal argument at an embassy party. The incident nearly got physical. Others intervened."

"And this was personal?" said Bill.

"Yeah. Some romantic conflict. But there was more to it. Maria handled field agents in a territory, and she believed Liliya was manipulating her agents and putting them in danger."

"What happened in the end?"

"The station chief told Maria to back off, which did not go down well. Anyway, I unexpectedly ran into Maria last month and grew concerned, so I warned Liliya."

A creepy thought crossed Bill's mind. Did Maria move to Wintergreen for the sole purpose of killing Lily Wolf? He did some mental math. Maria and Terry moved here four months earlier, shortly before Lily Wolf arrived. Maria may have planned it all from the start, or she might have come across Lily by happenstance and devised a plan to take revenge.

"So, you believe Maria Metcalf murdered Lily Wolf," said Emily.

Paul sat back with his hands in his lap and gave them a slight nod. "It's quite possible."

~

"What's your take?" said Emily.

Bill and Emily sat in her office. She had released Paul Jameson after the interview.

"These spies," he said, "are all good liars. I don't know."

"I think he's telling the truth," said Emily. "He was struggling with his emotions because he had feelings for Lily. Not romantic stuff. More like an uncle thing."

"An uncle thing?"

"A mentor with a problem mentee. He wanted to steer her in the right direction, but she wouldn't listen."

Could be. One thing was for sure: Bill needed to speak with Maria again. Maria had lied about the embassy party. She had known Lily Wolf quite well.

Emily and Bill planned the next steps.

"I don't want you interviewing Maria alone again," said Emily. "I'll send Mitch and Jose to bring her down here. And I'll ask Krista to verify Maria's alibi."

"Sounds good. Has Brendan figured out who hired the limo?"

"Not yet."

FORTY-SEVEN

"Hello. This is Krista Jackson with the Wintergreen Police Department."

"Oh, hi. This is Patti Barkley. You left a voice message?"

"That's right."

"I'm sorry I didn't answer earlier. I thought it was a spam caller."

After Krista returned from the property manager's office, Emily asked her to verify Maria Metcalf's alibi. Metcalf claimed she was with her sister in Richmond on the morning of the murder. Sitting in her cubicle, Krista examined her monitor. She had pulled up Patti Barkley's address on a map, a southern suburb of Richmond.

Krista explained why she was calling.

"A murder investigation! Like the CSI shows."

"Something like that."

"And you think my sister is involved?"

Krista hastened to calm Patti's fears. This was something of a formality. She went on to explain in detail what she wanted.

"I don't know," said Patti.

"Excuse me?"

"I don't know if my sister stayed here that night because I wasn't home."

Krista's heart rate jumped. She adjusted her headset to turn up the volume and asked Patti to provide more details.

"Maria joined the CIA forever ago, and ever since, she's been hot stuff in her mind. Whoop dee doo. Too good for the rest of the family. But now she's retired."

"Okay. Retired." Krista typed notes on her keyboard.

"All of a sudden, she called me last week. She wanted to come and stay the night. Was that okay? I said sure."

Krista detected more than a smidgen of hostility in Patti's voice. Some families could never get it right.

"Two days later, I remembered we were supposed to visit my husband's brother in Nags Head. The date was all set, so I had a conflict. I called Maria, but of course, she didn't answer. I left a voice mail."

"Are you saying your sister did not stay at your house that night?"

"I don't know. That's what I'm saying. I know someone drank most of a bottle of Sauvignon Blanc. And I know someone slept in the guest room. But I can't say for certain that it was Maria."

What a strange sibling relationship.

"Could someone else have stayed at your house?"

"Sure. My two brothers both know where we hide the spare key."

"But you believe it was probably Maria."

"Yes. But probably won't work in court, will it? This much I can say for sure. Maria called me the next morning to say she was sorry to have missed me. She was headed back to Wintergreen. Can't you guys verify her whereabouts using cell tower signals or something like that?"

Krista blew air through her lips. Patti Barkley was no great help. They would have to resort to cell tower signals. Or something like that.

She thanked Patti for her time and signed off.

Whew. What a day. But it could be worse. When Krista came in, she had seen Brendan working at the dispatcher station, a job she had enjoyed for years but did not want to return to. Her new role as a patrol officer signaled career progress, and so did her studies. She had recently completed an online course on interview techniques. Interesting stuff.

Emily would want an update. Krista double-checked her notes.

FORTY-EIGHT

Bill stood when Emily brought Maria Metcalf into the conference room. Maria glared at him. He offered a hand for her to shake, but she ignored it.

"Nice digs," she said. "The CIA should take decorating tips from you guys."

Emily frowned. She was not a big fan of uppity types.

"Two times in one day," said Maria in a voice heavy with sarcasm. "What a treat."

Yeah, Bill had definitely lost a friend. Oh well. If Maria had killed Lily Wolf and framed Kim for it, he didn't care.

He said, "We need to clear up a couple of items you shared with me earlier."

Maria dropped into a chair. "Let's get to it. The sooner I'm out of here, the better."

"First of all, we talked with your sister Patti."

"Lucky for you."

"Patti said she wasn't at the house. So she can't verify that you were."

"Yeah, Patti ditched me. We're not exactly the Waltons.

But I called Patti that morning, and my cell records will show I was still in Richmond when I made that call."

"What time did you leave to return here?"

Maria looked at the ceiling as if trying to reconstruct that morning's timeline. "I left there at seven thirty, leaving me enough time to get here and change for our pickleball game."

"Did you hire a limo?" said Bill.

Maria frowned. "A limo?"

"Someone hired a limo that drove them up here in time to murder Lily Wolf. Then the limo left."

Maria's eye twitched. They might have her. If Maria had used her credit card to book the limo, she had a lot of explaining to do. At the least, Kim would be off the hook.

"I didn't hire a limo."

"You lied to me about your relationship with Lily Wolf. You guys had a serious run-in at the Belarus embassy party you mentioned."

Maria pursed her lips. Bill grew concerned that she would stop sharing and demand a lawyer. But Maria wasn't done.

"You talked with Paul Jameson."

"Don't concern yourself with who we talked to. There must be a hundred people at the CIA who know you had a fight with Lily. It won't be hard to find more."

Maria snorted with derision. "Liliya Volkova. The pure wolf. Volkova was not worth crying over. You should drop this case altogether. Give her killer a medal. How about we do that?"

Emily's face turned dark, and Bill feared she might say something. At this point, the best thing to do was to give Maria all the rope she wanted.

"She was a traitor, Bill," said Maria, all worked up now. "Liliya manipulated people as a matter of routine. She got them to trust her, and then she gave them up. People died, Bill. People who had families."

"Lily Wolf had a family," said Emily.

Maria shot Emily a glare and turned her attention back to Bill.

"You know what they called her at the agency? The back-stabber. She couldn't be trusted. The only reason no one killed her earlier is because the higher-ups protected her. They said she had *strategic value*."

It was close to a confession but not a confession.

Push her. She's on the brink.

"So," he said, "you saw the opportunity, and you killed her."

Maria sat back and relaxed her shoulders. "Sadly, no."

"We have a video of you walking up the hill to plant Lily's phone behind the café."

"Do you, now? How good is the resolution?"

"Good enough."

She chuckled. "You better look closely, because it's not me. I wasn't there."

FORTY-NINE

After Maria's interview, Bill and Emily sat in the conference room and exchanged views. Emily believed Maria was guilty. Bill wasn't sure. Maria had seemed confident that her alibi would hold up.

But if not Maria, then who? Paul Jameson? Aside from Kim Wiley, Paul was the only suspect who had expressed compassion for Lily Wolf. Was that all an act? With his background as a spy, Jameson may have learned to lie convincingly. Still, at the time, Bill had been persuaded by his statement.

The video Krista had tracked down complicated matters further. Bill believed the killer took Lily Wolf's phone and hid it behind the café to frame Kim. That meant the killer knew the golf course well enough to avoid the home surveillance cameras but not the camera at the Overlook condos. Paul Jameson walked for exercise regularly. Did one of his routes include the golf course's third hole?

Then there was Nick Pappas, the rich and unfaithful jerk. Pappas had money to hire a professional to do the job. But that made little sense to Bill. Pappas was a reckless philanderer, and Bill suspected that Pappas's wife was already aware of his affairs with other women. If so, why would Pappas try to cover up his latest act of adultery with a murder?

Jessica Smith? She thought Lily Wolf was bad news for Kim. But would Jessica commit murder to erase Lily from Kim's life? Not likely.

Which brought Bill to Kim.

The lover's quarrel. The blue-handled knife. The phone. The evidence combined to form a big red arrow pointed directly at Kim.

Except for the limo. What was that all about?

The limo owner had yet to return Brendan's calls. Hmm. It might take a drive to Charlottesville to track him down. Bill would sort that out tomorrow.

Bill and Emily wrapped up their conversation, and he returned to his home. Once there, he took Max out for a quick turn around the condo, promised him a longer walk later, and then fixed a quick meal of a turkey sandwich and potato chips. After doing the dishes, Bill cracked open a local craft beer and called Cindy. She picked up on the first ring.

How was Cape May? Wonderful. They had rented a townhouse near downtown, and Cindy had fallen in love with the architecture—Victorian-style homes built in the late nineteenth century. And Congress Hall? Oh, goodness. What grandeur. They must return for their own vacation. Maybe next year. Had she gone swimming? No. Justin and his girlfriend didn't seem to mind the frigid waves, but it was much too cold for Cindy.

Cindy asked about the investigation. Was Kim still in jail? Yes, but they had several other suspects, and Bill hoped to have Kim out soon. Cindy said she was supposed to watch a Netflix movie with Justin, and their conversation moved toward an awkward close. Bill and Cindy were still not comfortable enough with each other to risk the big three words, and they settled for less consequential farewells.

"Take care, Bill."

"You too."

Sensing that his time had finally come, Max rose from his bed to stretch.

"Okay, boy. Let's go."

Bill glanced through the window and was surprised by the darkness. His conversation with Cindy had lasted longer than planned. Bill was reluctant to let Max run free in the dark, so the dog would get less exercise than Bill had intended. But they could go to the café and back and stay in lighted areas most of the way.

Outside, Max was frisky, scampering left and right as he sampled familiar and new scents. A heavy cloud cover hid the stars and moon. They entered the parking lot and briskly covered the first fifty feet up the slope toward the next building. Then Max stopped and stared into the darkness beyond the nearest street lamp's cascading light. Bill searched the area ahead. The lighted complex sign was on the right, the dumpster's outline in the darkness ahead, and the next parking lot up and to the left. Nothing appeared out of place.

Though equipped with extraordinary powers of smell, a dog's eyesight was not as good as a human's. Bill had witnessed this difference firsthand when Max would stare at a distant object as if confused. Bill would recognize the object —perhaps a boulder or a bike or a trash can—as harmless, but Max lived in a different world. If the wind were blowing toward them, Max had no problem identifying whatever lay ahead, but if not, sometimes Max froze.

Bill pulled on his leash.

"Come, Max. It's nothing."

As was his custom, Max hurried to lead the way once he had committed to move. They continued walking toward the next building's parking lot and drew near the dumpster on the right. On the other side of the dumpster, a wooded section separated the parking lot from Blue Ridge Drive. A sedan's headlights passed on the road. The headlights faded, and Max stiffened again. They were abreast of the dumpster, and it was nearly pitch black.

Max growled softly, deep in his chest. He edged forward until the leash was taut.

What's that? Something in the woods?

Max growled again, louder now, nearing a bark.

"Hold on, boy."

Max barked. Barked again.

Bill detected movement in the trees.

Oh, no. Is that a bear?

Max pulled forward, straining against his leash. Bill held on with both hands.

The figure moved again.

It's a bear. No, wait . . .

Max exploded in fury. Barking. Barking. Pulling at the leash. Bill struggled to hang on. Max pulled forward, dragging Bill off the parking lot and into the flower bed beside the dumpster.

"No, Max. No!"

Max ignored Bill. He barked constantly and dragged Bill forward. Bill stumbled and lost his hold on the leash.

Three things happened at once.

Max leaped forward, unconstrained.

A light flashed in the woods.

A loud ping sounded behind Bill, signaling that something had struck the dumpster.

A second flash from the woods. Another loud ping.

Gunshots! Silenced fire. Bullets hitting the dumpster.

Bill rolled on the ground to his left.

Max ran into the woods and wrestled with the enemy.

No. No. They'll shoot Max.

"Come, Max! Come!"

Bill struggled to his feet and lurched left to the parking lot.

"Come, Max!"

Max bounded out from the woods to join Bill. Bill ran up the parking lot in semi-darkness. Max ran ahead. Bill approached an SUV, and a side window in the SUV shattered. Bill ran past the SUV and turned left to the sidewalk.

"Come, Max!"

Max appeared out of nowhere. Bill ran in a jagged line to create a difficult target. He reached the end of the building and crossed the sidewalk into the shrubs. Max followed.

Bill continued running down the slope and beyond the building to the grassy area. He picked his way across a drainage ditch and turned briefly to look toward the parking lot above him. Nothing.

Bill turned and ran into the dark area behind the next condo complex. Max ran beside Bill.

"Come on, boy. Keep going."

Bill's lungs heaved, and his chest hurt, but he kept running, fueled by adrenaline.

On familiar territory, Max ran a hundred yards ahead and then returned to check on Bill. Lights from the condo buildings on the right provided scant visibility. Bill traversed the rear side of the Cliffs complex and the Ledges, and then he reached the Highlands. At the far end of the Highlands complex, Bill finally stopped running and turned around. He bent over to gulp air, then strained his eyes to see in the darkness. He detected no movement and sensed they had escaped their assailant. At Bill's side, Max panted calmly, ready to follow Bill's direction. It hit Bill then that Max had saved his life, and Bill knelt beside him to express his gratitude.

"Good boy, Max. Good boy. Let's go."

The Highlands Express ski lift was below them on the hill. Bill grabbed Max's leash, and they picked their way down the steep incline to the lift, then turned right onto a gravel lane that led through a wooded section to Wintergreen Drive. Once under the forest cover, Bill paused to formulate a plan.

He couldn't return to his condo. That was lunacy.

Should he call 911? They would connect him to Wintergreen PD, who would send every patrol officer on duty to canvass the area. What would that accomplish? If the shooter had left the scene, a night search would accomplish next to nothing. If the shooter was hidden nearby, someone might get killed. It was best to save the search for the morning.

But what about Bill and Max?

He had several good friends who lived nearby. They would come for Max and Bill if he asked. Phyllis Spooner. Frieda Chang. But their homes were too close to the incident for Bill's liking. No. He needed more distance.

There was one person. Someone who lived on the Blackrock Mountain side. A place no one would expect to find Bill.

He called Rachel Dunn.

She answered after three rings.

"My goodness. Bill O'Shea. Do you realize it's nine thirty? Time for me to get my beauty sleep."

"I need your help."

A pause. Not a long pause. Just long enough for the urgency in Bill's voice to register.

"What is it? What's happened?"

FIFTY

Bill and Max hunkered in the woods at the edge of Founders Vision Overlook on Wintergreen Drive.

He had asked Rachel to pick them up in the overlook's parking lot. It was on a wooded section of the road halfway between the upper mountain and the main lodge area. Bill and Max had made their way down from the gravel lane via the road's ditch. They had ducked into the overgrown grasses on the way to hide from two passing cars.

Headlights approached from the downhill side. A light-colored van slowed and then turned into the parking lot. Rachel. She steered in a rough circle and stopped near them. Bill and Max hustled to Rachel's van and jumped into the passenger seat together.

Bill struggled to buckle the seat belt with Max in his lap. Rachel reached to stroke Max's neck. Max licked her hand.

Rachel wore her blond hair up. She appeared ready for a fashion cover shoot in a tight-fitting, long-sleeved shirt and light makeup.

Bill swallowed.

Jeez. Rachel would look good shoveling manure in the rain.

"Who's this?" she said.

"That's Max."

Rachel leaned closer and touched her nose to Max's. Max sneezed.

"How are you, Max? Did big bad Bill get you into trouble?"

"We should go."

"Yep. Got it."

It took five minutes to get to Rachel's place, a home at the ski slope's edge on the other side of Wintergreen.

"A glass of wine?" she asked, leaning against the white kitchen counter. "I have an open bottle of Chardonnay."

"Yes, thank you."

"What can I get you, Max?"

Max stood at her feet, wagging his tail. He had a new friend.

"Max already ate. He would love some water if you have a plastic container or something similar."

Bill watched Rachel efficiently organize refreshments. She wore jeans and sneakers and was tall with an attractive figure. Bill had been inside Rachel's home several times in connection with other investigations. He realized he was more relaxed now than ever in her presence. A near-death experience put things in perspective.

They sat in the living room, with her on the couch and him in a side chair. Max curled up at her feet.

Rachel asked for more details about the shooting. Bill provided a moment-by-moment playback, which was good practice for the statement he would give Emily the next morning. Unfortunately, he had not seen the shooter well enough to identify them. Tall. Short. Male. Female. Any of the above. If he could interview Max, Max would identify the shooter. Too bad dogs weren't allowed to sniff a suspect lineup.

"You must be close," she said. "Whoever they are, the murderer feels threatened."

"Yes, I'm close."

But not close enough. Who of Bill's suspects would have come after him that way? The gun was silenced. The only sound Bill heard came from the bullet hitting the dumpster. That could be the work of Paul Jameson or Maria Metcalf. And though unlikely in Bill's view, it could have been a murder-for-hire ordered by Nick Pappas. Jessica Smith? No way.

They discussed the investigation a while longer, and then Rachel stifled a yawn.

"I'm keeping you up," said Bill.

Rachel smiled. "Sad to say it, but I'm not the party girl I once was, and I have an early massage appointment."

"Thank you, Rachel. I'm truly grateful. So is Max."

"Anytime."

Their eyes met, and for a moment, Bill wondered if Rachel had intended a hidden meaning in the word *anytime*. No. It was his imagination.

"Let me show you the guest room."

A hallway off the living area led to the bedrooms. Bill and Max would sleep in a sparsely decorated small room with a queen-sized bed, bureau, and closet. Rachel asked if Max required anything special. No, he'd be happy to sleep on the carpet as long as Bill was nearby. A doorway at the end of the hall presumably led to the master suite. Rachel pointed toward her room and said, "If you get scared or anything in the middle of the night, I'm a few steps away."

Then she touched Bill's arm, and tingles of excitement

ran up his shoulder. With great control, Bill maintained his composure, but after he turned toward the guest room, Rachel giggled under her breath. Feeling sheepish, Bill stepped into the room with Max and closed the door.

With a cheeky grin, Max eyed Bill briefly and then looked away.

"Max, get your mind out of the gutter."

Later, Bill lay awake in the darkened room and reflected on the case. He had viable suspects, but a few of the jigsaw pieces had the wrong shape. No matter how he tried to jam them into the puzzle, the picture came out wrong.

He kept coming back to Maria's interview at the Wintergreen police station.

You know what they called her at the agency? The backstabber. She couldn't be trusted.

The line echoed in his mind until his subconscious took over and switched the words around.

Couldn't be trusted. The agency. Backstabber.

His dark thoughts threatened a restless night; nevertheless, the day's fatigue eventually won, and Bill felt himself slipping into slumber.

Then his phone buzzed.

Bill rubbed his eyes and reached for the phone.

Brendan Baittinger.

"Hello."

"How are you, Bill?" The boy spoke hesitantly, as if he feared Bill. And for good reason.

"Brendan, do you realize it's after eleven?"

"Yes, sir. But the limousine service owner finally called me back."

Bill sat up. "Okay. Good. What did you find out?"

"The customer arranged the booking using the service's

website form. The charge for the limo was prepaid by debit card, but the name sounds odd. Brad Clooney."

Brad Clooney.

It took Bill a few seconds. "Yeah. That's definitely a fake name. Did you get an address for the pickup?"

"That's just it. There was no pickup."

"What do you mean? The driver picked someone up somewhere. Richmond. Staunton. Charlottesville."

"No. There was no pickup. The owner of the service drove the limo that morning. His instructions were to drive to the top of the mountain, circle around for two-and-a-half hours, and then drive back to Charlottesville."

Bill held the phone to his ear and tried to process the new information.

"Maybe it doesn't mean anything," said Brendan.

"How so?"

"Maybe it's a false clue. You know, like in those British mystery shows? What do they call it?"

"A red herring?"

"Yes," said Brendan. "Maybe it's a red herring."

Bill frowned. Max, who may have sensed Bill's confusion, nudged Bill's knee. Bill absentmindedly stroked Max's head.

"Bill?" said Brendan.

"Uh-huh. The limo might be a red herring. Anything else?"

"No. But while I have you on the phone, I wanted to say it's been a pleasure working with you on this investigation. I feel like I've learned a lot."

"Yeah. It's been great, kid. Keep up the good work."

Bill lay back down and stared into the darkness.

A limo with no pickup. A blue-handled knife. The back-stabber.

The jigsaw pieces swirled before him but still didn't fit. Something was wrong with the whole picture.

Bill grabbed his phone from the bedside table, tapped the screen several times, and called CIA John. The man answered on the first ring. Did he ever sleep?

Bill said, "I need to give you an update on the latest developments."

"Let's hear it."

After the update, CIA John said, "The limo with no passenger, what does that tell you?"

"The killer was trying to confuse us by casting suspicion on other suspects."

"Kind of a crude tactic, don't you think?"

"Yeah, maybe, but it worked for a while."

"The attempt to kill you puts the spotlight back on my guys. Who do you like for it? Metcalf or Jameson?"

"In terms of motive, I like Metcalf. But I think her alibi's going to check out."

"Which leaves us with Jameson, who was my first choice all along."

Jameson. After the interviews, Emily believed Paul Jameson was innocent and Maria was guilty. Bill was inclined to believe the same. But Maria had an alibi and Paul didn't. After the murder, the killer had hiked up the golf course to hide Lily's phone and avoided the surveillance cameras on the third hole. If Jameson was an avid golfer, it would have been enough to sway Bill's opinion, but Jameson got his exercise by walking on the street, not the golf course.

And that notion sparked another thought that Bill did not care for. Nevertheless, he forced himself to hold a new scenario up to the light.

Huh. Yeah, that could work.

"What do you have on Maria Metcalf's partner?" Bill asked.

"Partner? What sort of partner?"

"Her romantic partner, Terry Stinson."

The sound of CIA John typing came through Bill's phone.

"We don't have a romantic partner for Metcalf in the system. What's the name again?"

"Terry Stinson."

John typed some more and then paused.

"Oh, crap."

FIFTY-ONE

The next morning, Bill arrived fifteen minutes early for his pickleball date with Terry Stinson. Cindy was still in New Jersey, so the two men would play singles. Bill considered this fortunate, given the acrimonious nature of his last conversation with Maria.

A younger man had arrived earlier and was practicing his serve, presumably waiting for his playing partners to come. He was medium height and wore white shorts, a blue polo, sunglasses, and a Wintergreen ball cap. Bill and the man exchanged a few words, and Bill pointed to the court where he usually played. The man nodded, moved to a court on the opposite side of the playing area, and resumed hitting practice serves.

Terry arrived soon after that, and he and Bill shook hands. Bill had worried that Maria would tell Terry she was a suspect in a murder investigation. Judging by Terry's typically bright demeanor, Maria had kept that information to herself.

"What's this guy's deal?" said Terry, eyeing the younger man in the white shorts.

"He's waiting on some other players. They're up here for a conference and have the morning off."

Terry nodded good-naturedly, always eager to make a new friend. "Maybe they'll let us play in. A foursome is more fun."

"Definitely. Let's ask when the others come along. Should we get started?"

Bill and Terry hit practice shots, and Terry asked about Cindy's trip to Cape May. She was having a blast. It was a beautiful town with great restaurants, but the water was cold.

"Sounds nice," said Terry. "I'd like to go sometime."

They played as if evenly matched. Bill scored a few points. Terry scored a few points. Bill went on a run that took the score to nine–five, his lead. Terry came back and tacked another point on top: ten–nine, Terry's lead.

Bill bounced on his toes. His adrenaline was pumping because he wanted badly to win the first game. They exchanged the lead a few times until, finally, Bill won the game fourteen–twelve.

"Nice game," said Terry, and they bumped paddles at the net.

Terry's eyes rolled to the man in the white shorts, who continued practicing serves.

"I guess his buddies are late."

"Maybe they got the wrong time."

Of course, Terry had let Bill win the game. It was obvious once Bill knew what to look for. The slackened effort to return a lob. The intentional foot faults. Out-of-bound shots.

Oddly, though, even a false victory felt good that morning. You took the wins when you could.

Bill won the first two points of the next game and then glanced at his wristwatch. He rarely wore a watch, but at the moment, minutes counted. Better get to it.

"Hey, I have a question for you," said Bill.

"Fire away."

"Where did you say you worked before retiring?"

"I was a defense contractor."

Bill's next serve had a good spin on it and landed deep in Terry's court. Terry managed to return the serve, but his shot landed wide of the court on Bill's side.

Three–zero, Bill's lead.

"What area of defense?"

"Aviation. Pratt & Whitney was my main client."

"Gotcha."

Bill served again. Terry returned the serve easily. They both approached the kitchen, volleyed quickly four times, and then Terry won the point.

"I thought maybe you did more hands-on work," said Bill. "Given your service with the Army. You were with the Rangers, right?"

Before answering, Terry served again. He put a lot of spin on the ball, and Bill had no chance of returning it.

Terry approached the net. "What are you getting at, Bill?"

"I'm curious about one thing. When you moved here four months ago, you never gave the CIA your new address. How come?"

Terry's eyes tightened, not sure yet where Bill was headed.

"I was a contractor, not an employee. Contractors aren't required to report their every move."

Bill nodded. "You gonna serve?"

Terry hit the next serve even harder. Bill managed to make contact with the ball, but the ball sailed over the fence. Enough of that nonsense.

"The CIA didn't even know you were with Maria."

After edging toward the net a few paces, Terry said, "I

don't want those guys tracking me. And I didn't want people here to know I was in that line of work."

"What line of work is that? Killing people? Like you tried to kill me?"

Terry faked a laugh. "Have you lost your senses?"

"We've got all the evidence we need. But I'd still like to hear you say it."

Terry nervously glanced over his shoulder at the man in the white shorts, who was now sitting under the canopy checking his phone.

"Are you recording this?"

"Nope."

"You swear?"

Bill shook his head. "Not recording it. I promise."

"What evidence?"

"I should have figured it out sooner—as an avid golfer, you knew how to weave your way up the third fairway without triggering a surveillance camera. But you should have stayed on the course. When you switched to the trail through the woods, the Overlook cameras got you. It's a clear image. The phone in your hand is quite visible."

The last part was BS, but Bill had no problem with lying to a murderer.

Terry responded in a voice laced with skepticism. "A clear image in darkness from a distance? I doubt it."

"And there's the issue of you living up here and partnering with Maria without telling the CIA."

Terry snorted. "I've already answered those questions. Is that all you have? Let's keep playing, for crying out loud."

"There's the limo, of course."

"What limo?"

"You booked it to throw us off the scent. You used a prepaid debit card and a clever name, but now that we know what to look for, we'll find a paper trail leading back to you."

The smile left Terry's face, and he gripped his paddle with both hands.

"And then there's the hair the forensics team found on Lily Wolf's deck." Bill smiled as if he had Terry in handcuffs even though the hair story was a bald-faced lie. "The hair probably fell off your shirt when you struck the blow. At this moment, Nelson County is executing a search warrant on your condo. I'm sure they'll find the dye on your hair at home matches the one from the crime scene."

Terry's face sagged, and his remaining confidence appeared to escape him.

"You had me going," said Bill. "Round and round and round. Volunteering to keep the café open. That was a nice touch. Still, I was convinced it had to be Paul Jameson or Maria."

With a sneer, Terry said, "Jameson. That lightweight. He couldn't kill a gnat if it landed in his wine."

"I believed Jameson's story about his relationship with Lily. They were allies. That left me with Maria, but she said something that didn't add up yesterday. She said people in the agency used to call Lily Wolf the backstabber. If Maria had known the murderer's means, she would have never mentioned the term *backstabber* to me. But she didn't know because the police never released that information and Maria didn't kill Lily. Someone else killed Lily—you."

Terry sighed. Bill held his breath.

"No one will miss Lily Wolf," said Terry. "She was a despicable person. I knew those Polish agents. I knew them personally. They deserved justice, and I got it for them."

"By killing Lily."

"Yeah. I killed her. So what?"

The bastard. Bill didn't know everything Lily Wolf had done to save herself, but he knew she didn't deserve the treatment she got from Terry. Plus, Terry had set Kim up to go to prison. And Bill could not abide that.

"Your recorded statement should just about do it," said Bill. "Game over."

Terry's face grew dark with fury. "You promised."

"I didn't record your statement. He did."

Terry whirled to his right to find CIA John—the man in the white shorts—standing twenty feet away.

"Terry, this is John. I don't know John's last name."

John held up a small electronic device and replayed the critical line. **Yeah. I killed her. So what?**

Bill said, "John would like to hide you in a cell in Cuba or someplace similar for the next twenty-five years. But that's not our deal. Is it, John?"

"No, that's not our deal."

A rattling noise came from the fence behind where they stood, and the three men turned that way. A Wintergreen squad car sat parked on the shoulder of Blue Ridge Drive. Mitch had opened a locked gate and now stood a few feet inside the court.

"Your ride is here," said Bill.

Terry's eyes went from Bill to John and then over to Mitch. The main entrance to the courts lay a hundred feet in the opposite direction. Terry wrestled with mental calculations.

"Mitch was a linebacker," said Bill. "And he stays in top shape. You wouldn't get far."

Terry's shoulders dropped. His eyes locked on Bill.

"Don't give up on the handyman concept," Terry said. "We could have made it work."

"I'll keep it in mind."

FIFTY-TWO

Craig Beaumont's assistant showed Emily and Undersheriff Arnie Shields into the office. The commonwealth's attorney ignored them. Emily surveyed the office's decor, noticed the large portraits of white men in suits, and raised an eyebrow at Arnie. Arnie shrugged. They took seats across the desk from Beaumont, who was apparently arranging a dinner date for the weekend.

Emily had asked to join Arnie when he met with Craig. Arnie had no problem with that.

Craig put the phone down, nodded curtly at Arnie, and then studied Emily's face. His chin jutted forward. "Emily, is that you?"

"The same."

"All dressed up. I heard you entered law enforcement. Picked up a few pounds, I see. The donuts?"

"Three kids did that. How's *your* love life?"

Craig fidgeted nervously. "I'm divorced."

"Twice over, I gather."

Emily knew a cop who knew a cop in Philadelphia. Word

was Craig had trouble with the until-death-do-us-part part. Never mind. His exes were better off without him.

Craig returned his attention to Arnie. “I’m not dropping the charges against Ms. Wiley. The evidence stands. We’ll get an easy conviction.”

Arnie threw his hands to the sides. “You’re not making sense. We can’t keep her. The real murderer confessed. It’s on tape.”

“I’ve reviewed that recording. That’s the weakest confession ever. The guy’s a nut job.”

“He’s at the jail in a holding cell. We’ve already arrested him.”

“Arnie, you’re naive. If my mother confessed to the JFK assassination, you’d lock her up.”

Arnie leaned forward and scowled. “Have you lost your mind? This case is gift-wrapped. The murderer is ready to talk, but he wants a deal.”

“Wiley stays in custody.”

At that moment, Beaumont’s assistant re-entered the office and announced that Craig had a call. In a sharp tone, he told her he was busy.

“But it’s the governor,” she said.

Craig did a double take. “What governor?”

“Our governor. You know, the governor of Virginia.”

Sheesh, Emily thought, *those fed guys work fast.*

Earlier, Bill had related to Emily the details of his deal with CIA John. The agency wanted Terry Stinson locked up somewhere they could keep an eye on him. Bill didn’t care much about that, but he knew Beaumont might be a problem. Stinson had to be arrested by Nelson County to get Kim’s charges dropped. John said that was fair enough, but the feds might come in over the top later. Not much later, as it turned out.

Craig picked up, introduced himself, and listened for a bit. The voice on the other end was male and excited.

"We already have the guilty party in custody," said Craig.

The other voice grew louder. More forceful.

"But governor, I've already pressed charges against her because the evidence is compelling."

The outburst that followed forced Craig to pull the phone from his ear.

"Yes, sir."

More loud instructions.

"Yes, sir."

Then, a loud click.

"Sir? Are you there?"

Craig's face lost its color. He was in a tough spot because he'd already spread the word about Kim's pending conviction. Folks in the far reaches of Nelson County believed that a woman with wiry hair who hailed from Staunton had killed her lover in Wintergreen. Now, the truth would come out. Regular citizens still wouldn't know who Craig Beaumont was, but those who mattered would mark a black X by his name. That was fine with Emily.

"Go ahead," said Craig. "I'll drop the charges. Let her go."

"Thanks."

Arnie rose and left the room with speed. Emily took her time. Her eyes lingered on the portraits.

"You should swap these out, Craig. Get some diversity in here."

"I had them pulled out of storage last week."

"Idiot."

Craig examined the portraits and then nodded as if to give credit to Emily's point. "You're right. Some diversity. I'll work on that."

Emily made for the door.

"Say, Emily," he said. "Have you kept up with Georgia Longtree? I haven't seen her since high school."

Emily almost mentioned Lynchburg, but a better response came to her in a flash.

"She's in Alaska. Six kids and counting. I hear her husband is almost seven feet tall."

Craig swallowed hard. "Good to see you."

"The pleasure was all mine."

FIFTY-THREE

At ten o'clock the next morning, Bill sat at his counter lingering over a cup of coffee. He and Max had hiked three miles on the Appalachian Trail earlier. Max lay on the carpet, knocked out by all appearances. Then, without warning, Max rose suddenly and trotted to the front door. This usually meant someone had entered the building, climbed the stairs to their floor, and would soon ring the bell. Max waited calmly.

The bell rang, and Bill stepped forward. Hairs stood on Max's back. What did that mean? Bill opened the door.

Maria Metcalf.

Holy jalapeño.

Bill's heart rate jumped. He took one step back and looked at Maria's hands. They were empty.

She smiled at Max. "Is he going to attack?"

"That depends on your intentions."

"I come in peace."

Maria held her hand out for Max to sniff. He hesitated but then edged forward and licked her fingers.

"I smell coffee. Do you have an extra cup?"

"Yeah. Sure."

They sat across from each other at the dining table. Bill had eyed Maria's outfit. She wore jeans and a short-sleeved top. If she carried a weapon, it was tiny.

"We won't see each other again," she said. "I'm leaving in an hour. There's no place for me in Wintergreen now."

"I'd say I'm sorry to see you go, but your partner tried to kill me, so I'm ambivalent."

Maria frowned.

Bill said, "He didn't mention that during your visit with him at the jail yesterday?"

"It didn't come up."

Bill shared the story of Terry's nighttime assault.

She shook her head. "He completely lost it. You may not believe this, but I had no idea."

"Uh-huh."

Bill had slept little the night before, worrying over whether Terry had acted alone, fearing that he had missed something, something that proved Maria and Terry had planned to murder Lily before they moved to Wintergreen. If Maria maintained her contacts within the CIA—and there was no reason to believe she didn't—then one of those contacts might have told Maria in advance that Lily was headed to the Wintergreen safehouse. Given their mutual hatred of Lily, Maria and Terry may have seen an opportunity to settle an old score.

Maria sighed. "I had my suspicions, of course, when Lily Wolf was killed, but Terry swore he had nothing to do with it. The evidence piled up against Kim, and I convinced myself she was the murderer."

"Bullshit. You knew. Whose idea was it to help out at the café? Terry's, right? Because it was the best way to keep tabs on me."

Maria couldn't hold his gaze. Yeah, she knew Terry had murdered Lily. But was she in on it from the beginning? Bill had called CIA John earlier that morning to share his concerns, but John didn't want to hear them. As far as John was concerned, the case was solved. He would investigate no further, because the CIA had no interest in a larger scandal. A rogue ex-contractor was one thing. A scheme involving multiple parties was a front-page story.

Maria's hands gripped the table's edge. "After Terry left the Army, he applied to the CIA but he failed certain personality tests. That didn't stop them from hiring him as a contractor. The funny thing is he knew Lily Wolf in the field. They were lovers for a time. But then a foreign agent Terry worked with was killed, and Terry suspected Lily had divulged his secrets to the other side. He never forgot that.

"When I first spotted Lily here in Wintergreen, I mentioned it to Terry. I told him we had to let that go. We were retired, and it was time to move on. He agreed.

"Then Paul Jameson came to see me because he worried I would go after Lily. I told him I had no such intention. Let bygones be bygones. I don't believe Paul knew Terry lived here."

"The CIA didn't know because Terry never told them."

"I told Terry about the conversation I had with Jameson. Terry shrugged it off. But I should have known something was wrong when Terry suggested I visit my sister in Richmond."

Maybe Maria's version was the truth, but the way she studied Bill's face left room for doubt. She studied him as if trying to read whether he fully bought into her version. Then Bill realized that it was in his best interest for Maria to believe he bought her story. Lingering doubts might convince Maria she had a loose end that needed tying off. Bill nodded.

Maria covered her face with her hands and then slowly pulled them away. "Anyway, I'm getting the hell out of here."

"It's a good move. Move far away from Wintergreen. Try to forget it. Try to start over."

At the door, Maria offered her hand, and Bill readily shook it. He played his part. He acted as if he believed Maria knew nothing of Terry's intention to commit murder.

"You're a good detective," she said. "Without you here, Terry would have gotten away with it."

"Maybe. Maybe not. In any case, he'll be in prison for a long time, and that's where he belongs."

"Of course. You're right."

After Maria left, Bill breathed a sigh of relief. He told himself there was an excellent chance Maria would leave things alone. An excellent chance.

FIFTY-FOUR

"Man, you got some crazy stuff going down in Wintergreen," Ritchie said.

"Yeah," said Mitch, "it was a heck of a week."

Three full racks of spare ribs crackled on the grill. Mitch basted them generously and then flipped them. The sauce sizzled. He tested the heat with his hand and adjusted the flames.

Lulu's cousin Ritchie and Ritchie's wife, Sarah, were over for dinner. The women sat at a round wooden table drinking mocktails on the back deck of Mitch and Lulu's small rental home. Sarah was six months into her pregnancy.

Mitch and Ritchie stood at the grill and drank beer. The yard was small and backed up to a forested area. Tall wooden fences separated their yard from the neighbors on both sides.

Someday, when Lulu joined a successful dentistry practice, they would buy their own home. Until then, this, or something like it, would have to do. Mitch tried to imagine where he would put a swing set. Over there on the left next to that tree?

Ritchie told him about a call from the previous night.

There had been a shooting in the parking lot of a dance club. A bullet had grazed a man's foot.

"The shooter was long gone by the time the first squad arrived. Witnesses gave different descriptions of the shooter's ride. A truck. An SUV. Big. Small. They were trying, but it was dark, and almost everyone was high on something."

Mitch nodded. He had worked as a patrolman in Richmond for two years, so he knew the kind of calls that Ritchie worked every day. Disturbance calls. Wellness checks. The occasional adrenaline-pumping footrace chasing bad guys through alleys and backyards. Police work varied wildly between cities and rural communities. In the cities, bad stuff happened every day. In the countryside, the same things happened but with much less frequency. On the other hand, some aspects of the job were the same: the camaraderie, the paperwork, the training.

He'd been giving his job at Wintergreen a lot of thought after his conversation with Krista. He had to prioritize. Krista put family first, then career, which, according to Krista, left only scraps of time for her personal life. Mitch would adopt the same prioritization, but he thought about it differently. At that point in his relationship with Lulu, he didn't much care to do anything but hang out with her. His family was his personal life. He was never that much of a hobby guy anyway. Watch sports? Play video games? He'd rather go on a day trip with Lulu to one of the beautiful parks in Central Virginia. And if they brought a little tyke along, so much the better.

The only real problem they had was one of distance. Mitch had an hour-long commute. Lulu's daily drive was even longer. When their baby got sick, and the baby would get sick sooner or later, they'd have a full-blown crisis on their hands. And that didn't work.

A while back, Ritchie had arranged for Mitch to meet his sergeant. Charlottesville PD was hiring then, and the meeting had gone well. The sergeant offered to forward Mitch's name to the recruiting team, but Mitch declined. He enjoyed his work at Wintergreen—the people and the natural beauty. Plus, he and Lulu had planned to wait several years before starting a family. So much for plans.

Ritchie, a keen observer at all times, may have read Mitch's mind.

"My sergeant brought your name up the other day," he said.

"Oh, yeah?"

"He still wants you on the team."

Mitch confirmed that Lulu's pregnancy had heightened his interest in a Charlottesville-based position.

Ritchie grimaced. "Unfortunately, the hiring window is closed. Budget constraints."

"Damn. I'm always late to the party."

"But the window will reopen. We need more staff. No question about that."

"Cool. Let me know when it does. I'm ready."

FIFTY-FIVE

Krista and Skip checked into a hotel at the intersection of West Main and Ridge Street, convenient to the restaurants and bars of UVA's Corner and the pedestrian mall downtown. They ate fresh seafood at Public Fish and Oyster and then strolled to the downtown mall for window shopping. Skip bought a book on the evolution of humans. Krista picked up a historical novel set during the Civil War. With books in hand, they stopped for a drink at Miller's patio section. A gentle breeze blew up the brick walkway and chilled Krista's arms. She pulled on the light jacket she'd brought along.

"Gosh, this has been fun," said Skip.

Krista smiled. "The night's not over yet."

He chuckled nervously.

Hmm. What was that about? Skip had never shied away from suggestions of intimacy. Why start now? Unless he had something else on his mind.

Skip gazed at her fondly, and then his eyes moved past her shoulder to the next corner, where a busker played a reasonably good version of *Blowing in the Wind.*

Skip pointed in that direction and said, "He's not bad."

"Yeah. I've heard worse covers from famous singers."

His eyes locked on to a couple that strolled by them on the promenade. Then he studied his hands.

"What's up, Skip?"

"What do you mean?"

"You look like you're trying to decide whether to jump off a building, but we're sitting on the ground. So, what's up?"

Skip rocked his head left and right as if unsure how to respond.

"Out with it," she said.

"Okay, here goes. I'm trying to figure out where we are. And before you say we're in Charlottesville, I'm talking about you and me. Where are *we* in this thing?"

Oh, boy.

Krista had hoped to make it through the weekend without having this conversation, but obviously, Skip wasn't on the same page.

"You'll have to be more specific," she said. "What do you want from *this thing?*"

He put his hands forward as if reaching for something. "I want *more*. I want to spend more time with you. I want to be a bigger part of your life."

Krista took a deep breath.

Here goes.

"Skip, you're thirty-six, and I'm thirty-seven. We're not that young."

"We're not that old either."

"I guess that's true. Here's the real question. Do you want to have children of your own?"

She had already guessed the answer, and Skip's expression underscored her guess. He wanted the whole package—

marriage, house, babies, school, bigger house, more school, college, and retirement. And like most people who took that leap, he had no idea of how much work the journey entailed.

Krista squeezed her hands under the table. "There's really no easy way to say this. You should find another woman."

Skip pulled his head back. "What? Where did that come from?"

"Well, you started the conversation, and I want to be clear. I don't want to have kids with you. I don't want to get married."

Skip fell back in his chair with slumped shoulders.

"I'm sorry to cut to the chase, but I want to avoid any confusion between us."

"You don't want to get married again? Like never?"

She shrugged. "Never is a long time. Maybe, someday, in five or six years. But I'm certainly not ready to remarry now. Aside from marriage, though, the bigger issue is the kids. I love my boys. They're thirteen and fifteen. It's been a long, hard struggle raising them, but I wouldn't trade a day of it for anything. Now, though, I can see the light at the end of the tunnel, and I won't have any more babies."

Krista stopped then to let Skip process what she'd said. He didn't seem ready to respond.

"Skip, tell me the truth. You want to have your own children, don't you?"

He bit his lip, then said, "The thought had crossed my mind."

"I don't blame you. It's a wonderful experience."

"But I'm not dead set on it. The most important thing is to be with you."

Okay. That's what you're saying now.

But maybe Skip believed that, over time, he could change her mind. They would fall hopelessly in love, the real thing, and their love would be so strong they would naturally decide, together and spontaneously, that they must procreate.

Skip said, "You gave me hope by suggesting that marriage was possible in five or six years."

Jeez. Krista should have never said those words. Now Skip had her on a timeline.

"Maybe as a first step," he said, "we could move in together."

Krista could feel herself starting to frown. She tried to fight it off.

"How would that work?" she said. "Your job is in DC. Mine is a three-hour drive from there."

"We have a field office in Charlottesville. I could transfer, maybe. Or, you could move to northern Virginia. There are a ton of law enforcement opportunities. It would be a great move for you."

Krista's chest tightened. Already, Skip was throwing out decisions for them to wrestle over, stressful decisions she didn't have to face five minutes ago. She couldn't move to northern Virginia because Tyler had visitation rights. And, frankly, she didn't want to move to northern Virginia. She was recently promoted in Wintergreen and still had a lot to learn from her new job. Also, she had her ongoing studies in criminology. She needed the intellectual stimulation her career provided. And the excitement. And the action. Moving in with Skip entailed making many tiny decisions. Furthermore, adjusting her life, and the life of her boys, to the full-time presence of a new man would require the three of them to make many small and some large changes in their daily routine.

What impact would that have on her career aspirations? Some impact, certainly. To believe otherwise would be naive.

As her Uncle Charlie had advised her, *You can't do everything.*

Nope. This was not going to work.

"Why are you shaking your head?" Skip said.

"Because I'm worried about our future. I'm worried about where we are in this thing."

Skip tried to backpedal. "We're brainstorming possibilities. I'm not looking to make a decision right away. Let's enjoy the night. Listen, he's playing a Beatles cover now."

"No, Skip. We *can* enjoy the night. I *want* to enjoy our time together, but I also want to be *crystal clear*. At this point in my life, and for the foreseeable future, my priorities are my kids and my career. I don't want to move in together. I'm not getting married. And I'm not having any more babies. I enjoy our time together. We get away for one weekend a month, and it's fun. If we meet for dinner on another night each month, that's good too. We text. We talk on the phone a few times a week. That's all great. I love it. But don't think we're headed for more than that anytime soon."

"That's fine," he said hastily. "I'm fine with that."

Maybe he was. Maybe he wasn't. Time would tell. But she had done her part. She had typed it out for Skip in a crisp, clear font. And in truth, she didn't want to break up with Skip then. The night was young. The busker had talent. She had a nearly full glass of Malbec on the table and some possibly great moments of intimacy in her near future.

She lifted her wine, and they clinked glasses.

"I'm glad we had this conversation," he said. "Clear the air. I care for you. You know that."

"Yes. I care about you too."

FIFTY-SIX

The next day, Bill hiked up the hill to Café Devine and noticed Kim's black F-150 was parked in the lot. The bell hanging from the doorknob jingled to announce his arrival. He marched in and looked to the right, hoping to see Kim behind the register. No luck. A young woman with shoulder-length blond hair helped a customer with a purchase. In the kitchen behind them, Nathan wore a white apron and worked on something. Nathan smiled and waved. Kim was nowhere to be seen.

The café was busy, with the two indoor tables occupied and another six customers examining the various merchandise. Bill made his way to the wine racks and perused the French section. Cindy was due back later that afternoon, and he had in mind picking up a nice bottle for their reunion celebration. Oh, that's interesting—a forty-seven-dollar Châteauneuf-du-Pape. Cindy had a weakness for good French reds. A glass of that would get their evening off to a great start.

The woman at the register introduced herself as Molly, a

friend of Kim and Nathan's. She seemed comfortable behind the counter, and Bill got the impression she had experience in the field. Bill concluded his transaction, and then Kim appeared in the kitchen and approached the counter.

"Will wonders never cease," she said. "It's Bill O'Shea in the flesh. I thought I heard your voice."

Kim had bags under her eyes that had not been there a week earlier. And though her words resembled the old Kim's, she struggled to bring the same energy to her voice. Her mind knew what she should say, but her spirit refused to answer the call.

"It's good to have you back," he said.

"It's good to be free. Do you have a minute? There's something I want to tell you."

Bill nodded, and Kim suggested they sit outside on the patio.

Three women sat together at one table, so engrossed in their conversation that they didn't notice Bill and Kim coming through the door. Bill and Kim sat at a table on the other side of the small patio.

Bill touched her shoulder. "How are you, Kim? Tell me the truth."

She pressed her lips tightly together and then sniffed. "I'm sad."

He nodded that he understood.

"Of course, I'm happy to be out and no longer a suspect, but I'm grieving."

"Yes. You will grieve for a long time."

Kim Wiley wasn't the crying type, but her lips and eyes drooped as if they couldn't bear the weight of her loss.

"I know she wasn't perfect," Kim said, and then she chuckled. "Lord knows Lily had her faults, and she'd done some things no one could be proud of, but I loved her. And I will always believe that she loved me too."

Kim stopped talking and stared into space, as if she preferred to be done with it all, to not have to speak, feel, or do anything.

Perhaps a change in the conversation would help.

"What did you want to tell me?" he said.

She startled and then filled her lungs with fresh air. "Nathan's taking over the café."

"No kidding."

"Yeah. I need a break, obviously. But we've been discussing this possibility for months. Nathan has the energy and a new dream. He's going to make some big changes."

"What sort of changes?"

"He's bringing in a brick-style oven. He's going to make pies. Pizza. Pastries. All kinds of good stuff. Molly's going to help. Nathan and Molly have something going. Might be love. I don't think they realize it yet."

"Wow. Lots of changes happening."

"You bet. Nathan even has a new name for the café—Perfect Pies."

"Perfect Pies." Bill nodded his approval of the name, but he had concerns. "What about you, Kim? You're still coming up here to work, right? You're part of the community."

Kim twisted her lips into a bunch. "Sure. I still have a financial stake in the business. I won't be up here all the time, but I'll pull a few shifts every week."

"Okay. But I'm taking that as a minimum. The gossip line up here would go silent without you."

That earned Bill a laugh that sounded more like the old Kim. His chest grew warm.

She pointed a finger at him. "On that topic, I have a little something."

Bill's eyes sharpened. He sensed trouble.

Kim said, "Word's going around that a certain retired detective left Rachel Dunn's house at the crack of dawn a few days ago."

"Now, Kim, I can explain that."

"Uh-huh. I'm hanging on your every word."

FIFTY-SEVEN

Convinced that Kim was on her way to a full recovery, Bill made his way lightheartedly through the parking lots to the first Vistas building. With anticipation, he checked the lot of Cindy's building for her SUV, but evidently, she had not yet returned.

Once inside his condo, Bill placed the bottle of Châteauneuf-du-Pape prominently on the counter. Max rose from his nap and stretched expectantly. It was time for an afternoon walk, and Max wanted his due. If Bill didn't make a move soon, Max would begin his not-so-subtle routine of following Bill's every step.

"Let's take a look outside first," said Bill.

In the year since purchasing the condo, Bill had learned he must make an effort to enjoy the outstanding view. Otherwise, he could go an entire day without giving it the attention it deserved. So now, he opened the sliding door, and he and Max stepped onto the balcony.

Whoa! Even better than yesterday.

A light wind blew up the mountainside, rustling the bright green summer leaves. The sun was high and behind them, basking Nelson County in warmth and light. The mountain across the hollow rolled gently down to the left, and on the far right, a single car made its way along the curve of Wintergreen Drive. Far down in the community of Stoney Creek, sunlight bounced off tiny Lake Monocan. High above the hollow, three vultures circled slowly in search of a meal.

By his side, Max stood still and absorbed the view with a smile of contentment. Max tilted his head upward slightly and sniffed. Then he sniffed again. He had detected a scent Bill would never know. Max wagged his tail and turned slightly to explore the smell. Where did it come from? Max searched the immediate confines of the balcony and then turned his attention farther afield. Growing more excited, he lifted his nose toward the grassy area on the right. No luck. Undaunted, Max rushed to Bill's feet and searched left. Max next turned his attention to the area directly beneath their condo and was apparently rewarded, for his tail went into overdrive. He leaned his weight back on his forelegs, lifted his butt, and whined delightedly. What in the world did he smell?

Bill looked down and gasped. His chest filled with emotion, and his eyes grew moist.

Oh, my. It's Mr. Chips. At last.

Bill's furry brown friend nibbled lawn greens as if there was no time to waste. Instinct must have warned him of nearby attention because he dropped his greens, stood straight, and searched his surroundings. Evidently assured of his immediate safety, he adopted a pose of dignity and poise as might befit an English professor from long ago.

"Hello, Mr. Chips," Bill called.

Though he provided no verbal reply, the groundhog lifted his head to the balcony and studied them without reservation.

"Stay right there. I've got something for you."

Bill rushed inside and inspected the peaches he had laid

on the counter to ripen. He lifted the largest one and sniffed the stem. Perfect.

"Come, Max."

In record time, Bill haltered Max and led him down the stairs outside and around the building to the left. Bill paused. Mr. Chips had returned to his feeding. Bill held his breath and led Max closer. When they were twenty yards from Mr. Chips, the groundhog noticed them. He stood on his hind legs, turned toward them, and froze.

Max's eyes had caught sight of Mr. Chips. Bill could not be sure of Max's reaction to his furry friend, but he was comforted by Max's patient observation of the black bear several days earlier.

Bill dropped the leash, gave Max's back a reassuring rub, and then held his hand out with his palm down.

"Max. Stay."

With his tail still wagging, Max sat on his haunches.

Then Bill lifted the peach high with his left hand.

"See here, Mr. Chips? I have a nice juicy peach for you. Hang on."

Expecting Mr. Chips to take the fruit from his hand after a long winter of separation was more than Bill could hope for, but perhaps he could get a bit closer. The groundhog's burrow hole from the previous year was no more than twenty feet from where Mr. Chips now stood, and so far, he showed no sign of distress. Bill edged his way toward Mr. Chips. One gentle step. Then another. Fifty feet. Forty feet. Then thirty.

Bill breathed deeply. That would have to do. Mr. Chips eyed him curiously, still frozen. Bill could guess his thoughts. He wanted that peach.

Bill lowered his weight and soft-tossed the peach to close half the distance to Mr. Chips. The groundhog flinched. Bill caught his breath, but Mr. Chips stood his ground.

Then Bill began a slow retreat. He reached Max again, then stopped and waited. Max stood and wagged his tail, his attention locked onto the groundhog. Mr. Chips considered the peach for what seemed an eternity. Then he hurried forward ten feet and stopped.

Max whined, lowered his weight onto his front legs, and wagged his butt. The message Max sent was clear—he wanted to make friends. How had Max made such an extraordinary decision? Surely, he would have adopted a different approach as a hungry stray. Bill shook his head. What a remarkable dog, with wisdom beyond most dogs and many humans.

Suddenly, Mr. Chips made a commitment. He scampered the final few yards to the peach, snatched it up, and greedily gnawed at the fruit.

Max barked a friendly greeting and jumped vertically. Then he barked and jumped again. Max behaved that way whenever he encountered one of the friendly neighborhood dogs, and the spectacle warmed Bill's heart.

"I swear," said a familiar female voice, "that dog's as crazy as you."

At long last, Cindy had returned. She stood on her third-floor balcony wearing shorts and a T-shirt with her blond curls dangling about her shoulders. One foot lifted lazily behind her. Bright flowers bloomed in the railing planters at her side.

Bill waved, then said eagerly, "Hey! Mr. Chips has returned. And so have you."

"Obviously."

"Come over when you're ready. I have wine."

"The best words I've heard all day. Let me shower first. Thirty minutes?"

"Yes. Yes. Yes."

Cindy left, and Bill returned his attention to the grass. His exchange with Cindy must have frightened Mr. Chips, for he was nowhere to be seen. Bill and Max ventured to the groundhog's burrow hole, where Bill leaned forward.

"See you tomorrow. Sleep tight."

Passersby would agree with Cindy's assessment—he and Max were foolish to befriend a groundhog—but Bill didn't care. With Max at his side, he straightened and filled his lungs with clean mountain air. Puffy white clouds floated motionless in the azure sky.

And, for the time being, all was well with the world.

THE END

ALSO BY PATRICK KELLY

Thank you for reading *Murder at Dawn.* If you enjoyed the mystery, please tell your friends. Word of mouth is the best form of marketing.

And now, on to book five, *The Humpback Rocks Murder!*

There is no time to waste – important questions will be answered.

1. Why does Cindy's ex-husband, Kevin, believe she will come back to him?

- He's smarter than Bill.
- He's better looking than Bill.
- He's going to inherit fifty million dollars.
- All of the above.

2. What does Bill feed Ms. Betsy to distract her?

- A half-eaten hamburger.
- A candy bar.
- A quart of vanilla ice cream from Black Bear Creamery
- A fresh pie from Chiles Peach Orchard in Crozet.

3. Who murdered the missing cousin?

- Roddy Evans - an aging banker with a young wife.
- Lucy, the young wife of Roddy Evans.

• Kevin Quintrell, Cindy's ex.

• Cindy.

• Ishaan Dhar, the missing cousin's former fiancé.

• Sandy Anderson, the twin who always lived in the shadow of the victim.

On October 10, 2024, *The Humpback Rocks Murder* will be available in the print edition on Amazon and in the ebook version at all major online stores.

In the meantime, join the Readers Club and get your free copy of the *Wintergreen Mysteries Primer.*

Dear Readers,

I'm excited to introduce *The Wintergreen Mysteries Primer,* which is exclusively available for free to Readers Club members. Whether you're a long-time series fan or a newbie, the primer includes great content for you:

• A hand-drawn map with Scene-of-the-Crime markers for Books One through Five

• Thrilling short scenes from each novel

• The Bill O'Shea Detective Stories (Unavailable Anywhere Else)

• A stray dog story told from the dog's point of view

• Five Ms. Betsy the Black Bear encounters

Peruse the Table of Contents, pick your favorite topic, and jump right to it.

Go to my website and check out the Readers Club!

www.patrickkellystories.com

ABOUT WINTERGREEN

Several years ago, we bought a condo in Wintergreen, Virginia, to escape the hot Texas summers. Not by coincidence, our condo is in the same location as the one owned by Bill O'Shea. Groundhogs scrounge greens from the lawn beneath our balcony. Sadly, the groundhog named Mr. Chips is a fictional character. Black bear sightings and funny stories are common.

Most of the places and establishments mentioned in the story are real; however, the characters and events are all fictitious. The Wintergreen Police and Fire & Rescue teams do a fabulous job of protecting the community. The police procedures depicted in the novel are from my imagination and undoubtedly an inaccurate portrayal of how real law enforcement professionals go about their business. As a writer, my interest lies primarily with the mystery and the interaction of the characters.

As always, my wife Susie tried to help me write a better book. She is the love of my life.

ACKNOWLEDGMENTS

Sleepy Fox Studios designed the book cover. Liz Perry of Per Se Editing edited the manuscript.

Several Wintergreen residents were kind enough to read an early draft and give me feedback, including Emily Ferguson, Valerie Calhoun, and Terri Brooks.

A special thanks to Wintergreen Police Chief Dennis Russell, who generously shared tips on how the police use surveillance cameras to keep the community safe. Despite his best efforts, my depiction of surveillance cameras undoubtedly includes inaccuracies. I am entirely to blame for those errors.

Thank you to the many people who work hard to make Wintergreen a wonderful resort community.

KEEP IN TOUCH

If you enjoyed meeting Bill O'Shea and his friends, join the Readers Club, and I'll send you an email when the next mystery is released.

www.patrickkellystories.com

Follow me on:

www.goodreads.com/patrickkelly

Instagram: pkellystories

Facebook: patrickkellywriter

Made in the USA
Columbia, SC
30 May 2025